Feel It All

Mollie Goins

Copyright © 2023 by Mollie Goins

All rights reserved.

No part of this publication may be reproduced, distributed, or transmitted in any form or by any means, including photocopying, recording, or other electronic or mechanical methods, without the prior written permission of the publisher, except as permitted by U.S. copyright law. For permission requests, contact Mollie Goins.

The story, all names, characters, and incidents portrayed in this production are fictitious. No identification with actual persons (living or deceased), places, buildings, and products is intended or should be inferred.

Paperback ISBN: 979-8-8229-1562-6
eBook ISBN: 979-8-8229-1563-3

To myself and everyone who needs to hear that it's a battle worth fighting.

Disclaimer

Feel It All contains references to mental health issues that can be raw for some readers. The main female character struggles with general depression, severe anxiety, and suicidal thoughts. I want all of my readers to know that you are not alone, and I hope that Winry's story helps you find strength in your own journey. If these topics are too raw for you, that is okay, I would recommend skipping chapter 12.

Having struggled with suicide myself, I want everyone to know that you are worthy, brave, and strong. This battle is extremely difficult, but it is worth fighting. You are worth fighting for. If no one has told you today, let me be the first…you are loved, you are important, and you are irreplaceable.

If you or anyone you know struggles with suicidal thoughts, I would encourage you to reach out to the Suicide and Crisis Lifeline at 988.

Contents

1. Winry — 1
2. Graham — 13
3. Winry — 18
4. Graham — 29
5. Winry — 35
6. Winry — 44
7. Graham — 54
8. Winry — 67
9. Graham — 83
10. Graham — 88
11. Winry — 109
12. Graham — 131
13. Winry — 161
14. Winry — 178
15. Graham — 197

16.	Winry	216
17.	Graham	226
18.	Winry	240
19.	Graham	247
20.	Winry	259
21.	Winry	267
22.	Graham	275
23.	Winry	284
24.	Graham	291
25.	Winry	297
26.	Graham	300
27.	Winry	308
Epilogue		313
Acknowledgements		318
About the Author		320

Chapter 1

Winry

Chapter 1

"Oh, bless your daddy's heart." That's it, that's the line my sisters and I have heard over and over. Apparently, having three daughters calls for blessings and prayers for the father. "Didn't get his boy, did he?" That one was my favorite. Griffin Bennett was a proud girl dad and never regretted not getting "his boy" for one minute. He probably wouldn't turn away prayers though. My sisters and I were forces to be reckoned with and total daddy's girls.

We have had him wrapped around our fingers since birth. I'm the oldest at 24, then Waverley, then Wyla. I am two years older than Waverly, and our parents got down to business after because there is only a year between Waverley and Wyla.

We get this comment so much that when we do something to which anyone would say "Oh, bless your heart," we tease, "Bless your dad's heart." And it's being used today too, to my own dismay.

Today, my sisters and I are at my home away from home: my store, Crossroads Books & Café. We have met here every Sunday morning since I opened last September with my business partner and best friend, Ivy. There aren't many people outside of my family I connect with, but my girl Ivy wiggled her way in the first day of kindergarten. We have dreamed of opening a joint bookstore and coffee/pastry shop since sophomore year of high school. Last year, we finally made our dream come true, and we could not be prouder of Crossroads. Ivy is the master barista and pastry gal, and I manage the books and the business side of things.

"Win, did you tell them your 'bless your dad' moment?" Ivy beams as she passes our table. I told her this morning about the most embarrassing night of my life last night. I knew I would have to tell my sisters but hoped I could eat my muffin first.

"Oh, you have a moment? And you weren't going to say anything!" Waverley snaps as she slaps my hand away from my muffin.

"Ow, jeez, thanks, Ivy." I stare dagger at her as she walks away cackling. "Ugh, this one takes the cake for sure. So, you know how Huck has moved into a living facility?" Huck is my neighbor—well, former neighbor now. My sisters nod. "Well, his niece has been staying for the past two nights getting it emptied and cleaned for the new renters. Flynn was over last night, and we were, you know..."

"Having sex," Waverley blurts out as she sips her coffee.

"Yes, okay but I wasn't going to say that aloud in my business," I say, which gets me eye rolls from both my sisters.

"Keep going," Wyla whisper-shouts.

"Well in the middle of our...activity...we hear pounding on the door. Naturally, we freak out because it's like two in the morning, so when I go to open the door..."

"Wait, wait, why didn't Flynn answer the door? You said it was two in the morning, right? What if it had been a murderer?" Wyla interrupts. Neither of my sisters is a fan of my current boyfriend, Flynn. To be honest, I'm not sure how big of a fan I am either.

"Because he started freaking out and being chicken shit, saying it's my house so I should be the one to answer the door. That's not even the worst part. When I open the door, it's two city police officers who said they had received a call for a woman in distress."

"What!" my sisters say in unison.

"Yup."

"No!" again in unison.

"Yes, that bitty called us in saying that I sounded like a woman in distress. And the worst part is I was overcompensating my noises because if I don't Flynn gets all paranoid and weirds out like I'm the reason he can't make me come."

At this point, my sisters are practically in the floor in a laughing fit, gasping for air with coffee coming out of their noses. "Oh, what happened next, what did the officers say?" Wyla breathed in between laughing.

"They busted out laughing just like y'all are right now. They made Flynn come out after they finally caught their breath just to make sure everything was okay, but ultimately it was mortifying, and I wanted to die. I mean, I got lucky one of the officers was Owen West. I threatened to feed him his balls if he told Dad."

Our dad is the police chief in Aster Creek, which always has us worrying about him. Mom used to stay up all night listening to the police radio on nights that he would patrol. Dad eventually made her get rid of it because she would never sleep.

"You were right. This is the best 'bless your dad' moment ever," Waverly exclaims, looking satisfied by my nightmare.

"In all seriousness, Winry, please tell me you are planning to break up with Flynn soon. I mean, come on, Winry, if the sex isn't good what is even the point?" Wyla questions.

"I know, I know. I am going to do it. You know how I am; I hate stuff like that. I am a people pleaser," I shuffle in my seat. Hard conversations have not always been my thing.

"It would be great if he pleased you for once," Waverley mocks and takes a bite of her scone.

Wasn't that the truth. I have been dating Flynn for three months. Wait, maybe it's four, if that gives you any indication about how attached to this relationship I am. He's not a bad guy. In fact, he seems good on paper. He is attractive and has a decent job, a good family, and a nice house. There is just no heat, no chemistry. I know I need to end things, but I have such anxiety about it. Granted, everything makes me anxious and overwhelmed, so I really should just get it over with.

"They are right, Win: It's time to cut things off with Flynn," Ivy chimes in as she brings me my favorite of her coffees, a Snickers iced latte with whipped cream.

"I'll do it, I swear."

"Soon," Wyla adds.

"I will, but let's move on to better things. Wav, tell us about the school where you start this fall." Waverley shares our mom's passion of teaching and just got her degree in Middle School Education. She starts teaching sixth grade this August at Aster Creek Middle School. Wyla is still indecisive on what she wants to do officially but is getting her basic credits right now at Aster Community College.

Waverley starts beaming at the now topic of conversation, "I am so excited—I will actually get to teach kids.

Years of school later and I will finally be doing what I have been dreaming of since we were kids. Plus, I get to decorate a room however I please, which is really one of the best parts. You two obviously will be helping me put it together."

"Oh joy," I mutter.

"I will gladly help you," Wyla says honestly. Wyla is the sweetest of the Bennett sisters, never snarky like Waverley and I are.

"Thank you, Wyla. Winry, you're helping whether you like it or not."

"I am just so jealous! You guys are both doing things you love, and I still have no idea what I am going to do. I finish my core requirements this fall—what am I going to do then? I'll be living with Mom and Dad forever," Wyla says looking like a lost puppy.

"You'll figure it out, Wyla, you still have time. You've been volunteering a lot; have you found anything you enjoy there?"

"I enjoy volunteering; it feels good to help people at the soup kitchen and I love the animal shelter, but I want to take every little helpless creature home. I brought home Poppy already and Mom nearly had a stroke." Poppy is Wyla's German shepherd mix she brought home a few months ago. She was a tiny little abandoned puppy, and I had to stay the night when she brought her home to help bottle feed her because Wyla had to study for an early test and couldn't be up all night before.

"Hey, why don't we have a Bennett sister sleepover tonight at Mom and Dad's? I could use some sister time, and it will help me avoid meeting my new neighbors," I suggest, hoping to lift Wyla's spirits. I hate when my sisters aren't feeling their amazing selves.

"I'm in," Waverly agrees.

After breakfast, I head straight over to our parents' house. With last night's incident and the new neighbor today, I'm feeling off my game. If I met them today, I would most likely say something awkward and stupid. I tend to say whatever comes to my mind at times. I would like to push off the new neighbor for as long as possible. I don't know why it bothers me so much, but I suppose it is just change in general. The new neighbors force me to get used to a new normal, and I have had so much on my plate between managing Crossroads and my daily routine that it just feels heavy at times. Don't get me wrong, Crossroads is doing well, but this is our first year, and I want it to be amazing. So I have been putting my heart and soul into it.

I walk into the house where I grew up, and it instantly brings me peace. I love this place. My whole childhood is packed in this house, so much so that it is practically bursting at the seams. With only 1,500 square feet and three bedrooms, we had to be a close family. There was literally no hiding from it.

For a while, just Waverley and I shared a room, but when Wyla got old enough, we decided to cram all three of our beds into one room and made the other room our walk-in closet. Mom always made us share everything anyway, so there was no point in trying to separate it out. "Hello," I holler as I walk in the door, "your favorite daughter is here."

"Wyla?" I hear my mom mock.

"Ha, ha, very funny."

"I couldn't pick a favorite of my girls, even if you forced me," my dad says while bringing me in for a suffocating hug. Dad's hugs are like that. They encase you and somehow bring you this comfort that you didn't even know you needed.

"That I believe. Me on the other hand, it changes daily." Mom confesses as she walks up to greet me. "Hi, Honey, what brings you over?"

"We decided to have a girls' sleepover tonight. Wyla ran to get the essentials, and Waverly is meeting us here around dinner. I didn't feel like going home, so I thought I would see my favorite people. Well, second favorite people, sisters first."

"That's exactly right," Mom agreed. She never had siblings, so that's why I always felt like she forced us to be close. And yes, "forced" is the right word, but it worked out. If one of us went somewhere, the others had to follow; there was no doing anything without each other. And there was no not sharing clothes either. They honestly never bought us clothes individually; it was always understood that anything Mom or Dad bought was ours to share.

"I'm glad you're here, moon baby," Dad says dearly. He has called me "moon baby" for forever. I was born on a full moon, and I have just always loved the nighttime. Even to this day, I don't sleep great; something about night just feels good to me.

"I am too," Mom butts in, "and it is a perfect night for a sister sleepover. Looks like a storm is rolling in, so y'all can do your usual sleep pile in the living room."

"Your favorite daughter is home!" we hear Wyla holler. We really are sisters. As soon as Poppy hears Wyla, she takes off to greet her. She lay in her dog bed when I got here, didn't even flinch. Little brat.

"Hi, Pops. Win, why don't you help me with this stuff?" Wyla has her hands full of bags full of absolute junk. "I bought stuff for you to make your homemade cookie dough, and the best part—look at what movie I found...*Aquamarine*!"

"Ah, no way. It's shaping up to be a perfcct sleepover. Mom said we can destroy her living room and make our signature sister pile." I take some of the bags from her and take them to the kitchen. I dig around in the kitchen until I find everything I need to make the cookie dough.

Over the next few hours, I make the cookie dough and put it in fridge to set, then I help mom with dinner. Ivy may technically be Crossroads's signature baker, but I'm not too shabby in the kitchen if do I say so myself. Waverley shows up just as we plate the spaghetti for dinner.

"Let's get this party started," Waverley says while carrying in each of our favorite bottles of wine. I am a Riesling girl, Wyla is a Moscato, and Waverly is a Zinfandel. "Oh, yes, Mom's spaghetti. She really does love us."

"I know what my girls like."

"Winry, I got you two bottles of Riesling. It seemed like you needed it after, you know," Waverley adds, wiggling her eyebrows and smirking.

"What, why? Winry, what's wrong?" Mom barely takes a breath in between questions. She always worries about us, but especially me. She knows I got her anxiety and then some. I stare at Waverley, mentally stabbing her for even insinuating about my night last night in front of Mom and Dad. "It's nothing, Mom, Waverley just knows I have had my plate full at Crossroads."

"You have so much on your plate; what does your therapist say? You know Dad and I can help you out, so you don't have to work so hard all the time."

"Mom, really, I am fine. My therapist has been impressed with my progress over these past few months. Can we please just eat?"

"Okay but promise you will tell us if you need help. Please."

"I promise, Mom," my mental stability has always been a tough subject. Hell, it's a tough subject for anyone. I know my family wants to ask more about why I take the medications, see a therapist at least once a month if not twice, and always stick to my routine. I have always been the dependent one and always appeared happy. I got the superlative "most bubbly" every year in high school. Mom knew I worried, but it has always been more than just worrying. My family didn't need the burdens of my mind, which is what therapy is for.

After dinner, my sisters and I start on our pile of blankets, pillows, and stuffed animals—anything remotely comfortable goes straight into the pile. "I cannot believe you found *Aquamarine*, Wyla. I am so pumped." Waverley says, popping the DVD in.

"I am just glad Mom and Dad are still old school and had a DVD player." We are all about halfway through the cookie dough and bottles of wine, and we haven't even started it yet.

"Okay, hush, it's starting," Waverley snaps. We cuddle together watching our favorite childhood movie, and it is blissful. Maybe it's the wine, but I feel at peace in this moment, and that's not something I feel often. Wyla and Waverley pass out right before it ends, so I turn it off and drift off soon after with a smile on my face.

Chapter 2

Graham

Moving is the biggest pain in the ass, but it's long overdue. My mom would have trapped me in Rosewood if she could. I stayed long enough, and it was time for me to do something for me. So when my buddy from the police academy told me about an opening in his town, I took it—no questions, no hesitation.

Don't get me wrong, there is nothing outright bad about my mom, but she can be overbearing and controlling to say the least. And for me to be a police officer was a nightmare for her. She never understood my career choice; my father was a police officer too and they divorced when I was about six. I wouldn't say it ended amicably, but they did their best—well, semi-best—to hide it from me. Again, nothing bad about either of them, but I wouldn't use the words "big, happy family" to describe mine.

Mom made it her personal mission to make sure I did not turn into my dad. Dad's mission was that I never get married. Neither of my parents re-married after the divorce. They dated, but it never worked out. I know that the fact that it did not work for them does not mean that it won't work for me, but relationships required work, and I just never felt the need to put forth the effort. I have a few exes but never really made it past a couple months. They would always end it because I was "emotionally unavailable." Oh well, maybe I am, or maybe I am just an ass, but either way I was not heartbroken by any of the relationships ending.

"Where do you want these boxes, Taylor?" Owen hollers from the living room of my new apartment. I found this place at a total steal, and considering I'm now on a police salary, I'll take what I can get. It's a small loft with the living room to the left and stairs to the bedroom and main bathroom to the right of the door. The kitchen and half bath are toward the back, and two sliding doors open to a covered porch.

"Just in the living room for now. I want to get everything in first; it's starting to look like a storm is rolling in."

"Sure thing."

I met Owen West in the academy. He is one the of best guys I know. He is a good cop, tough but fair. He also could make light of any situation, which can come in handy in this line of work. You would never think it by his appearance and jokes, but he was the top of our class in the academy. I was a close second though.

We carried in all the furniture and boxes in a couple of hours. I didn't have much, just the essentials. While I work on getting stuff separated, Owen perks up, "Oh, I forgot to tell you about your new neighbor. I didn't realize this was going to be your place or I would have warned you." He says this all with the biggest smile on his face—that's how I know I really am not going to like this.

"Great, haven't even unboxed all my stuff yet and I am already wanting to pack it back up. What about my neighbor? Are they annoying or something?" I pause looking through boxes.

"Oh, you wish. Your new neighbor is none other than your new boss's daughter, Winry Bennett. She is just a couple years younger than us, but she's pretty cool. Although, last night I got a call to her place, and oh you'll love this—I got called because she was being too loud with her loser boyfriend. She threatened to feed me my balls if I told her dad about it."

"I'm sorry, she got called for what?" I must have misheard.

"You heard right, my friend. Our boss's daughter, and your new neighbor, is a freak. I can't wait for you to meet her. She is just your type too. I would describe her, but it wouldn't do her justice." Owen starts shuffling through some boxes.

"Hey, if Chief Bennett hears you talking about his daughter this way, I think he really will feed you your balls." Chief was an intimidating guy. I interviewed with him, and I had never been more stressed in my life. He was tough, asked hard questions, and gave hard situational ones too. He wasn't doing it to be an ass though. You could tell he took every single aspect of being a cop seriously and he did not have room for anyone who did not do the same.

"Winry would too—I am more scared of her. Chief maybe a hard-ass at work, but he melts when his daughters are around. He would commit murder if someone hurt his girls."

"Well, it's a good thing she is just my neighbor." I can feel Owen smiling at me like I have just said something humorous.

We move and unbox things for a few hours, then Owen leaves before the rain starts. I continue to unpack some things but decide to take a break and have one of the beers that Owen brought on the covered porch around midnight. Every cop in Aster Creek starts on night shift, so I am having to stay up all night to prepare.

The rain is beating down on the covered porch and thunder rolls in the distance. I take a look around; I will have to remember to get some chairs to put out here. It is a decent-size porch, and I could get some good outdoor furniture and a grill out here. As I take a swig of my beer, I look over at the neighboring porch. She's not home—hasn't been all day. Not that I am looking for her. I just want to know who I am living next to, that's all. Her porch looks homey and makes mine feel even more empty. She has a couple of plants spread out in different places, an outdoor couch, and in one corner it looks like workout stuff. Hmm, wonder if she works out on her porch often.

Nope, not entertaining that thought.

I quickly finish my beer and head back inside to finish unpacking. I have nothing better to do and I have to stay up for a few more hours so back to it I go. Around eight in the morning I finally have every single thing I own unpacked and in its place. Just as I crash on the bed, I hear someone knocking at the front door.

Chapter 3

Winry

The neighbor—neighbors? I am not really sure—should be all moved in now. I should go over and introduce myself, but I hope I can make it inside to freshen up before I go over there. Oh, and maybe I should take some pastries from the store for a welcome present. My unease about meeting the new neighbors came back on the drive over. I guess that's anxiety for you. No real rhyme or reason, just the feeling of walls closing in around you. My apartment is my safe place, and it's my own fault for thinking I would always have it like it is. I live in the most adorable tiny duplex; it has a very modern farmhouse style, a white exterior with rich wood accents. The best part is it has a beautiful flower bed in the middle of the entryways and opposing sides.

When I pull into our driveway, I see them outside in front of their door. A tall, dark-haired man whose features I can't make out for the blonde women whose curves I saw as soon as I rounded the corner onto my side of the driveway. Mentally, I am kicking myself for not putting any effort into my appearance today. Not that I am insecure in myself—I rock—but if I am going to meet them for first time, I wish I just looked a little more put together. So, I take my time getting everything out of my car. Maybe if they won't notice me, or if I carry in everything at once I can hide behind my junk and they won't give me a second glace.

Yeah, right. Wishful thinking, Win.

And I am so not eavesdropping while I am stalling…I hear the man say, "I'm sorry but can we do this another time?"

"Please Graham? I just want to come inside for a little bit. Maybe get some breakfast together."

"Claire, I have been here one day, and I work night shift tonight. I have been up all night and I just want to sleep. Can I just call you later?"

And at that she scoffs; I am picking up the awkward tension all the way from my car. So they aren't living together? It sounds like he wants her to leave but "no" doesn't seem to be in her vocabulary from how their conversation continues.

Let it go, Win. Not your problem.

This is a prime opportunity to sneak into my apartment unseen and meet him later, but do I do that? No. I stay pretending to get my stuff together at the car listening to their conversation.

"Claire, if you could just, please..."

And before I can stop myself, I blurt out, "Graham, thank goodness I ran into you. I desperately need your help again." This is a prime example of saying whatever comes to your mind.

Now that I am no longer hiding behind my car, I can finally take him in...and holy hell. Even though it looks like Claire just forced him out of bed, he is still breathtaking. With dark brown wavy hair, six feet tall at least. I notice that his gray sweatpants and white tee both have "ACPD" on them. I should be thinking about how annoying it's going to be having one of Dad's cops right next door, but all I can think about is how he will look in his uniform. I come back from that daydream and they both stare at me like I have three heads. This plan very well may blow up in my face, but I cannot help but pick up the vibe that he wants her to leave. So, he should just follow along and we will be fine.

"My AC went out on me again this morning. Whatever you did yesterday fixed it for a couple of hours. The landlord is coming by this afternoon, but it gets so hot during the day. Do you mind coming over and doing it again, please?" I try to stress the come over part so that he hopefully gets the hint.

It's like I can see the wheels turning. Finally, he understands what I am doing, and perks up, "Oh yeah, um, I can do that. Really quick though, then I have to get some sleep."

He turns to Claire, "I will call you later."

And with that, he races over to my side without giving her a chance for a rebuttal. We shuffle in my apartment, and I do give myself a gold star for picking up my place the other day. It's like the Lord knew I would use it but did not give me the heads up to look cute while doing it too. Damn, that girl was pretty, and I am trying to not dwell on my post-sister sleepover attire of maroon yoga pants and one of my dad's oversized beer t-shirts. I lean to look out the window and see Claire shoving her designer purse in her car.

"Is she gone?" Graham asks over my shoulder. It takes me a minute to process that he is talking to me. His voice is smooth and smoky at the same time. I just want to hear him speak again.

"Um, yeah, just drove off. Ha, who knew I was such a good actor?" A "humph" is all I get in return.

Okay...keep it cool, Win. This is one of your dad's employees.

"I am Winry, by the way. I'm sorry if I misread the situation, but it just seemed like you wanted her to leave, and she didn't seem too keen on the word 'no.' I just kind of started talking and..."

"No, I did want her to leave. Sorry, I am exhausted. I'm Graham."

He holds out his hand out for me to shake and it is almost laughable how tiny my hands look in his. I do not mean to stare at them, nor do I mean to hold on slightly longer than necessary.

Shit. Get it together.

Gah, he was attractive. Up close, I could see his features better. He had dark chestnut brown eyes, with a strong jaw, obviously. He was clean shaven and his hair, man I wanted to run my fingers through it. He towered over my 5′2″ stature, had to at least be a foot taller than me.

"Right," I jump back. "It seemed to work, so I will let you get some sleep." We held eye contact for a moment, studying each other. Why did it feel so comfortable? I hated eye contact. It usually made me want to crawl in a hole, but right now I could not drag my eyes away from his. Graham broke away first. He ran his hand through his dark waves and looked down at the ground. Was he nervous?

"Yeah, thank you for rescuing me. I guess I'll see you around, Winry."

I opened the door for him and 100% checked his ass out on his way over to his place. I have no shame, especially when it looks good enough to bite into in those sweatpants. Man, just imagine it in a police uniform.

I was dying to ask if Claire was his girlfriend. I was playing devil's advocate in my head about it. I mean he wanted her to leave, but then said he would call her. No, let it go. One thing I know for sure is he isn't mine, technically he is more my dad's than mine. He is just my neighbor—hot neighbor, though. Nope. Let's not focus on that.

I make my way back inside. It is one of my rare days off from Crossroads. Last month, we hired a college student part-time, Abigal, to help the cover some of the shifts so Ivy and I are not working ourselves to death. We still try though. Neither of us really likes being away. It's our baby; we can't help it.

I go through my normal routine of tidying up around the house and watering the plants. I usually keep my place pretty neat; it is decorated in creams, tans, and dark greens. I have plants everywhere. Growing up, I had the worst brown thumb; I even killed two cacti once. Do not ask me how, I swear they just gave up on me. Despite the many tragedies through the years, I have finally achieved my green thumb. I make my way to the back porch to water my outdoor plants when I am attacked by a black bundle of fur.

"Hey there, Blackjack, you haven't been by in a few days. Are you cheating on me or something?" he rubs up again my legs and purrs in response. "You hungry? Let me go get you something to eat."

Blackjack showed up the day I moved in meowing like crazy at my back door. He was a skinny little thing, so I took him to the vet for a checkup and some shots. They checked for a chip, but there wasn't one, so I went to the store and bought all the stuff I would need to bring the little guy inside.

It lasted one good day and Blackjack was over it. He constantly pawed at the back sliding doors, desperate to escape. I tried not to take it personally—was living with me that bad?—but I have accepted that Blackjack is just a free soul, and he comes and goes as he pleases. I still feed him and take him to get his shots when the time comes.

"I met the new neighbor today, Blackjack. Between you and me he is quite the looker, but you can't be leaving me for him, buddy." He ignores me as he gobbles up every bit of food I set out. "Well, if you are just going to ignore me, then I am going to go back inside."

My phone starts ringing just as I sit down after finishing my daily tasks. I reach for it and see it's Flynn calling.

"Hey, Flynn."

"Hey, babe. Listen, a group of us are going to Bluebird's tonight and you are coming with."

"I don't know, Flynn; it is my only day off…"

"Exactly, it is your day off, so no excuses. I will pick you up at six; wear something hot." *Click*.

Well, I guess I am going out tonight. Bluebird's was the only local bar in town. On the weekends, they do karaoke, which was fun, but it was Monday so no karaoke and it would be with Flynn's friends. It is not that I don't like them, they are just—well, I don't like them. They all are pretentious, and I don't think they really like me either.

I honestly do not even know how Flynn and I are still together, or really how we got together to begin with. I guess we have just always known of each other; he was two years ahead of me in school. We never really talked though until one day he came into Crossroads and asked me out, and here we are three—no, four months?—later. Man, I really should work on that.

A knock at my door came at exactly 6. Flynn was never late. I did decide to wear something hot. For myself though, not him. I put on a black silk dress, with a chunky belt to help accentuate my waist, and my kick-ass combat boots. I had my hair down in loose curls and a silver layered chain necklace. To finish the look, I put on my favorite red lipstick. Nothing made me feel more confident than red lipstick; don't know why, but this outfit gives "fuck off" vibes and I liked it.

"Whoa, went a little heavy on the black, didn't we?" Flynn states as he looks me up and down.

"What? You said hot, and I think I look hot," I throw back. I don't need his approval; I feel good and that's what matters.

"Well come on, let's go," he says flatly, completely unamused with my answer. Just as I head toward his car, I hear a door open and close. It's Graham. He's in his uniform, and I am pretty sure I am staring. Graham gives an awkward nod and half wave as he gets into his car.

Okay, not sure what to think about that.

"Um, hello? Are you getting in or not?" Flynn sneers.

"Right, yeah. That is my new neighbor, he is new to town and one of Dad's new cops.'

"Mhm, that sounds great," he replied, clearly not listening to me.

Bluebird's is just about a ten-minute drive from my apartment, and when we get there, we grab a table with his friends, whose names I definitely cannot remember. A girl named Sara, maybe, has been talking nonstop throughout the whole dinner. She keeps finding ways to not-so-subtly touch Flynn. It should bother me, but it doesn't. I have made up my mind, I have to end it with him, tonight. Just not here; I will do it tonight when he drops me off.

However, my plan to end thing starts to look further and further away, just like Flynn's consciousness. He is on his sixth drink, and he is not holding up well, and neither are his friends. I head over to the bar; Lacey is working tonight thankfully or we probably would have been thrown out by now.

"Sorry Winry, I am going to have to cut your friends off," she says with a half-smile.

"That is perfectly fine with me, I just came to get some waters for me and Flynn."

"I know you are good to drive, but I will call cabs for the others."

"Thanks, Lacey, you rock." I make my way back over to our table, happy the night is nearing its end.

"Looks like we have been cut off guys. Lacey is going to call some cabs. Flynn, I can drive your car to my place, and you can sleep it off there."

"That's bullshit. Why are we cut off," a guy who I have been calling Chad in my head all night starts ranting.

"Seriously, babe, that's ridiculous. Tell Lacey we need another round," Flynn retorts.

"No, I am not telling her that. Look, I do not care where the rest of you guys go as long as you are not driving," I tell the group. "But we are going back to my place so you can sleep this off."

"What if he doesn't want to go with you?" Sara chimes in now.

"Oh, come on now, Sara, if Flynn wants to go home with the goth chick, let him."

Goth Chick? Let him? Do they not remember that I am his girlfriend?

"Like I said, I don't care where you guys go. We are leaving." I'll drag Flynn out of here if I have to. I give Flynn a look that means I mean it and he gives in.

"Looks like I am out of here, going to go have me some fun with my goth chick."

Yeah, he wishes.

By some miracle we make it to the car without Flynn falling over. I hated leaving that group in there for Lacey to throw out, but I was over the night, and they weren't my responsibility.

"Come on babe, let's get home so I can get you naked." Flynn is slurring even worse now. He starts digging for his keys, but when he finds them, he does not hand them over.

"Fat chance bucko. Hand me the keys Flynn."

"Oh, come on, you thought I would let you drive my BMW," He snarls. "No way, I am fine."

"No, you are not. Flynn, I am serious. If you do not want me to drive that is fine, we will take a cab, but you driving is not an option."

And that was all it took to get the argument started.

Chapter 4

Graham

Today is my first patrol in Aster Creek. Somehow Owen talked our Sergeant into letting him be my training officer, so I will be riding shotgun with him until they think I am ready.

"Hey, bud, ready for you first patrol?" I meet Owen at the front of the department, and he has that same stupid grin on that he always does. I have a feeling he will not be my T.O. for long.

"As ready as I'll ever be," I huff. I am still exhausted from moving and then the unwelcomed visit from Claire. I am sure my mom had something to do with that. I ended things with Claire before I left. I did not move far, only a half an hour away, but I did not have any intentions of telling her that. She and my mom had formed a quick bond the one time they met. They both wanted the same thing, for me to settle down. It is not like I am out there going from one to the next, I just do not really care for relationships right now.

"You look like hell; did you stay up unpacking all day?" Owen pulls out of the parking lot.

"No, I had Claire show up at my door demanding to see my new place and talk," I shudder at the word. I knew I would have to call her eventually and make sure she understands that this is just not going to work out, but I will worry about that another day.

"Oh man, that sucks. How did you get rid of her?"

"I didn't. Actually, Winry did," I whisper the last part.

"Winry, really?" I fill him in on Winry's little stunt that actually worked. At first, I thought she was crazy, but somehow in my sleep-deprived state I figured out that she was trying to help me.

"So, any thoughts on her?" Owen asks, all too giddy to hear my answer.

"Who, Winry or Claire?" I deflect.

"You know which one," I don't have to look at him to know he has a ridiculous smile on his face.

"Let's just say I hate it when you are right," and right he was. Winry was just my type. Medium-length hair, just a shade away from being jet black, big round hazel eyes that actually had little flecks of blue in them. She also had an adorable dimple chin that I really wanted to touch my thumb to. She was petite but not scrawny. When I saw her for the second time in that dress, I wanted to fall to my knees—she was gorgeous. And that red lipstick—that really did it for me.

"I knew it. You are in so much trouble," he taunts.

"I am not, she is just my neighbor, nothing more. I am not stupid enough to think starting something with Chief's daughter is even remotely a good idea."

"Sure buddy, I believe you." He claps me on the shoulder.

"Whatever, man."

"So sensitive."

We drive around for a couple of hours; it seems to be a pretty slow night. A few traffic stops, and we give them all warnings. Owen said he is feeling gracious tonight, and I am not complaining; tickets are a pain. We make our way back into town when I notice a similar black dress and what looked like a guy yelling at her.

"Pull in here, looks like this couple is yelling at each other." I point them out to Owen.

"Yeah. Hey, that is Winry and that tool-bag boyfriend, Flynn."

I immediately feel this instinct to protect her, but something tells me she can hold her own. We pull up and I can hear his yelling.

"You know you always do this; you are so boring. I try to bring you out with my friends, and you act like you couldn't be bothered. It wouldn't hurt you to actually have a personality," he berates her, and it is almost like I can see her flinch.

We come up behind her, "Hey, what seems to be the problem?" I interject.

She turns to face us. If looks could kill, hers right now would do it. "It is nothing, guys, I can handle this."

"Hey, you are her neighbor! What, Winry, are you sleeping with him or something?"

"Oh, don't be ridiculous, Flynn. You are drunk. You need to get a cab home and cool off. I am not sleeping with him; he is my neighbor. Plus, you have girls that are friends, you do not see me accusing you of sleeping with them."

"Oh, to the contrary. I am sleeping with them and most of them are a hell of a lot better in bed than you are."

"Okay, that's enough," I want to rage at him. "You need to..."

"Hold on, Graham, I got this," Winry holds up her hand to pause me. "I know you think this is going to have some sort of effect on me and make me want to beg for you to stay with me, but I am not that girl. I honestly don't give two shits that you have cheated; I have wanted to end things with you for a month now. And *I'm* bad at sex? Please, you couldn't find a g-spot even if I gave you a map."

Owen and I are really trying to hold it together, but damn, it is good to hear her stick up for herself.

"So, unless you want to have these guys take you in for public intoxication, I suggest you take the cab they are going to call for you home because we are done." She crosses her arms and stares daggers at him.

"Fine by me, you—"

"Don't even finish that sentence, asshole," I barked at him, she said her piece, and I was not about to let him speak another word to her. Owen pulls him aside and calls him a cab, which leaves me alone with Winry. "Are you all right?"

"Just peachy." We stand silent for a minute. She has her arms crossed still and is in defense mode. I try not to stare at her. She does not seem like she will take me trying to comfort her very well. "Sorry, you haven't done anything. I don't mean to take it out on you," she finally says looking a bit more solemn.

"You are fine," a few more minutes of silence elapse, and a cab finally arrives.

"He is in a cab. Why don't you let us take you back to your place? It is a slow night, and it is not a far drive."

"Okay, that's fine."

Owen makes his way back over and we get in the patrol car. I hated putting her in the back, but I hated the idea of not getting her home safe more. We ride the whole way in silence. I can feel a mixture of fury and sadness resonating from the back. We reach our apartments, and she finally speaks.

"Thank you for your help. Um, could you guys do me a favor and not mention this to my dad?"

"Sure thing, Winry. Have a good night," Owen replies with a half-smile. And before I think about it, I get out to walk her to the door.

"You do not have to walk me to the door, Graham."

"I know you are perfectly capable; I want to do it."

"Okay," she grumbles, and we walk to the door.

"So, are you going to be okay?"

"I will be fine, Graham. This is not my first break up and probably won't be my last, so let's not dwell on how shitty this one was." We reach her door. Why does the look on her face make me feel like I have been hit in the gut?

"Right, well good night," I say, not sure of what else to do.

"Good night Graham," She gives me a half smile and closes her door.

I make my way back the car, and I am dreading it. I tell myself it's because I won't hear the end of this for the rest of the night from Owen, and not because I am leaving her. "I do not want hear one word," I say as I climb in.

"I wasn't going to say anything," he says as he throws his hand in the air in defense.

Chapter 5

Winry

When I am back in my apartment is when I finally allow myself to feel anything other than pure anger. I meant what I said, I was not upset about Flynn cheating, but to say his words didn't sting a bit would be a lie. I try my best to not let them affect me, but they do. Am I really boring? No personality? Am I really bad in bed? I do not want to let the voices in, but they are here, and they are screaming that I will never be good enough.

Deep breaths. In and out. In and out.

No, I am in control here, not my thoughts. When my sisters and I would go through a breakup in high school, Mom would allow us only three days to wallow, cry, and be a complete mess. It's a practice I have put in place even out of high school, but this time Flynn does not deserve three of days of my happiness. I will wallow tonight, and that is all the power I will give him.

I make my way into the kitchen and pull out a bottle of wine, and a pack of cookie dough. Tonight, I allow my demons in, on a leash that is. I won't let them take over, and in the morning, I will be all better. I turn on some *Friends,* pour a giant glass of my favorite wine, eat half the pack of cookie dough, and allow myself to cry a little.

I barely sleep, but by seven in the morning I have decided to end my pity party. Thankfully, it is my later day at Crossroads, so I do not have to be there until ten. So I throw on my favorite burnt orange workout set and head to the porch. A good workout to kick my butt is exactly what I need. I roll out my mat, turn on some jams, and start my go-to full-body workout. Halfway in I am drenched in sweat and out of breath. Damn South Carolina heat. Even at seven in the morning it is humid as fuck.

"I see you are doing all right." I scream and jump in response. I turn and see Graham standing on his porch, still in uniform, still looking hot as hell.

"Goodness, you scared me." I place my hand over my chest, trying to steady my heart rate.

"Sorry about that. I just got home from my shift, and I heard music. Thought I would check it out."

"Sorry, I will turn it down." I pause the music.

"It's no problem, I was just checking…"

"You do not have to check on me, you know. I am a big girl; I can take care of myself." I may have had a pity party last night, but he doesn't need to know that.

"No, I know you are, I was just...I didn't mean...um, I'm sorry." He runs his hand through his hair and looks down at the ground.

"It's all right, Graham. How was your first night?" I ask, leaning on the railing.

"Good, uneventful, mostly. Just some traffic stops. I should probably get some sleep soon though; I work again tonight."

"Yeah, the five on, two off schedule. I know it well. What are you doing this week? Schedule-wise I mean." I hope that didn't come off as weird as it sounded.

"This is my five days on week, and night shift for the foreseeable future."

I give him a light smile; it is tough schedule. I remember how hard it was for dad growing up. He always adjusted his schedule when he could so that he never felt like he missed anything, but it takes its toll. Dad moving to day shift was a total game changer for our mom. She hated not sleeping at the same time Dad did, but I secretly loved it. The nights when he would stay up were my favorite. I have always had a hard time sleeping, and Dad would never force me to sleep. I think he enjoyed the company just as much as I did.

"It is not for the faint of heart, that is for sure. I will let you get some sleep," I glance down at my watch; I am running behind to get ready for work. "I have to get ready to go into work myself."

"Where do you work? Sorry, I know you need to go."

"No, it's fine, I always love talking about my work. I own a café and bookstore with my friend Ivy. It's called Crossroads. You should come by. We have the best coffee in town, and I recommend the best books." I smile with pride.

"Is that so? Well, I will have to come check it out. I will see you around, Winry," he smiles back. Man, his smile makes my stomach turn in knots; I want to learn more about him, but I have a feeling that will lead to a whole lot of trouble.

I make my way back inside and quickly get ready. I push off calling my sisters about what transpired last night. They will be glad it's over with Flynn, but I do not feel like answering the million questions they will have.

I get to work right at ten. Ivy and Abigal have been here since we opened at seven. "Hey, beautiful ladies," I holler as I walk in; Abigal is at the front desk, so I make my way to the kitchen to find Ivy.

"Hey, you look rough," Ivy calls out my lack of effort in my appearance yet again.

"Gee, it's like a hug," I set my stuff down and hop on the counter next to Ivy. She is currently mixing up some frosting for some of her signature strawberry cupcakes.

"I call it like I see it, babe. What's wrong?"

"I broke up with Flynn last night. We got into a screaming match in the parking lot after he got wasted at Bluebird's." I fill her in on all of the details of our argument.

I conveniently leave out the part about my extremely sexy neighbor coming to help me.

Ivy stops in the middle of mixing, and with an astonished look on her face says, "My goodness, Win. Are you good?"

"Yeah, I'm good, I actually am. I had a pity party, but I feel better. I knew he was not the one, so it is good that it is over."

"Well, good. I didn't like him anyway." She goes back to mixing.

"Yes, I am aware."

"Have you told your sisters yet? I have a feeling they will be a mixture of happy and wanting to riot for him yelling at you."

"I haven't told them yet; I have not had the energy that that requires."

"Ha, I am sure. Want to lick the spoon?"

"Obviously. Let's move on to better topics, like what we are going to do for our one-year anniversary of Crossroads in September."

"Winry, it is the middle of June. We have a couple months," she rolls her eyes at me. What can I say? I like to have a plan. "Why don't we plan something for your birthday first," she retorts.

Now it is my turn to roll my eyes. I have never enjoyed my birthday. I like to plan but not for my birthday. Something always goes wrong. So far, I have been dumped twice, gotten in a car wreck that resulted in a broken leg, and was literally left at a park at Disneyworld for a couple of hours. "Why don't we save ourselves the trouble of that monstrosity and pretend it is a normal day and maybe the sky won't start falling?"

"You are so dramatic. So you have had a few bad birthdays."

"A few? Ivy, one birthday, my whole party got food poisoning from some shady bakery that Mom found."

Ivy shudders at the memory, "Yeah that one was pretty bad."

"Exactly, July 20th is better off alone," I jump down from the counter. "I will stay in my apartment alone like I have for the past few years. I will make cookie dough, drink my wine, read a good book, maybe do some writing, and let the day go on."

Ivy calls me a party pooper on my way up to the front desk, where Abigal is checking someone out with one of our "blind date with a book" books. I got the idea off TikTok, and it has been doing well. "Thank you; come back and let us know how you like your book."

"Hey Abigal, I am here if you want to head out early." I offer.

"Really? That would be great, I have got a test today and I would like to review my notes."

"Yeah, it is no problem. Good luck on your test."

The rest of the day goes pretty smoothly. We have been getting more and more regulars coming back, and it is so good to see. Crossroads is right in the middle of town, so we get good foot traffic. The space is perfect for us. We have the books to the right on shelves that my dad made, and we have some tables in front with some specials like the "blind date with a book," a spicy section, and sales. Then the bakery is set up to the left with the kitchen in the back. For the furniture, Ivy and I ran all over South Carolina thrifting couches, tables, and chairs. It gives off a very hodgepodge boho vibe that is a perfect mixture of me and Ivy.

When our day comes to an end at six, I decide to do a joint call with my sisters to fill them in on what transpired last night on my drive home. I will again leave out Graham's involvement. They will see right through me and try to push me to get with him. I start calling, and they both answer almost immediately.

"Hey, Win," Wyla answers.

"What's up, good looking?" Waverly adds.

"I just wanted to fill y'all in that Flynn is no more."

"Praise the Lord," Waverley sings. "Give me the details, honey."

"Well, we may have got into a small argument in the parking lot at Bluebird's when he got wasted and tried to drive home. It's okay though. I ended it, and he took a cab home." I try to keep it short and simple.

"Oh, gosh, Winry. Why didn't you call us last night?" Wyla asks, I can hear the concern in her voice.

"I am good, guys, really. I'm not even sad; it needed to end. Do I wish it ended a little more amicably? Yes, but I am just relieved it is over," and I really was. Last night's pity party really helped me feel better. Sometimes you just need a good cry. My sisters stay silent for a beat, but then they jump straight into "we hate Flynn" mode. They both hammer out some good curse words to describe Flynn and threats of what they would do if they saw him out in town.

"All right, down girls," I interrupt their rants. "He is an asshole, but let's not breakout the voodoo doll yet," I tease.

"Okay, but now it is time to get you a real man, Win," Waverley exclaims.

"No, no guys, consider this my loving-being-by-myself era." I need to be by myself for a bit after this. These last few days have made me reevaluate my mentality. I want to stand on my own two feet better. I need to.

"I love that, Winry. Let's do girls night this week," Wyla suggests.

"Yes, karaoke at Bluebird's Saturday," Waverley loves karaoke, and Wyla and I do it for her, but we aren't terrible singers either.

I end the call and decide to treat myself to some enchiladas from our local Mexican restaurant. By the time I make it home, Graham's car is gone, and for some reason I am disappointed I won't get to see him tonight. I scarf down my food, and naturally I am still restless. I decide to do some yoga on the porch and then decide to do a little reading before I fall asleep right there on the couch.

Chapter 6

Winry

The week passes in a blur. I keep myself busy at Crossroads, and Graham and I pass by each other a few times, but we just wave and go on with our days. I know it is for the best, but I can't help but be downhearted about it. I know his off days this week were Wednesday and Thursday because I may have checked for his car a few days, so that meant he was working this weekend.

Ivy and I take turns leaving early over the weekends, and thankfully Saturday is my early day, so I sneak out by three. I make my way back to my place and start my usual daily chores: the dishes, some laundry, check on my plants. I go out back to tidy up the porch, and Blackjack does another sneak attack.

"Hey there, Blackjack. We need to go over how you greet people in the South." He starts to meow and rub up against my legs. "Okay, buddy, let's get you some food."

"So, do you always talk to cats or just this one?" I jump and scream, startled by Graham for the second time. "Sorry, I really do not mean to scare you," he tries to sound apologetic, but I definitely sense amusement in his tone.

"No, you are fine, I am just jumpy. And yes, I talk to all animals when I can." I smirk.

"Hmm yeah, I can see that. Who is this little guy? I thought it was a no pets apartment."

"Technically he is not an official pet. I tried, but Blackjack is a free cat. He likes coming and going, so I just feed him when he comes around and take him to the vet every October for his shots."

"That sounds like a pet, Winry," he laughs, and I love it. "Why Blackjack?"

"Well, he is all black for starters, and my family loves playing blackjack."

"Oh really, a chief who gambles," he is smiling again, and it makes me feel all warm inside.

"Well, if you count using coins as gambling, then yes. I am pretty good if we are being honest, I have wiped the floor with my dad several times," I say cockily.

"Now that I would pay to see."

"Are you working tonight?" I ask, as if I do not already know the answer.

"Yeah, start at seven." He runs his hands over his face, then yawns. "What do you have planned for this weekend?"

"Let's see, tonight is sister karaoke night at Bluebird's, and sister time will continue into tomorrow because we meet every Sunday morning around nine at Crossroads."

"Winry doing karaoke. I changed my mind; that is what I would pay to see."

I can't help but blush, "Hey, I am not too bad, but my sister Waverley is really the star when it comes to karaoke."

"Well, I am sad I will miss it tonight."

We fall silent. So I couldn't date this man—it would be too complicated—but we could be friends. I could settle for friends, right? He speaks up first, "I will let you get back to it, Winry. I will talk to you later."

I know he means that we will eventually talk later—we are neighbors—but I can't help but feel like a giddy little schoolgirl about it. "Right, talk to you later."

I meet my sisters at Bluebird's at seven. It feels a little weird being here. Everyone in town comes to Bluebird's, and I do not want to have a run-in with Flynn, especially with my sisters around. I scan the bar to find my sisters, and thankfully no Flynn.

"Winry!" Waverley yells from the back of the bar, waving. I laugh and make my way to their table. Karaoke is already in full swing; a couple is up on stage now doing

"You're the One That I Want" from Grease. They are not too bad, but they are taking it way too seriously. Karaoke is all about fun; if you aren't absolutely making a fool of yourself, you are not doing it right.

"Hey guys," I give both my sisters a hug and kiss.

"You ready to sing some of The Chicks? I am feeling 'Goodbye Earl' tonight. I already put our names on the list," Waverley is thrilled to be here right now.

"Oh yes, that one is one of my favorites," Wyla says, just as eager.

"Sounds good to me, but I am definitely going to need a celebratory shot for no more Flynn in my life."

"Brilliant," Waverly jumps up. "I will go get three shots of whiskey from the bar."

"So are you really okay, Winry?"

"Yes Wyla, I promise I am fine. Us breaking up was a good thing." I take my seat across from her.

"I know that, but that does not mean that it can't suck also. I mean, you didn't even wallow for the standard three days."

"I swear I am good; I gave myself the night to feel sad for myself, and I decided that was all he was worth." I dust my hands of him.

"Okay if you say so." I know Wyla wants to push more. My whole family likes to tiptoe around my mental health like it's a ticking time bomb or something. Thankfully, I do not have to dwell on that thought long because Waverley returns with the three shots.

"Here we go, sisters. To being single and living our best lives with or without men." She passes them out then raises her glass.

"Amen to that," I say as I raise my glass then throw it back.

"So, Winry, have you met your new neighbor yet?" Waverley asks with a post-shot look on her face.

"Um, yeah, I have. He is actually one of Dad's new officers, but I have not really seen him much. You know, police schedule and all." It is only half a lie really; I mean, what defines "much"?

"But you have seen him, right? What does he look like, how old is he?" Waverley has always been the nosey one.

"I do not know, I mean I guess he is kind of attractive, he seems a little older than us," I do my best to deflect.

"You guess? Kind of? Winry, come on."

"I am serious, look, I have hardly spoken to him," I lie.

Before they can ask any more questions, my saving grace comes. The DJ calls our names for us to head up to the stage. We head up there and, to put it lightly, we kill it; as usual, we have Waverley to thank. Something about her energy is infectious, and it spreads out to the crowd. We get so caught up in our night that, thankfully, the topic of Graham doesn't come up again.

The next morning, I meet my sisters again, but this time at Crossroads, and we all seem to be suffering a bit of a hangover. I technically work today, but Abigal is going to cover the morning shift with Ivy, and I will take over after my sisters leave.

"Someone remind me whose idea it was to take shots of whiskey last night," Wyla asks while rubbing her temples. "Because I hate them."

"It was Winry's idea to take shots," Waverley accuses me like she was an innocent bystander.

"Um, I believe it was your idea for them to be whiskey," I fire back.

"I hate you both then," Wyla groans.

"You love us," I challenge her disdain for us.

"I guess, but never again will I drink whiskey." We laugh knowing that we will all drink whiskey again. Sometimes you just need the strong stuff.

"Anyway, I was thinking we should—" Wyla starts to change the subject, but Waverley cuts her off.

"Who is that? Oh, come to momma, that man is gorgeous."

I turn to look, and I see Graham, looking just like Waverley said, gorgeous. Why does this man have to be so attractive, and why must he always be around when I put so little effort into my appearance? I am wearing pink biker shorts and an oversized t-shirt. It's our short day open here, so I didn't even bother to put on makeup. Granted, he is just wearing jeans and a t-shirt, but still he looks too good. Graham spots me almost immediately. Crossroads is not very big, and it is not like I can climb under the table and hide from him.

"Winry, he is looking at you," Waverley interrupts my mini panic attack, "Oh, he's coming over."

"Hey, Winry, I thought I would come see your place before I crashed for the day," Graham says as he reaches our table.

"Yeah, I am glad you stopped by," we hold eye contact and again it doesn't feel weird. It's like his eyes just suck me in. Waverly kicks me under the table to snap me out of it.

"Right, these are my sisters, Waverley and Wyla. Waverley, Wyla, this is Graham, my neighbor."

"Oh, this is your neighbor. Hmm," Waverley gives me a look that says I will have some explaining to do when he leaves.

"Um yeah, I am her neighbor," I know he can pick up the weird vibes that my sisters are giving off. "So, what should I order?"

"Well Winry's favorite is an iced Snickers latte with whipped cream," Wyla replies with a smile matching Waverley's. They are enjoying this way too much.

"I'll walk you over to Ivy, our master barista," I say, wanting to pry him away from my sisters.

"It was nice to meet you, Graham," Waverley purrs.

"Yeah, y'all too." He nods at them, then follows me. "So those are the infamous Bennett sisters," Graham smiles.

"Yup, we are a unique bunch," I laugh lightly.

We walk up to the front desk, where Ivy and Abigal are, and I swear their jaws drop at the sight of Graham. "Hey Ivy, this is my new neighbor, Graham. He stopped in to get some coffee."

"Yeah, Winry tells me you make the best in town." His smile is genuine and there is that warm feeling again.

Ivy blushes, "I sure do, what can I get you?"

"I think I will take the Winry special, iced latte with Snickers and whipped cream, right?"

"Yup, that is it. Coming right up, and you should also get a banana chocolate chip muffin, those are also her favorites," Ivy says winking at me.

"Sounds great."

She gets Graham his drink and muffin and we walk back over to the table where my sisters are anxiously waiting.

"Goodness, Win, this drink is going to make me have a sugar high. How am I supposed to sleep now?" Graham says while sipping his coffee. He sets down his drink and muffin to pull my chair out for me.

Do not think too much into it, Win. It's a southern thing.

"Thank you," I smile at him, trying my best to not look at my sisters right now.

"I'd better take this to go and let you guys get back to it. I will see you later, Winry. It was nice to meet y'all."

"Nice to meet you, Graham," my sisters practically sing.

As he walks out, I feel the blatant stares coming from my sisters, and I notice Ivy is making her way over to our table now and pulls up a chair.

"I'm sorry. I believe the words used last night in reference to your new neighbor were, 'I guess, kind of attractive.' Now tell me, what sane person would call him 'kind of attractive'?" Waverley demands.

"Okay, okay. So I may have not mentioned that my neighbor is quite possibly the hottest guy I have ever seen." I continue to fill them in on the day we met, how he tried to step in during the Flynn fiasco, and how we chat on the back porch every now and then. By the end of it, Waverley is smacking my arm as punishment for keeping all of this a secret.

"Why didn't you tell us?" Wyla asks.

"I don't know, because I knew you guys would and will push for me to pursue him, but that will never happen. He works for our dad, and he lives right next door. It's just too messy. Plus, I just talked about making this an era of me, not me and Graham."

"Well, we would push because you need to get laid and actually have orgasms this time around. Something tells me that Mr. Guy Next Door can get the job done, and I mean, come on, Winry, the man practically stared at you the whole time you were here," Ivy gives me a little shove.

"Winry, we just want you to be happy, that's all, and you deserve the best. We don't want to see you push it away because it could be messy," Wyla adds.

"I know y'all do, but I have accepted that with Graham it will just be a friendship and y'all should too," I retort, feeling satisfied that I ended the subject.

"You could be naked friends," Waverley teases.

Chapter 7

Graham

Winry lies next to me in my bed, her dark hair cascades down the pillow. She looks so peaceful and sexy in just one of my t-shirts. I can't hold back anymore, so I pull her into me; her round ass snuggles up against my already hard dick. Why is she so sexy; I just want to hold her here and never let go. Suddenly I am flipped over, and Winry climbs on top, straddling me. She has got a smile on her face, and her lips are demanding to be kissed. I try to pull her down to me, but she places her hand on my chest, pausing me. She grabs the hem of her shirt and begins to lift it over her head and...

Buzz. Buzz. Buzz.

I am pulled from my deep sleep, cursing whoever is calling me right now and interrupting one of my now recurring dreams involving Winry.

Buzz. Buzz.

I begrudgingly reach for my phone and immediately regret it.

"Hi, Mom." I don't even try to hide the fact that I just woke up.

"Oh, am I waking you up? I figured you would be up; it is two in the afternoon Graham." I can hear the judgment in her tone.

"Well, in case you forgot, Mom, I worked nightshift last night. It is going good by the way; I am all settled in. Thank you for your concern." I throw a judgmental tone back.

"Oh, the dramatics, Graham. What I really want to know why you turned Claire away and you have not returned any of her calls or texts all week. Really, Graham, I raised you better than that."

"Mom, Claire and I are not and will not be together. How did she even get my new address?"

"I gave it to her, because my disrespectful son decided to run away to be a police officer and left her behind without any warning."

"I didn't..." I take a deep breath. Arguing with her will just be a waste of time, so I try again. "Mom, listen to me, I will not be getting together with Claire. We were barely together to begin with, we went on a handful of dates, nothing serious."

"Ugh, I don't know how you turned out to be so much like your father, when I tried so hard. That man never worked for our marriage, and he ruined all my plans. Now he is messing you up also." I can hear in her voice that she is about to threaten tears. "I mean you are practically following in his footsteps."

This is her M.O.: disapprove, blame Dad, then cry. "Mom, don't cry, I have barely had any sleep and I don't need the be-better-than-your-father talk. I get that you want me to get married and 'have a better life,' but marriage is not the answer for me. Maybe one day, but not now, and not with Claire."

"I don't understand you sometimes, Graham, I don't know where I went wrong," she cries.

"Okay great talk, Mom, I will talk to you later. Goodbye." I hate being harsh with her, but she doesn't listen to me. Everything is always on her terms. Despite what she thinks, I am not my father. My parents only got married because Dad got her pregnant with me. Getting married because of a pregnancy isn't a bad thing, but it is better when the couple actually love each other. And even though Mom would argue with me, I don't believe they were truly in love with each other. She is right though that Dad never worked for it. If I get married, I will give it my all.

I wish I could go back to sleep and restart that dream with Winry. I have had one every night since the night she broke up with that asshat, but after that phone call I am worked up and frustrated. I put on my running stuff and decide to run a few miles around town. I have gotten a good idea of the town now from riding around all night with Owen, but I haven't really seen it during the day other than going into Winry's place this morning. Without even really thinking about it, I start to head in that direction.

I noticed on the door that they close at three on Sundays, and it was almost that time. I don't know why, but I feel comfortable with her. But I imagine most people do—she just gives off this energy that is infectious. I come up on Crossroads and notice her friend Ivy locking up the store. I look around, but I don't see Winry.

Damn. I missed her.

I try to wave off the feeling of disappointment. I mean really, what is going on with me? I have never wanted to be around someone so much, and I don't even really know a ton about her. I need to let this go. I know I can't pursue her, and Winry seems like the type to want the whole package. I definitely am not that. My parents didn't completely turn me off from the idea of marriage and a family, I just didn't know if they were things I wanted. They are a bunch of work, and I want to focus on my career right now. I am finally doing something I enjoy. So it is decided: friends only with Winry. It is for the best, for both our sakes.

I make my way back to my place, and I am drenched in sweat and on the verge of a heat stroke. It's the middle of June, and it is hot. I head straight for the shower; I don't need anyone to tell me that I stink from that five-mile jog. I let the water run over me and my mind wanders off to that dream I had earlier. Didn't I just agree to stop thinking about her so much? But it was too late. I was already hard, and judge me all you want, but I knew I wouldn't be able to have the real her, so what is the harm in this? I grip my dick and brace myself against the bathroom wall and pick up where my dream ended off. It doesn't take long to find my release. As soon as I get out of the shower, I check my phone, and man was that a mistake.

Dad: Your mom called me yelling and crying blaming me for how you have grown up to be just like me. Can't please that woman. Never get married, son.

Mom: I'm sorry I cried, but you need to settle down, Graham, you are not getting any younger and neither am I. You will regret letting go of Claire, so call her.

Claire: Your mom called me and said you wanted to have dinner but have been busy. I will bring over some take out tonight. Be there around 5. <winky face emoji>

Oh no, no, no. What time is it, and then I hear the doorbell.

Well shit.

I throw on some sweats and a t-shirt. This is not going to end well. Why would my mother do this? Scratch that, I know why. Still, I can't believe she actually took it upon herself to talk Claire into coming back here. I make my way to the door and when I open it, I am met with warm hazel eyes and a dimple chin. All of my frustration immediately dissipates.

"Hey, I realized that I never brought over a welcome-to-the-apartment gift. So I made some of my homemade cookie dough and thought you would like some." She holds out a container and I take it from her.

"You didn't have to do this. You made this from scratch? I thought Ivy was the Crossroads baker."

"Yeah, I'm not too bad in the kitchen, but it's not very hard. I will have to teach you sometime," she gives a nervous laugh. I want to keep talking to her, but just as she is about to say something else Claire pulls in.

"Oh sorry, I didn't know you were going to have company. I will get out of your way." Winry's voice changes from her usual honey-sweet tone to something flat.

"No, it's not like..." I want to tell her nothing is going on, but I am interrupted.

"Graham," Claire hollers. "Can you help me carry in the food; I got your favorite lasagna from the Italian place back home."

"Yeah, I'm coming." Winry goes to walk away, but I grab her arm. "Why don't you join us?"

"What?" both Claire and Winry say at the same time.

"Yeah, stay. I mean we ought to get to know each other, why not over food?"

"Um, Graham, I only got food for me and you," Claire says, completely unhappy with what I have suggested.

"Yeah, I am not going to intrude on your night, Graham."

"No, I insist. I'll share my food, the to-go orders are always too much anyway," I shrug.

Winry looks at me confused; she thinks Claire is here for a date and I am not okay with that. Claire is staring absolute daggers in the side of my head, but I hold Winry's gaze.

"Um, okay," she agrees.

"Great. Winry, this is Claire, a friend from my town where I grew up. Claire, this is my neighbor Winry." Claire looks at me like I just shot her. I feel a little bad about doing this; she didn't know that my mom orchestrated this whole thing without me knowing.

"Hi, it's nice to meet you," Winry holds out a hand for Claire, but she doesn't return it.

"Right, well, we'd better get this food inside," Claire replies tightly.

The awkwardness is so thick I think I could cut it with a knife. We walk into my apartment and get the food unloaded on the coffee table. I grab an extra plate to share my food with Winry. I lied when I said I wouldn't be able to finish all of this lasagna. Claire was right that it is my favorite. I don't mind sharing with Winry though, but I know I will still be hungry later.

I take my seat on the couch, I set Winry's plate next to mine, and before Winry can make it to sit, Claire slides right into the spot I wanted for Winry. She gives Claire a fake smile and grabs her plate to take it over to the side chair, literally as far away as she can sit from me, and I hate it.

"So, Graham, your mom said you have been working a lot this week. Will you always work this much? When will we ever see each other?" Claire set her plate down on the coffee table. She never really ate much when we were together, and that bothered me; I wanted to tell her to eat. But I knew she wasn't here for that; she and my mom had one goal for tonight, and it did not include eating or Winry.

"No, it can be a weird schedule, so it's five on, two off. One week I work five days and the other I only work two days. It rotates every weekend too."

"Oh, so you will be off this weekend, right? So, you could come home, and we could have dinner with your mom too. She would love that." Claire places her hand on my thigh.

"Sorry, Claire, I already have plans this weekend." I look over at Winry, who has not made eye contact with me since we came inside. She is just eating her food, avoiding my stare.

"Really? What are they?"

"Winry's dad is the Chief of Police here, and he is having a barbecue this weekend, so I will be going to that."

"You're coming?" Winry asks. Why does she have that deer in headlights look?

"Well, it is for the police department, and I am one of his officers." I say it out loud to remind myself also.

"Right. So, Wendy, what do you do?"

"It's Winry, but thanks for asking, Carol." I really do try to hold in my laugh, but one slips out and Claire gives me the evil eye. Winry finally looks at me and gives a small smile then continues, "I own a bookstore and café in town. It's named Crossroads if you are ever back in town."

"Yes, I will have to come check it out. Graham, will you take me?" Claire asks, and just like that Winry stares back down at her plate and starts eating again.

The rest of the night mostly involves Claire talking about any and every date we ever went on, which was only four by the way, but Claire somehow made it seem like we had a full-on relationship going for months. It didn't help that she knew so much about me from my mom, so I am sure to Winry it seems like we are a couple. She has barely spoken, and she still won't look at me.

"Well, thank you for having me for dinner. It was…nice, but I am going to get back over to my place." Winry gets up and places her empty dish in the kitchen. "It was nice to meet you, Claire, and I guess I will see you this weekend, Graham." She gives a tight smile and heads for the door.

"Winry, why don't you let me walk you over?" I don't want her to leave like this; I want Winry to always be happy.

"It is just next door; you could probably hear me open and close my door. I will be fine, Graham."

"Yeah, Whitney will be fine."

"Her name is Winry, Claire." I give her a look saying cut it out, and she seems to heed my warning because she doesn't object when I stand to walk Winry to her side.

Once we are out the door, I decide it's best to start with an apology. "Hey, I am so sorry I dragged you into that. I know it was awkward."

"It's fine, Graham. Really you don't have to walk me over. I thought we had covered that I'm capable of taking care of myself." The shy smile she gives me makes me feel at a little more at ease, but I want to see it like it normally is. The one that made me completely enamored with her.

"I know you are, but I want to."

"Okay."

How do I tell her that there is nothing between me and Claire? She made it sound so convincing. Why am I so concerned about it? I mean we aren't together, so why do I feel like I need to explain myself? I have this internal conflict for the fifteen steps it takes to get to her door.

"Here we are, thanks for the food. Good night." She opens her door and walks in; she looks over her shoulder for a moment and gives me another shy smile.

"Um, yeah. Good night."

On the short walk over, I kick myself for not stopping her and explaining what happened tonight, but first I need to straighten things out with Claire. It wasn't fair that my mom was filling her head with ideas that we would get together. I needed to be honest with her; Claire isn't a bad person and needs someone who will give her the attention she deserves.

I walk in the door, and Claire is still sitting on the couch but now has a bottle of wine on the table and two glasses.

"Oh, I hope you don't mind I brought some wine and thought we could have some together."

"That's fine, listen I do want to talk to you about some things."

"Can't it wait, Graham? I want to enjoy this time with you."

"No, Claire, that wouldn't be fair to you. I need you to know…"

"Graham, stop. I know what you are trying to say," I take the seat next to her and she takes my hands, "but please, why won't you give us a chance?"

"I'm sorry. I really am, but it's not fair to lead you on, and my mom has not been helping. It is just not going to work out, I don't want a relationship right now."

"Oh, please. I saw how you were looking at her all night Graham. If you are going to break up with me, at least be honest about it."

"I am being honest. For one, there is nothing going on between me and Winry." She scoffs. "And two, there never really was an 'us.' We went on a few dates; I told you before

I left that I did not want a relationship. I'm sorry my mom has been filling your head about us getting together, but it's just not where I am at right now."

"Sure Graham, whatever you want to tell yourself to help you sleep. Do you not see how embarrassing tonight was for me? To come all this way, with your favorite food just for you to invite your neighbor over, and you literally stare at her the entire time. I mean, she didn't even speak, and you were captivated by her. Why can't you look at me like that? We could be so good together, but you won't even try." Tears threatened her eyes. Oh no, I'm not good with tears.

"Claire, look I think you're great I really do, it's just…"

"Not going to work, I get it. I am not her. You know what, I am going to go. I hope you have a good life, Graham." We both stand, and I walk her to the door.

I don't know what to say. I feel like anything I say will just make it worse, so I just leave her with a last "I'm sorry." She doesn't acknowledge it and I don't blame her. She gets in her car and drives off.

I need some air. And a beer. This night was brutal. Claire was right, I'm interested in Winry. I can't help it, and it sucks because there is no way I can date my boss's daughter. I just know I want her around, and maybe just being friends will be enough.

I grab one of the beers out of the fridge, and head out to the back porch. I have got to get my mind off Winry. I am out there for five minutes, and then somehow, I find myself at her front door.

Chapter 8

Winry

I enter my apartment after what was one of the most awkward nights of my life.

Wine. I need wine.

I make my way to the kitchen and grab a glass and the bottle from the fridge. While I'm in there, I notice the bowl of cookie dough and my mood immediately picks up. I settle in on the couch and turn on the TV but decide to call my sisters first.

"Hey, Win," Wyla answers first.

Then Waverly, "Hello, dear sisters."

"So, would you guys like to hear about how I just spent my last two hours?"

"Of course we would," Wyla answers.

"So, I decided to make some cookie dough and thought I would take some over to Graham."

"Oh, is this going to get steamy? Please tell me it gets steamy," Waverley begs.

"It goes the complete opposite of steamy." They both groan in despair. "I go over there, and we are talking, things are going well, but then Claire, his girlfriend, shows up."

"No, he is not supposed to have a girlfriend," Waverley cries.

"Well, he does, and I just spent the whole dinner listening to her call me the wrong name and tell me all about the dates he takes her on." I take a big sip of my wine.

"Oh Win, that must have been terrible," Wyla sympathizes.

"It totally sucked, but I mean why am I so bothered by this? I mean..."

Knock. Knock.

"Hold on someone is at my door." I set down my glass and stand up.

"Keep us on the line, what if it is a murderer?" Wyla whispers like someone else could hear her.

"Wyla, why would a murderer knock?"

"I don't know, just keep us on the phone."

"Okay, okay." I reach the door and hesitate to open it.

Damn it, Wyla.

I shake those chills off and open the door to find Graham standing on the other side.

"Hey, I'm sorry, is this a bad time? I didn't know if I could talk to you for a bit," Graham rambles.

"Um, yeah. Hey, guys I will call you later, okay?"

"Who is it? Is it Graham? I bet it's Graham." I try to hold in my smile while Waverley rattles off, "Winry Ann Bennett, you'd better call us when he leaves."

I open the door wide, motioning Graham to come in. "Okay I got to go; I love you both."

"Love you," they sing in unison, and I hang up my phone.

I turn to Graham, who is acting fidgety in my living room, "What's up, Graham? Is everything okay?"

"Um yeah, I, um, I just wanted to clear the air about dinner. Can we sit?"

"Sure." We both sit on the couch, but I am careful not to sit too close.

"First, Claire is not my girlfriend. My mom told her I wanted to have dinner with her but have been too busy and to just show up because it was my day off."

"Okay..." I don't really know how to respond to that. "Graham, you don't have to explain yourself, it was an awkward dinner, it's no big deal."

"No, it is, I asked you to stay and put you in that position so I wouldn't have to be alone with her and I should not have done that. You barely looked my direction the whole night."

"I'm not mad at you, if that is what you are worried about. Look, why don't we just start this night over?" He watches me as I stand and walk into the kitchen grabbing an extra spoon. "Do you want a beer or a glass of wine?"

"Uh, beer please."

I grab the beer and head back into the living room. "Here you go," I say, handing him the beer as I sit back down next to him. I lean up and grab the bowl of freshly made cookie dough. "All right, hey, Graham I made some cookie dough as a welcome to the apartment gift, would you like some?"

His smile is something I don't think I will ever tire of, and he is smiling at me right now. I have a need to clench my legs together, feeling aroused instantly.

Is it hot in here?

"Yeah, I would, thanks. So, what are we watching?" He has relaxed now; it feels natural for him to be here.

I look at the TV where I had it paused to call my sisters. "I was watching *Friends,* but I have watched this show start to finish at least ten times, so we can watch something else."

"You have watched it at least ten times," he says stunned.

"Oh, at least ten, if not more. My mom loved this show, has all the DVDs, so my sisters and I watched it constantly. It's my comfort show." I press play.

"So, tell me, cookie dough or ice cream?" he asks as he passes me the bowl.

"If it is not already obvious, cookie dough hands down," I say as I scoop out another large scoop.

"I normally would say ice cream, but cookie dough is starting to rival it."

"Oh really? What is your flavor?" I pass back the bowl.

"Chocolate. It is a classic." He takes another bite, and I try not to focus too much on his mouth.

"Okay, I can respect that, I wouldn't have been able to accept something like mint or vanilla." I say as I bring my legs up on the couch, getting more comfortable.

He laughs. His laugh only adds to my want for him. "Really, that is where you draw the line? Mint and vanilla?"

"Yes, I cannot stand mint or like peppermint, especially in dessert form. And vanilla is just too plain, it needs something else to pair with it to be good."

"Good to know," he smiles at me, and I stare at his lips. I wonder what it would be like to kiss him. The need to know is so strong that I almost lean in.

No, Winry. Friends, remember.

I pull my gaze away. "So how are you liking Aster Creek? I know it isn't too far from Rosewood, but do you miss home?"

"No, I don't really miss it. It wasn't like there was much holding me there, you know? I think I will like it here much better; I know this great place in town that sells coffee and books, it is one of my new favorite places," he teases.

"Oh, is that so?" I raise my eyebrows.

"I do know the owner, so maybe I could even get a banana chocolate chip muffin on the house for you." He winks and butterflies flutter in my stomach.

"Those are one of my favorites. What is your favorite go to sweet snack?"

"Fudge Rounds, one hundred percent."

"The little Debbie?" I snicker.

"Absolutely, don't hate on fudge rounds. Not everyone can make cookie dough or have a café with delicious muffins."

"That's fair." We grow silent and turn our attention to the TV.

I want to ask so many more questions. I want to know about his family, what his childhood was like. I need to know more, but I don't want to pry either. We haven't even clarified what this is between us.

"Man, it is midnight, I'd better get out of here and let you sleep. I'm not going to force my night schedule on you."

"It's okay, I wouldn't be sleeping right now even if you weren't here. My dad calls me his moon baby because I would never sleep. I still don't sleep very well. Plus, I don't work on Mondays. You can still go if you want to though." I try not to sound too clingy, but I want him to stay. I like him being here.

"Yeah, okay. I'll stay." He looks at me and I feel everything: the butterflies, the heat—our chemistry is tangible.

"Okay, good." I force myself to turn away from his gaze. It's for the best, I remind myself.

We watched the TV for a couple hours. I don't remember drifting off, but I woke up the next morning on the couch covered up with a throw and Graham was gone.

I check my phone. It's eight in the morning, and I already have several messages from both of my sisters. I push off replying to them. I want to enjoy how I feel this morning. I have never fallen asleep so easily. Usually I am tossing and turning until I tire myself out. Even after I fall asleep, I usually don't sleep that deeply; my bed usually looks like I did flips all night.

I am in such a good mood, I get all of my daily to-do list done within the hour and then do an hour workout on the porch, while Blackjack sunbathes next to me. Around midmorning I hear another knock at my door. I know it is not likely Graham, but my heart beats a little faster at the idea of seeing him again so soon.

I answer the door and it is none other than my sisters and mom in tow.

"Hey, I didn't realize we were having a party," I say as I let them in.

"Well, we didn't actually plan this, I actually pulled up at the same time as your sisters. I was in town and wanted to get some Winry time. I don't know what these strays are doing here."

We all gather in the living room; Mom and I take the couch, and my sisters take the love seat by the window.

"Oh, Winry knows what we are doing here. She keeps ignoring our texts. Why is that, Winry? Is there something you don't want to tell us about last night?" Waverley has always been the pusher of the group, always so nosey.

"What happened? Are you okay?" Mom panics.

"I'm fine, Mom. There is no need to worry. Waverley is just being a brat."

"But something happened last night?" The panic still hasn't left Mom's tone.

"It's nothing really, Waverley is making something it's not, Mom. My neighbor Graham just came over last night and hung out. Nothing happened."

"Her neighbor that is beyond gorgeous and totally likes her," Waverley sings.

"But remember, Waverley, he has a girlfriend. Right?" Wyla looks at me for confirmation.

"Well, actually he doesn't. He came over here last night to tell me they weren't together and apologize for how terrible that dinner was." I try to contain my smile by biting my lip, but it slips.

"Hold on, I feel like I am chapters behind. Winry, aren't you still with Flynn?"

Poor Mom, I hadn't told her about any of this because I knew she would worry, and she can't keep a secret from Dad. I knew she would end up telling him about his new cop that his daughter is interested in. I spend the next ten minutes filling Mom in on everything that has happened this past week.

"Well, first, I am glad things with Flynn are over. He just wasn't the one; your dad and I knew it right away. And second of all, Winry, why don't you pursue thigs with Graham, I agree with your sisters that he likes you too. If you are worried about your dad, don't be. You are both adults, Win, he wouldn't be weird about it."

"I would be weird about it. I mean, let's just say we do get together..."

"Which you should," both Wyla and Waverley say.

"Even if, what if we break up? We live next to each other. It's not like with Flynn where I may run into him in town once in a blue moon. No, there is a high chance that I would run into him every day. Plus, with him being one of Dad's guys...Mom, you know Dad, he would so be weird about it, especially if we broke up. The man can't hide his disdain for someone well. We still can't talk about Genevieve Lewis without him talking about how he doesn't like her because she didn't invite us to her tenth birthday party."

"That is a good point," Wyla agrees.

"Thank you."

"Listen, honey, I get it. You're scared to put yourself out there, but you can't live your life off of what ifs." Mom holds my hand and gives it a squeeze.

"Guys, I am not going to pursue Graham, we will be friends, and that is all."

After my declaration of friendship, we changed the subject to lighter topics, such as Waverly's classroom, and Wyla tells us crazy stories from volunteering at the vet clinic. We laugh and overshare. We can talk about anything and it's not weird. Want to talk about sex? No problem. Want to talk about your body? Go right ahead. Open and honest is my family. You need people you feel at home with and who lay it all out there.

The next few days go by fairly quickly. I hang out with Graham again Tuesday night. He claimed he didn't mean to order so much Chinese food. I didn't mind, though. I wanted to hang out with him too. So far, I have learned that his favorite color is blue. He likes to run, go to comedy shows, and watch baseball. He also has his bachelor's in business but hated his nine to five, and he loved a law class he took in college so decided to go to the academy. We stayed up talking until one in the morning, and I had to force myself to leave then. It felt like Graham didn't want me to leave either, but maybe it's just what I want to believe.

It's Thursday night, so he is working now. I hadn't seen him yesterday or today. After dinner, I decide to do one of my nightly workouts with yoga on the porch. I usually do one if I really want to sleep a little better. Something about working out under the moon and stars brings me peace. At the end of the workout, I decide to take a moment to appreciate the night sky. There are some little moments that I have learned to appreciate. One is take in the wind on a warm summer day. Two is always look up at the sky and admire its beauty, especially on a full moon.

I crawl into my bed and wrap myself in my many blankets. I somehow manage to fall asleep around midnight and as soon as I drift off, I hear my door open and slam close. My eyes shoot open, and alarm bells start to go off in my head. Surely, I must have misheard. I thought I had locked the door, but then a thud came from downstairs. I quietly make my way to the rail overlooking the living room. I am both relieved and enraged to see a very drunk Flynn fumbling around. I throw on a pair of sweatpants, grab my phone just in case, and head downstairs.

"Flynn, what are you doing here?" He spins to look at me as I enter the living room, and he nearly falls over his own feet. He looks a mess, his face is all blotchy, and he reeks of vodka. I need to get him out quickly. I don't want a repeat of the last time he got drunk.

"Winry. Hey. I miss you, baby. Don't you think we can start things over?" His words slur and he tries to walk over to me.

I take a few steps back, "Flynn, I'm sorry but you need to leave. You're drunk. Please tell me you didn't drive here."

"No, don't start this again, Winry, I am totally," he burps, "good. I want us together; I know you miss us too." He takes more steps toward me, backing me up against the door.

He is so close now that I can feel his breath on my skin, "Flynn, back up please. Let's just talk for a minute, okay?"

Something in my gut tells me something is off. I slide my phone out of my pocket; holding down the lock and volume buttons, I click on the emergency call option. I slide my phone back in my pocket, knowing that they should send a car out for a suspicious call. I don't want to antagonize him more by letting him know I have called the police.

"I don't really feel like talking, Winry. Honestly, this is part of why we broke up to begin with. You could never just let go and enjoy the moment. Why don't for once you just relax and be quiet?"

"Flynn, I won't tell you again back up." I feel like I could throw up, but I have to give the appearance that I am strong. This looks like it is going to go south, so I pray that they have already sent someone over to check it out.

Before I have time to do anything Flynn takes my face in his hands and crashes his mouth to mine. He pushes farther into me, pinning my legs so I can't lift them up to knee him in the balls. So I take my only option of shoving him as hard as I can manage. Once there is enough distance between us, I deck him in the face just like my dad taught me. Blood starts pouring from his nose.

"You bitch," he barks. I go for the door handle, but he grabs me before I can get out the door and slings me back into the living room. I fall backward and bang my head in the floor.

Shit. I have got to get out of here.

I seriously don't understand what is happening right now. He has never acted to this extreme before. Granted, I never really had been around him when he drank. The only time he really drank around me was when we got into that fight. How did I not see this? I don't have time to dwell on that right now. I roll over and try to get to my feet to race out the back, but Flynn is on top of me before I can reach my feet.

"Why do you do this, Winry? You ruin everything good. I just told you we could get back together. Why are you acting this way?"

"Flynn, let me go," I cry. I am fighting him as hard as I can, but Flynn isn't a small guy. He flips me over, grips my chin hard, and spits on my face.

Everything happens so fast; I don't hear my door bang open, but in an instant Flynn is lifted off me. I can hear them wrestling in my living room, but I can't bring myself to open my eyes. I bring my hands up to my pounding head and try to wipe the mixture of spit and blood off my face. When I finally bring myself to open my eyes, I see Graham and Owen trying to get Flynn in cuffs.

"Graham," I say holding back a sob. He turns to look at me and he looks absolutely feral, but then he softens.

"I got this, go check her out," Owen orders, and Graham rushes to me.

"Winry, are you okay?" He gently puts his hands on my cheeks.

I can't help it, I burst into tears, and he wraps his arms around me as I cry. I feel his grip tighten, pulling me in closer.

I cry for a good minute, and I know I am on the verge of a panic attack.

Okay, Winry, focus. Calm down.

In therapy, I learned that one way to come out of a panic attack is to do a five senses count down.

What can I taste? Some blood in my mouth where Flynn spit on me.

No, keep going, focus on something else.

Okay what can I feel? Graham's warm body holding me tight.

What can I see? Graham's warm chestnut eyes staring down at me.

What can I smell? Graham's body wash. It smells like cedarwood and vanilla.

What can I hear? Graham telling me I am safe.

My breath starts to steady, and my tears slow.

"Do you want to go outside to get some air, or sit on the couch? Owen has him in the patrol car, and we have a paramedic on the way to check you out."

"Couch...just please don't leave me, okay?"

"I won't, Winry, I promise." He helps me stand and we walk over to the couch.

It's this moment I decide I don't want to be just friends with him anymore. I can't ignore my feelings for him. I don't want to.

"Are you okay to tell me what happened, Winry?" Graham holds my hand in his.

"Yeah, I think so," I go through the series of tonight's nightmare and let him know about hitting my head. I have a pounding headache and I'm dizzy; I'm sure I have a mild concussion.

The paramedics arrive as I finish telling him everything. They check me out and confirm a mild concussion. Graham stays with me the whole time, other than to get me a rag to get the blood off my face. Owen comes in to check on me but then leaves to make a phone call. I am positive one is to my dad. I know threats won't work this time to keep this from him.

Just as I suspected, my dad and mom come rushing in my apartment. Mom has pure fear in her eyes, but Dad's have a mixture of fear and fury. Graham stands and lets my parents sit on either side of me.

"Winry, sweetie, are you okay?"

The tears threaten to come back, but I hold it in. "I'm okay, Daddy." I grab his hand; I need someone to ground me, or I will lose it again.

"What happened?" Dad is trying to hold in his anger the best he can.

"Griffin, just give her second. Why don't you talk to the officer and paramedics and find out what happened?" Mom uses her soothing voice to soften Dad's intensity.

Dad gives me a tight squeeze and turns to Graham to be filled in. Thankfully, they walk outside. I don't want to relive it again.

Chapter 9

Graham

I meet Owen at the start of my shift at the station. We make our way through town giving a few tickets that Owen makes me do because "I need practice" apparently.

We make it through town, and a call comes out for a suspicious call that possibly could be a domestic, and when the address is given, my stomach drops.

"That's your address, Taylor." Owen confirms my fears and then he punches the sirens and races to my apartment.

We get there in three minutes flat, and I jump out of the car immediately, running to her door.

Her door is ajar, but I can't really see anything. "Flynn, let me go," is all I need to hear, and I bust in the door. I never really gave much thought about my worst nightmare, but there it is in front of me. Flynn was on top of her, pinning her down, she had blood on her face; her eyes were squeezed shut, and she is doing her best to fight him off.

I yank him off of her and wrestle him to the ground. My sole focus right now is getting cuffs on him and getting him out of here. I'm afraid if I look at Winry, I will lose my cool, and that's not what she needs right now. But when I hear her say my name, I look at her and every fiber of my being just wants to hold her.

"I got this, go check her out," Owen orders.

When I reach her, she lets it all out. My heart feels like it's exploding listening to her cry, so I pull her in closer.

Once her breathing calms, we move to the couch. I need to hold her somewhere, so I take her hand in mine. She is shaking like crazy, and I squeeze her hand tighter. She tells me everything that happened and that when he threw her, she hit her head. When the paramedics get here, I immediately have them check her out, twice. I know that dick will also need to be seen; I'm pretty sure Winry broke his nose. That thought brings a small smile to my face.

I stay glued to Winry's side like she asked. I know Owen called her dad, and it takes no time at all for him and Winry's mom to come screeching in on two wheels. They come barreling in her apartment. I stand up to give them some room, but I don't go far. I don't think I can; it's like I need to see that she is breathing.

They talk for a minute, then Chief Bennett turns to me and pulls me outside and over to where Owen was helping the paramedics look at Flynn, who has all but passed out, he is so drunk.

"What happened?" Chief barks.

"They broke up last week and tonight he decided that was a mistake, so he broke in and when she refused him, he attacked her. Paramedics say she has a mild concussion. They are looking at Flynn now. I think Winry broke his nose."

A smile similar to mine threatens his face at the mention of her breaking his nose. Once Flynn is checked, we get our statement from Winry and are clear to take him in. But the thought of leaving Winry makes me sick. I walk in and lightly knock against the door. Winry hasn't moved, and her mom has her wrapped up in blankets.

She turns to me slowly. "Graham," she says as she stands up and walks over to me.

"I just want to let you know that we are taking him in. I wanted to make sure you are okay."

"Yeah, I think my parents are going to stay here tonight. Thank you for saving me and then staying with me the whole time," and unexpectedly she wraps her arms around me and nestles her head in my chest. I know her dad is watching, but I don't care. I pull her in tightly and breathe her in. She always smells fruity and sweet, like peaches and honey.

Finally, we release each other. "I'll check on you tomorrow, okay?"

She nods as I walk out the door.

The rest of the night drags by, and I can't focus. All I can think about is her face when she first called my name. After tonight I don't think I can push back my feelings anymore. I like Winry, and I want to do something about it.

When I get off work Friday morning, I go check on Winry. I knew I wanted to ask her out, but it seems that her parents are still here and one of her sisters answers the door. So, I decide to push it off.

"Oh, hi. Winry, Graham is here," Waverley hollers.

"Waverley Dawn, I told you to stop yelling. Your sister has a headache," her mom whisper shouts.

Waverley steps aside as Winry comes to the door. She looks effortlessly beautiful in the same beer t-shirt she wore the first time we met, a pair of pajama shorts, and fuzzy socks. "Hey, I wanted to check in and make sure you were doing all right."

"Well, how sweet is that, Win?" Waverley says with a giant smile on her face.

"I think I will talk to you out here." Winry steps out the door, pulling it closed behind her.

"Thank you for coming to check on me. I love my family, but they are driving me crazy."

"I know the feeling," I give her a sympathetic laugh. "Are you okay? I heard your mom say you have a headache."

"Just a small one, I took some medicine, and I am having Abigal cover my shifts at work today and tomorrow."

"Good, good." I shove my hands in my pockets and rock on my feet. "So, listen..."

"Oh Graham, you're here. Great." Winry and I both turn to see her dad standing at her door. "So nice of you to come check on Winry. I didn't know you were neighbors." His tone is neutral. I can't tell if he appreciates that I am here or hates it.

"Dad," Winry looks like she could kill him.

"Are you coming to the cookout tomorrow?" He avoids her glare and stares solely at me.

"Yes, sir. I will be there," I reply. Why am I sweating?

"Great," he says flatly. "Winry, your mom has finished breakfast, why don't you come back in?"

"Okay. Graham, would you like to come in for some breakfast?"

I look at her then look at her dad, my chief. Why does he look like he likes me and hates me at the same time? "Um, that's okay, I should probably get some sleep. I just wanted to make sure you were okay first."

"Thank you, Graham. I'm feeling okay, I promise."

"Okay, good," I study her for a moment. I want to reach out and touch her, but I don't. I step back, give her dad an awkward nod, and make my way back to my apartment.

Chapter 10

Graham

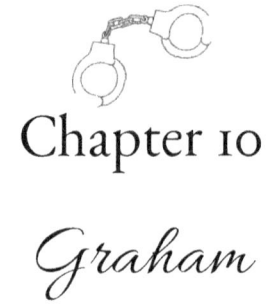

I make it through the night Friday without sneaking over to Winry's place. I'm dying to see her again, but based off how many times I looked out the window for their cars to leave, Winry's parents stayed the night again. By morning, I can't stand it anymore. I have to talk to her before I can even think about sleeping. I shoot off a message to Owen.

Me: Think you can get Winry's number for me?

I wait for what feels like forever for a reply.

Owen: Okay, I got it, care to tell me why you want it? <smiley emoji>

I roll my eyes. Why does he have to be so nosey?

Me: I just wanted to check on her, and her parents still haven't left.

Owen: Scared of her parents or something? I mean, if you are going over there with pure intentions what would be the harm?

Me: Send. Me. Her. Number.

He finally sends her number; I save it and send her a message.

Me: Hey, it's Graham. I got your number from Owen. I just wanted to check on you.

Winry: I'm good other than my family won't leave my house. I feel fine now, no headaches or dizziness but I can't even walk to the kitchen without them being my shadow.

Me: Are you still coming to the cookout tonight?

Winry: Yeah, I will be there. My parents won't let me drive, so I will ride with them. Will you take me home? I love them but I can't handle them at my place anymore ha.

Me: Of course. I'll see you tonight.

I smile at her message; I am way too excited for this cookout to end and it hasn't even started yet.

I arrive at the Bennett home right at six. They live about ten minutes away; that's ten minutes alone with Winry at the end of the night. The house is small, but when I walk around the back there is a nice back porch, and the yard is pretty big. I'm greeted by Winry's mom first.

"Oh, Graham, I don't think I have officially introduced myself. I'm Isabel, Winry's mom, but I'm sure you knew that part. I am so glad you could make it." She opens her arms wide and wraps me in a hug. "Listen, I wanted to thank you for taking care of Winry the other night. I think it shook her up more than she cares to admit. I know it helped you being there."

"Hey, Mrs. Bennett, I was there too. Where is my hug?" I see Owen making his way toward us.

"Owen West, you are a mess. Come here, sugar." She wraps him in a hug too. "All right now boys, you have a good time. Graham, I think Winry is over there at one of the tables," she walks away winking at me.

"See, everyone can see it," Owen smirks.

I give him a light shove in response and make my way over to where she is. I see her sitting with her sisters over on the opposite side of the yard. I take a moment to take her in. She is wearing some black high-top Converses, cutoff shorts, a white ACPD t-shirt, and has a black flannel tied around her waist. Her hair is down in her usual waves, with one side tucked behind her ear. She throws her head back laughing at something her sisters say, and I am mesmerized. I want to hear her laugh and see her smile all the time. I know she can feel me staring at her; she turns to me, still smiling, and waves me over.

I walk over and take the seat next to her, and Owen pulls a chair over next to me. I was so wrapped up in looking at Winry that I didn't even know he was behind me.

"Hello, ladies," Owen greets the sisters.

"Owen, what are you doing here?" Waverley snaps.

"Oh, come on now, firecracker. You know you missed me."

"I told you to stop calling me that," Waverley snaps back at him.

"All right, I feel like I am missing something," I lean over to Winry.

"Well, their relationship is complicated," she replies.

"No, no, no relationship here, I just can't stand him," Waverley says, annoyed. Her arms are crossed and gives Owen her best evil eye.

"Wav here is just upset that she can't have me," Owen teases but Waverley is not amused.

"No, like I said, I just can't stand you."

"Okay, children that's enough," Wyla cuts in. "Owen likes to push Waverley's buttons, and Waverley is holding a grudge because last Fourth of July a group of us went out to the beach and were going to shoot some fireworks. One of the fireworks fell over and went off right at Waverley. Owen tackled her so it didn't hit her, but when he did, he accidentally untied her swim top so she flashed the whole group."

"It wasn't an accident, and it was so embarrassing. We are not talking about it anymore."

Owen gets ready to either defend himself or say something stupid, most likely both.

"All right, we won't, Wav," Winry says, hushing Owen and making her sister relax just a little. "Let's talk about how Wyla and I are going to win the annual cornhole tournament like we do every year."

"Nope, not this year. I am finally going to beat you two." Owen claps my back, "I have a new partner this year."

"Like that will help. You are the one who sucks," Waverley jabs Owen.

"Yeah, Wyla and I kick your ass every year," Winry adds. "What about you, you any good?" She nudges me and I'm tempted to pull her into me.

"I'm not too bad; I think you may actually have to work for it this time," I nudge back.

We fall into casual conversation. Several people from the department are here. Winry says that her dad likes to do this every summer and whoever can make it makes it. Chief Bennett has been on the grill the entire time I have been here, but every now and then I can feel him staring a hole in my head. I know I should probably move around and socialize with more people in the department since I am new and all, but I can't help it. I don't want to leave her side.

After eating, they announce that the cornhole tournament is going to start soon. They have two games set up to help move things along. Winry and Wyla are dominating at the first setup, and I carry Owen round after round on the second. I knew I wasn't terrible at this game, but I have never played this well before. I guess when the stakes are playing against Winry, I step it up.

Owen and I win the first four games. We just have to beat one more team, and we can play Winry. Our new opponents walk up, and it's Winry's parents. Mrs. Bennett comes up to stand on my side with a warm smile.

Thank goodness.

"Actually Isabel, I play better on this side. Why don't you stand by Owen?" Chief says, walking up to switch with her.

Well, shit.

"How are you doing, Taylor?"

"Good, sir, having a good time." I have never really had to give much thought to girls' fathers before, mostly because I knew I would never meet them. This time I guess I want to go all out and date my boss's daughter.

"Great, that's great." Awkward tension fills the air. I want this man to like me and not just as his employee. I want him to see me as someone good enough to date his daughter.

"Winners go first," he says, motioning me to start.

I throw and manage to get two in the hole, but then Chief sinks two in behind me. Well, this is not going to be as easy as I had hoped. We are up, then we are down, now we are tied. I hear squeals of joy and laughter at the other setup. Winry and Wyla are jumping up and down and doing a victory dance for beating the last opposing team. I must have been staring for too long because chief says, "You aren't going to win if you keep staring at my daughter, Taylor."

"Right, sorry sir," I reply sheepishly looking down at the ground.

He throws his sack and sinks it, "So you like Winry, huh?"

I try to remain calm, but I am panicking, I haven't even told her I like her yet. My immediate instinct is to deny and deflect, but I know he will be able to see right through me, and I think lying to him will just make it worse. "Yes, sir, I do," I say as I sink in my next one.

"Little bold, don't you think? Coming into a new job and trying to date the boss's daughter," he sinks another.

"It wasn't my intention, sir," I throw, and I miss. "I don't want to do anything that will jeopardize my position as one of your officers. I enjoy my job, but I like Winry. It would do me no good to lie to you."

"I respect that," he throws his last sack and also misses. Owen and I are now down two points; the score is 19 to 17. They just need two more points to win. Mrs. Bennett isn't as good as Chief, but she is better than Owen. Winry and Wyla come up next to their mom to cheer her on; whoever wins here plays them next.

"Come on, Mom, kick his ass," Winry shouts.

"My daughters mean the world to me; I didn't care for the last guy she dated, and I didn't say anything about it, and look how that turned out."

"I would never hurt her," I add quicky because I would never ever hurt her.

"I know that you would never hurt her physically, Taylor. It's emotionally I worry about; Winry likes to put on that she is strong and nothing gets to her, but it does. More than you probably think it does. I won't tell you about her struggles; that's hers to tell. However, I raised her to be independent. She doesn't need some to take care of her. She needs a rock, a constant, someone to be her partner and biggest supporter. You two are adults; I won't stand in your way. Just think about what you have to offer her before you do anything about it."

I give him a nod. I don't want to think about that right now, mostly because I'm afraid of the answer. Mrs. Bennett makes her first two sacks on the board and Owen misses his first two, which means if he doesn't make at least one on the board, we lose.

"Come on, Owen, just one on the board," I yell.

"Hey, I got this," but, in fact, he did not; he misses his last two and we lose. The girls jump up and down, ecstatic for their parents.

Chief claps me on the back. "Good game. Think about what I said, okay?" He walks over to his wife, picking her up and twirling her.

Winry walks over to me, "Chin up, sugar. Don't worry, Wyla and I will take them down." I manage a fake smile. She places her hand on my shoulder, "You all right?"

"Yeah, I'm good, just bummed I don't get a chance to take you down a peg."

"In your dreams, buddy," she smiles, but I know she can tell that my mood has changed. My original plan was to ask her out on our way back home, but now I'm not so sure.

Just like Winry said, she and Wyla take their parents down 21–15. It was brutal. Watching it put me in a slightly better mood, seeing her so focused and determined to win. She was just attacked by her ex and had a concussion, but here she was just as happy as she could be, and absolutely killing it at cornhole. By the time the tournament ends, it's starting to turn dark and they get a fire going for s'mores.

"Hey, I made you a s'more," Winry says, with two s'mores in her hands, and sits next to me.

"Awesome, thank you." I take the s'more and nearly eat the whole thing in one bite.

"So, you have survived your first Bennett family cookout. What did you think?"

"I think that your dad makes the best burgers, always have you as my cornhole partner, and never have Owen as my partner ever again." I laugh.

"Ha, yeah, you carried his ass the whole time. Are you still good to take me back home? If not, that's okay. I can see if Waverley can take me," she stammers.

"No, I can take you. Are you ready to go?" I finish my s'more, and she's on her last bite.

"Whenever you are is good with me."

"Okay, let's head out." I stand and pull her up.

"Let me just tell everyone bye."

We walk back to the porch where her family is.

"Okay, we are leaving," she says as she starts giving out hugs.

"Who's we? Are you leaving with your sister?" Her dad asks as she hugs him.

My palms start to sweat.

"No, Graham is going to take me; you know, since we live in the same building." Winry rolls her eyes at him.

Chief gives me a look that I can't read, "I can take you home, Winry."

"Griffin don't be silly—they live right next to each other. Graham, you'll get her home safe, right?" Mrs. Bennett gives me a warm smile.

"Yes, ma'am, it's no problem really." I walk over to her dad. "Thank you for having me, Chief, Mrs. Bennett." I reach my hand out and he shakes it, thankfully.

"Glad you came, Graham, give me a hug," Mrs. Bennett stands and gives me my second hug of the day.

"All righty, we are leaving. Love you all," Winry cheers.

"Love you," they shout back to her.

We climb in my car and head for home. I don't know what to say. My original plan was to ask her if she would let me take her out some time, but after what her dad said, I am not very confident. Every single girl I've dated comes to mind; they all said I was too emotionally unavailable, and they were right. I never put much emotion into the relationships. They were just casual things that I knew would never really go anywhere. I couldn't do that to Winry.

"Are you okay?" Winry asks, drawing me out of thoughts.

"Yeah, yeah. Sorry, just focusing on the road."

"Okay."

Yeah, it was a lame excuse I know, but what was I supposed to say? Your dad told me to think about what I have to offer you and I have realized that in no way am I good enough for you. We make it back to our apartments without much conversation.

"Hey, why don't you come inside, and we can hang out for a bit?"

I want to say yes, but I need to say no. But the moment I look at those big hazel eyes, it's like the word "no" has left my vocabulary. "Yeah, I'd like that."

"Okay great. It's nice tonight. Why don't we sit on the porch for a little bit?"

"Okay, sounds nice."

We settle in on her small outdoor couch. She is so close I breathe in her fruity smell and blood instantly rushes to my dick. She brings her knees up to her chest then grabs a throw and drapes it over her knees. I take advantage and adjust myself so she won't be able to see my current situation.

"Let me hear your best joke." She leans into me for a moment then pulls back.

"A joke? Okay, why didn't the two skeletons fight?"

"I don't know, why?" She presses her lips together, fighting a smile.

"Because they didn't have any guts."

Winry's head falls back in laughter. "That is your best joke? Come on, you can do better than that."

"Hey, you laughed, didn't you? Okay, your turn, tell me a joke. Let's see if you can do any better."

"All right, why was the mermaid wearing seashells?"

"I don't know, why?"

"Because she grew out of her b-shells."

We both break out in laughter. It's so easy being with her. In this moment, I'm not thinking about anything other than her.

"There we go, feeling better?" She shakes my shoulder.

"I don't know what you are talking about; I'm fine," I deflect.

"You are fine now, but you have been acting weird ever since that last game with my dad. Did he say something to you?"

"What? No, he didn't say anything." Deflect. Deflect.

"Oh yeah, that was convincing. What did he say?" She presses.

"Nothing, Winry. Don't worry about it."

"So, he did say something. Graham, you can tell me."

I avoid her gaze, "Win, let it go. Come on, ask me something else."

I can tell she is dying to fight me on this, but she doesn't. "Okay, tell me something about yourself that not many people know."

"Oh man, bringing out the big guns. Well, let's see. I have a completely rational fear of birds, especially ducks and geese."

She tries but fails to hold in a laugh. "I'm sorry, it's not funny. Fear of birds, noted."

"All right, giggles, tell me something about you that not many people know." I unintentionally scoot slightly closer to her.

"I love to write."

"Oh yeah, what do you write?"

"Anything really. Poems, short stories, or just about my day. I have journals full of them." She stares at her blanket, twirling the tassels between her fingers.

"I think that's great, Winry. Would you let me read some?" I reach out and put my hand on her knee.

"Maybe one day. You've got to earn it." She gives me a small nudge with her knees.

"Oh, I intend to."

She stretches out her legs in my lap, and before I think too hard on it, I place my hand under her thighs and pull as close as I can without pulling her in my lap. I bring my hand up to her face and tuck her hair behind her ear. I want nothing more than to lean in and kiss her. Still not thinking about what I am doing, I lift her chin and put my thumb in her dimple like I wanted to do the first time we met. Her breath hitches, and her lips part slightly. We just stare at each other, unwilling to move from this position.

"Graham," she says breathlessly.

I start to lean in when suddenly my conversion with her dad comes screaming back, and I pull away.

"I'm sorry. I didn't...sorry...I wasn't thinking." I take her legs off my lap and stand up, needing some air and space.

"Graham, it's fine really."

"I'd better get going."

"Graham, come on, you don't have to go. Why don't we just go inside and watch some TV?"

I run my hands over my face. What was going on with me?

"I'm sorry, Winry, I think it's best that I head home."

Her face looks so hurt. Damn it, this is exactly what I wanted to avoid and what her dad told me would happen. I don't want to be the one to hurt her in any way, so why am I screwing this up so badly?

"Okay, if that's what you want." She stands up and we both walk toward the front door silently. Gah, I am such a dick.

"Winry, I'm sorry."

"Why are you sorry exactly? Are you sorry because you almost kissed me? Because you didn't want to, or you're not attracted to me?" She has a hip stuck out and her arms crossed; if she only knew how I was dying to rip every piece of her clothing off her and absolutely devour her right here in her living room.

"Win, that's not it."

"Then why are you running out of here?"

"Because I'm not sure I have anything to offer you. I like you, Winry, like really like you, but I don't know how to be in a relationship. I think my longest relationship lasted a month, tops. You deserve so much more, and I don't want to lose you. I have already fucked it up enough tonight."

Her face softens, and she uncrosses her arms at my words. Understand, please understand, I silently pray.

"It's okay, I get it, but you don't have to run away. I just don't want you to leave." She grabs my hand and intertwines our fingers. I look down at her and she has the sultry look in her eyes.

Don't be an asshole.

"Winry, you're killing me."

"Good." She goes up on her tip toes and catches my face in her hands pulling me down and crashing her lips to mine. She tastes sweet, like the s'mores we had earlier. My arms wrap around her waist pulling her in closer to me, then lowering them down to cup her ass. More, I need more.

Moving my hands down to the back of her thighs I lift her up and her legs wrap around me. I push her up against the wall, and she groans in satisfaction. Her lips part and I dive in, deepening the kiss. Her hands are now running through my hair, and she grinds her hips against me.

"Graham," she moans as I kiss down her neck. "Please."

I pause for a moment and study her face; she is the most beautiful woman I have ever seen. Her lips are swollen from our kiss, and her eyes are begging me for more.

"Winry..." my dick rages against my jeans for me to give in to this.

"I don't need you to offer me the world, Graham, I'm just asking you to give us a shot."

"I want to do that, but what if..."

"No, no what ifs. Not right now. Do you want to be with me?"

"Yeah, I do." A lot, actually.

"Good, now take me upstairs," she demands.

"Are you sure?" I need know that she is good with this, with everything that just happened, I need this confirmation.

"Yes, I'm sure." She leans back in for another kiss.

I carry her up the stairs to her room, kissing her the whole way. Once we reach the top, I set her down. I need her clothes off now. Yanking at her top, I pull it over her head. She is wearing a skimpy black lace bra. I can't resist; I palm one breast with my hand and take the other in my mouth. Her hand goes to the back of my head, steadying her, then pulling me in close.

"Oh god," she whispers.

"Naked. Now," I demand as I pull away to rip my shirt over my head. She unclips her bra, tossing it to the side, then unbuttons her shorts, and they fall to the ground.

"Win, have you not been wearing underwear all night?"

"Can't say I ever cared too much for underwear." All she is wearing is a sexy smirk on her face.

I want to fall to my knees right then and there, "You will be the death of me, Winry Bennett."

I lay her on the bed, and she props herself up, watching me. I take my time unbuttoning my jeans. I want to memorize how she looks right now, every inch, every curve. The room is dark, but her curtains are open and the moonlight shines in highlighting her body perfectly.

"You always smell so sweet and fruity; I'm dying to know if you taste the same."

I climb on top of her. I give her a slow gentle kiss, then kiss down her body until I am between her thighs. I tease her a bit, kissing her thighs and everywhere around where she wants me to.

"Don't you think you have teased me long enough?" She bites back a moan.

"Buttercup, I have had many dreams about this, I'm taking my time."

Finally, I give in and to start to circle her clit with my tongue. She tastes even better than I expected. If I could have one thing to eat for the rest of my life, it would be her. I take a finger and slide it in her. She is drenched. When her legs begin to shake, she begs for more. I insert another finger. She's so tight, I can only imagine how good it will feel to be inside of her.

"Graham," she pants, "I'm so close, don't stop."

A few more strokes are all it takes. Her hands dig into my hair, her back arches, and her hips thrust against my tongue riding out her high. I continue to lick her slowly as she comes down.

"That, that was amazing," she says breathlessly.

My cock is demanding to be inside of her, "Please tell me you have a condom."

"Nightstand, middle drawer."

I climb off of her and go to the nightstand.

"Oh hello, what do we have here?" I pull out a pink vibrator.

She rolls over onto her stomach to face me. "It's a vibrator, Graham. I have no shame about it." She gives out a small laugh.

"And you shouldn't; we will most definitely be using this in the future," I say, dropping it back in her drawer. I grab a condom and rip it open with my teeth. I quickly take off my underwear and put it on.

Winry watches me the entire time, biting her lower lip.

"Something pique your interest?"

"Oh yeah, I think next time I get to enjoy a taste," she says as she gets up on all fours and crawls toward me. I fist a handful of her hair pulling back so she is looking up at me and give her pouty lips another demanding kiss. When we break apart, seeing her on her hands and knees nearly does me in.

"I think I like you in this position, don't move."

Climbing on the bed behind her I grab her hips and yank them back against me. My dick teases her entrance. "Last chance to back out, baby. I don't think I will be able to stop once we get started, and I don't intend on going easy on you."

"Fuck me, Graham. I need you to fuck me like you want me."

"I love it when you talk like that, say that again."

"Fuck me, Graham, now."

"Ah even better." I plunge inside of her, my rhythm hard and full of need. Needing to be inside her, to claim her and ruin her for anyone else. I continue pounding in and out, and she begins to push back against me. Oh hell. I don't even think about it and smack her perfect round ass. She yelps in a mixture of pleasure and pain and pushes back against me even harder.

Damn, it has never felt like this, this is pure bliss. My thrusts get quicker, I am getting close, and I can tell she has one more in her. "I'm going to need you to come one more time for me, babe."

"I don't know...oh yes just like that." I continue that rhythm and decide to give her ass one more smack, and that does it. Her arms give out, and her pussy squeezes my cock. When she cries out my name, I fall over the edge too. My orgasm hits me so hard I nearly fall over, but I catch myself before I crush her. I collapse to the side and pull her toward me.

Still on her stomach, she looks up at me, "I don't think it has ever felt that good, nor have I ever orgasmed twice in one go."

"No, it has never felt like that for me either," I say, still trying to catch my breath. She nestles her head in my shoulder, and I lean in, kissing the top of her head. "Let me get rid of the condom. I will be right back, and so help me, don't you dare put clothes on."

Chapter 11

Winry

"I wouldn't dare." I roll on my back, giving him a full view of my naked body.

He takes me in. "You are so beautiful, Winry."

A smile a mile wide spreads across my face, "Thank you."

He leans down and gives me a tender kiss and heads to the bathroom. I revel in how I feel right now; my skin is buzzing. Energy is coursing through my veins. It's after midnight, but there is no way I will be falling asleep anytime soon.

Graham comes back, and his naked body is everything I dreamed it would be. He is built beautifully, with nice, sculpted muscles and abs that I want to trace with my fingers. He has the right amount of chest hair that makes him look even more manly. Don't even get me started on his ass. "Bitable" is all I have to say.

Climbing back onto the bed, he wraps me in his arms, and I nestle back into his chest. His body is so warm, like a furnace. I breathe in this moment. This feeling is euphoric; I don't think I will ever get enough.

He lightly runs his fingers up and down my back. "Tell me about your tattoos. I noticed a couple of them while you know, rocking your world."

I give a snicker at his boasting. "Um, let's see. I have few small ones." I sit up so I can point them out. "I got my rose on my shoulder first, on my eighteenth birthday. It's my mom's favorite flower. The moon on my ribs is for my dad since he calls me moon baby. I have got an arrow on my wrist because I liked it. Oh, my hip is the best one. It's a dragonfly, but I didn't actually pick this one out." I turn so he can see the black dragonfly on my right hip.

"What do you mean you didn't pick it out?" He runs his hand over the tattoo, sending a shiver down my spine.

"Well, if it isn't obvious, I am really close with my sisters. I would trust them with my life. So, one time we saw this video where a couple picked out some tattoos for each other and they got them tattooed without the other knowing. We thought it was a cool idea, so we did it. Wyla and Waverley came up with the idea of a dragonfly and I didn't know what it was until it was already on me."

"What? You are insane. Did the rest of them do that too?"

"Just Waverley. Wyla is too big a chicken to get tattoos. We still let her help pick out the tattoos though. For Waverley, we did a little bouquet of wildflowers because of her wild and free personality."

"Why did they pick the dragonfly for you?"

I lie back down, snuggling next to him. "Well, dragonflies are supposed to symbolize our ability to overcome our struggles and reconnect with our happiness." I hope he accepts that as a good enough answer. We just slept together; now is not the right time to talk about my struggles with anxiety and depression. Not even my sisters know the full extent of my struggles with my mental health.

He rolls over so we are face to face and surprises me when he says, "We don't have to talk about it, Win, you can tell me more about it when you want to." He brushes my hair out of my face and kisses me lightly.

"Thank you. So, what about you? I didn't see any tattoos while, you know, you rocked my world."

"Don't patronize me, buttercup." He brings his finger up and taps my nose. "But no, I don't have any. My dad has a ton of them, and my mom would keel over if I got one."

"You don't talk about your family much. What are they like?" I hope I'm not prying. What if he doesn't like to talk about them like I don't like to talk about my mental stability? He was just so sweet about it and here I am pushing. "Unless you don't want to," I add.

"Well, not much to tell: parents divorced when I was six and they never remarried, so it's just me. But I would really rather not talk about my parents while I have you naked." His hand starts to explore my body, moving up and down my side and then back to cup my ass.

I bite back the smile that has been permanently glued to my face.

"Would you want to stay over tonight? You don't have to; I know you need to stay up at least a few hours more, so your schedule isn't too messed up. Just don't feel like you have to stay, but I'm not kicking you out…"

"Winry," he interrupts my rambling, "I am not going anywhere."

"Good." I stare into his eyes; they are warm and inviting. He then starts to pepper me with kisses on my face and neck.

"What do you have planned for tomorrow? Are you back to work?" He asks in between kisses.

"Yeah, Ivy will cover the morning while I have breakfast with my sisters, then I will take over until three." I respond begrudgingly. I would much rather stay in bed with him.

He stops kissing my neck, much to my dismay. "Do you need to get some sleep? It's almost one in the morning."

"I'll sleep later, right now I am wide awake." I throw my leg over his hip and push with the other so I am now straddling him. I can feel him hardening beneath me. He places his hands behind his head and stares up at me. I give my best sexy smirk and run my hands over his muscles.

"You know, I had a dream just like this once." He sits up, so we are chest to chest. He places his hands on my ass and starts to kiss my collarbone.

"Oh yeah, how did it end?" I am getting wetter with each kiss, and I moan when he starts play with my breasts.

"Unfortunately, I woke up before I got to the good part." He takes one of my nipples in his mouth and continues to massage the other.

"Well, I think we will just have to rectify that, won't we?"

We stay up talking, kissing, and touching each other for almost the whole night. I feel so safe and comfortable in his arms, and we drift off right before dawn. The sleep is so deep and peaceful.

"Well, well, well. What do we have here?" Waverley says loud enough to stir us both. I lean up on my elbows to see my sisters walking up by my bed. I lay my head back down and cuddle into Graham's warm body.

"What are y'all doing here?" I ask groggily.

"Hmm, what time is it?" Graham asks, still foggy from sleep. He sits up and I groan at the loss of his warmth.

"Winry, you were supposed to meet us for breakfast an hour ago." Wyla says as they both plop down at the end of the bed.

"What? No, I had an alarm set." I roll over to my nightstand to check my phone. Damn, I must have snoozed it in my sleep. "I'm sorry guys. I swear I had one set."

"Oh, don't be sorry, I personally am glad you missed or else we wouldn't have gotten to see the show. So, what have you two been doing?" Wyla asks, all too happy about this.

"Nothing, leave us alone." I throw a pillow at my sisters.

"Nothing, really? I just couldn't help but notice that you don't seem to be wearing any clothes. Nice abs by the way." Waverley winks at Graham and I throw another pillow at her.

"I'm only teasing," Waverley says throwing the pillow back at us.

"Okay come on, Wav, let's let them get dressed. Win, we brought your favorites. Sorry, Graham, we would have brought you something had we known. I am sure you are both hungry from all that nothing you have been doing." Wyla snickers and pulls Waverley down the stairs.

Graham falls back down on the bed taking me with him. "How are you this morning, buttercup?"

"I feel good, happy. How are you?" I place my hand on his face and use my thumb to caress his cheek.

"Same. Do we have to go downstairs? If we stay here long enough, they will leave and we could stay naked in bed all day."

"Oh, that does sound good, but there is no way they would leave. Plus, I'd better go into the store for a little bit, and you need to get some sleep so you aren't messed up all week."

Graham groans when I break apart from him. I throw on some black leggings and a t-shirt then head to the bathroom to wash up and throw my hair in a high ponytail. When I come out, Graham is fully dressed, his hair is all messed up from where I kept digging and running my hands through it. He smiles at me when he sees me; a look has never made me feel beautiful, but right now, how he is looking at me makes me feel like the most beautiful girl in the world.

"Come here," Graham reaches for me and wraps me in his embrace. I can't resist, I climb up him, wrapping my legs around his back and give him a kiss of need and hunger. I can feel him harden against my core. He gives a low growl when I bite his lip.

"I'm going to need you to stop right now. Your sisters are downstairs, but I don't care enough to not throw you back in that bed."

I'm tempted to call his bluff, but I just give him a wicked smile as he sets me down. "Come on, let's go, there is no telling what they are tearing up down there." I tug him down the stairs.

My sisters are chatting in my kitchen, sipping their coffees. "Look, it's the happy couple," Waverley beams.

"Wav," I shoot a warning look—we haven't really clarified what this is. I hope it is something, but last night he mentioned not knowing how to do a relationship, so I don't want to push. Thankfully, Graham looks unbothered by Waverly's "couple" comment.

"Here is your coffee and muffin, Win." Wyla hands me my usual iced latte and muffin.

"Oh yes, I'm starving. I'll split this with you Graham." I dig into the bag, pulling out the muffin.

"You don't have to, Win; I know they are your favorite."

"I want to." I halve the muffin and hand it to him. My sisters stare at us like they are trying to read our minds.

"So, are you guys going to tell us what is going on here, or are you just going to make googly eyes at each other?" Waverley asks casually while she sips her coffee.

"Waverley, don't ruin their moment." Wyla gives Wav a little push.

"What, it is a fair question. I feel we should know if they are together or just sleeping together."

"We are together," Graham says, surprising me. I look up at him, I guess with a wide-eyed doe look because he gives a quick kiss on my forehead. "I mean unless you don't want to."

"No, no complaints here." I know I have a cheesy smile on my face.

"Aw, Win." Waverley claps her hands together. "Ugh, I want a hot boyfriend." She pouts.

"Okay, I think I'd better go back over to my place and leave y'all to it. Holler at me when you get home from work, okay?" Graham places his hand on my lower back.

"Okay." I walk him out and give him a kiss that still lingers as I go back into the kitchen.

"Um, I am going to need every detail," Wyla demands.

"Ooh start with how was it? No, how big is it? Tell me when to stop." Waverley holds out her hands and starts to spread them out.

"Waverley, stop it. I am not telling you how big it is. I will tell you it was life-changing but you will have to wait for more details because I need to go into work. I haven't been in since the Flynn incident."

"Ivy said you could have the day off if you need it. What happened was traumatic. No one would blame you for taking today off. Have you gotten an update on what is next with Flynn anyway?" Waverley asks, her tone less giddy at the change of topic.

"Dad told me Saturday he got bailed out. We have a protection order, so he is not supposed to contact me in anyway." I feel a chill go down my spine just thinking about that night. "I'll most likely have to see him in court to tell my side of the story, especially since I broke his nose trying to get him off of me."

"See, you need the day off. We can talk about better things, like, you know, your new hunky man." Wyla looks to be genuinely trying to brighten the subject.

"No, I need to go in, I'll be off tomorrow. Why don't we do dinner here tomorrow? I'll cook, and we can talk all about my hunky man." I hold out my hands imitating the size of his dick.

"Oh lord almighty. I need one of those." Waverley fans herself.

"You are going to make us wait that long, no way. Why not tonight?" Wyla raises her eyebrows, fully aware of why I don't want to do it tonight, but I know she just wants me to say it out loud.

"Because Graham is off again tonight before he works for the next two days so I was hoping..."

"You could have life-changing sex again." Waverley says with her typical bluntness.

"Yes, I admit it. Now get out of here, I have got to go. I will see you tomorrow." I push them out of my house and head to Crossroads.

FEEL IT ALL

Crossroads was buzzing all day, and as soon as the last customer leaves, I lock our doors and turn off the neon "open" sign. I head back to the kitchen, where Ivy has been holed up the whole time baking cupcakes. At peak rush we got an order for five dozen of her strawberry cupcakes.

"Where do you need me, Ivy? Give me something to do to help."

"Here, will you start scooping out the batter into this tray? And I will start the filling for the ones I have finished." Ivy looks like she has gotten into a fight with the flour and lost.

"Ives, you got some flour on your face." I try to hold back a laugh. I know she is stressed, but if you don't tell your friend when they have something on their face, what kind of friend are you?

"Oh glory." She takes a rag and cleans up her face. "Who orders five dozen cupcakes the day of an event? You order ahead of time, not hours before."

"I know, I know, but I'm here for you, babe." Nothing can ruin my good mood today; a smile has been permanently locked on my face all day.

"All right, spill, why are you smiling like that? You have been unusually happy today. I could hear that hateful guy making snide comments about our spicy book section from back here and you were just as nice and bubbly to that man like you were to everyone today." Ivy stops filling her cupcakes and gives me the spill-your-guts look.

"I am just in a good mood, that's all, and I wasn't going to argue with him about our spicy books; it would have been a waste of breath. He clearly is too insecure if he is threatened by a spicy book." I wave her off.

"Uh huh, and this wouldn't have anything to do with Wav and Wyla finding you in bed with Graham this morning. Hmm?" Ivy raises her eyebrows up and down. "I told them to text whether you were good or not, turns out you were doing really good."

"They have such big mouths. If you knew, why didn't you start with that, you little brat?"

"Oh, I'm the brat? You are the one not telling your best friend about getting down and dirty with her sexy neighbor." Ivy whips her towel at my butt.

"I'm sorry, I was going to tell you, it just happened. Honestly, I am afraid this is like a concussion-induced dream and I will wake up." While I have had a smile plastered to my face, there is a small voice in the back of my head telling me it's too good to be true.

"Those aren't a thing, Winry. Tell me everything, how big is it?"

"Oh, my word. You are just like my sisters, could you guys be normal for once." Leave it to my sisters and bestie to ask about dick size.

"Hush, quit being a prude, just tell me all the nitty gritty details." Ivy does a little shimmy.

"Ugh, it was so good, Ivy, and as far as the size, I am just going to say impressive. I orgasmed twice the first round."

"Twice? I was sure that was a myth. Man, I need to get laid," Ivy cries.

"It's a wonder how you and Waverley aren't sisters, she asked and said the same things." I finish scooping the batter and pop it in the oven.

"Ha, it's part of why you love me so much. I fit in just like a Bennett. So, does this mean you guys are together now?" Ivy asks as I start on the next batch.

"He said we are. He told Wav and Wyla this morning we were together when they asked." I give a very half confident shrug.

"But you aren't sure?"

"No, I want to be with him, he just said last night that he wasn't sure what he had to offer me, then this morning it just felt different. I don't know, you know how I am, anxious about every little thing in my life, and he doesn't even know anything about that. I'm trying not to be in my head about it but it's hard. I really like him; I don't want to mess this up."

"Win, don't get too wrapped up in that, I could tell the day he came in here that he liked you. You can tell him about that stuff when you are ready, but I know it won't matter to him," Ivy reassures me.

"I hope you are right, but come on let's knock this order out." I pop the next tray in. "What next?"

"In a hurry for something Winry?" Ivy winks.

"You know I am not even going to lie, yeah, I am."

We finish up the order and I feel like I drive a little bit faster home than I normally do—sue me, I am excited. I debate with myself whether I should call or text Graham; he just said to holler at him when I got home. I don't want to wake him up if he is still sleeping though, so I will just send him a text letting him know I am home.

It doesn't take long, and there is a knock at my door, which I am all too eager to answer.

"Hey…" is all he can get out before I am on top of him. We only make it to the couch by the time clothes are being ripped off and lots of touching starts. By the end, we are sweating and trying to catch our breath.

"Hey," I finally say back to him.

"I hope that I get that greeting every time I come over," Graham huffs.

"I am just glad you brought that condom in your pocket; I was too excited to make it upstairs." We both laugh and he pulls my naked body in his lap.

"I missed you, is that weird?" He asks, I can hear hesitation in his voice.

"No, I missed you too. I had to stay late and help Ivy and I thought I was going to go insane."

"Me too," Graham leans his head back against the couch. "Have you eaten? I'm starved, do you want to order something delivered?"

"Yes, please. Can we do Mexican?" I reach for his t-shirt and pull it on.

"Anything you want, buttercup." He gives me a squeeze and kisses my temple.

I maneuver my legs so I am straddling him and wrap my arms around his neck. "If that's the case, I need to take a shower, so why don't we call it in and while we wait on it to get here, we take one together."

"That sounds like a great idea." Graham gives my ass a good squeeze.

"Okay, you order the food, and I'll get the shower started. Just order two of whatever you get, I like it all."

"Sure thing." Graham gives my ass a light smack as I make my way toward the stairs.

I start the shower and the steam starts to fill the bathroom. I love a steaming hot shower. I close my eyes, taking in this moment, and let the water fall over me. Strong hands grip my hips, pulling me out of my haze.

"I hope you like your showers hot," I tease.

"Bring it on, baby." He gives a seductive smile.

I let Graham under the water. Watching it drip down his body is so erotic that I drop to my knees in front of him. I grab the base of his shaft and lick the tip, looking up at him.

"This has to be the sexiest thing I have ever seen. Now be a good girl and keep going," he commands.

Yes, sir. I don't waste any time. I move my hands to his hips and take him in. I panic a little because he's bigger than I have ever had before, but I remind myself to breathe, and I adjust my angle so I can take him as far as I can. Keeping a good rhythm, I continue to suck greedily. I don't know why, but I feel powerful knowing that he is at my mercy.

"Fuck, Winry."

He braces himself against the wall with one hand and the other grips the back of my head. He begins to thrust his hips, gentle at first, testing how I can handle it. When I moan, he loses all control and picks up his pace, going hard and fast.

"Now is your time to pull out if you need to, buttercup."

I look up at him and then tighten my grip on his hips in response. I need to taste him. He is so close I can feel it, so I bring my hand up to give his balls some attention. Graham lets out a low growl and a string of curses. Then I feel the hot and steady stream of his climax going down my throat. I stand with a wicked smile, feeling pretty proud of myself.

"Shit, Win, you are something else." He crashes his mouth to mine with a needy kiss. "I think I ought to return the favor."

"Later, big guy, our food is on the way, and I haven't even washed my hair and body."

"Fine," he grumbles, "but I call dibs on washing your body."

"Deal."

We wash up and what should have taken five minute takes ten because we can't keep our hands or our mouths to ourselves. Thankfully we make it out right as the food arrives. Graham throws on his clothes and goes to grab it while I brush my hair and get dressed.

"What did you order us?" I walk into the living room where there is a feast laid out.

"I got you some burritos, rice, salsa, and cheese dip. I like to mix the salsa and cheese dip."

"Seriously? I do that too. It drives Waverley insane, but she is picky anyway." I take a seat next to him and am practically drooling over the food in front of me.

"How did things go this morning after I left? Your sisters looked like they were dying to ask a million questions." He mixes up our salsa and cheese dip combo and takes a bite.

"Oh, they tried. I had to kick them out so I could get to Crossroads, but they are coming over for dinner tomorrow, and I am sure I will have to answer the questions they didn't ask this morning."

"What questions did they ask this morning?" Graham asks while unwrapping his burrito.

"Hmm let's see. How big was it was Waverley's choice," I say plainly.

Graham nearly chokes. "She asked how big my dick was?"

"Yeah," I laugh. "I know it's weird, but we have always been close, we really don't have a filter around each other anymore."

"I just need to know if you said all good stuff or if I need to step up my game." He gives me a wink then goes back to his food.

"Oh, all good stuff...all big stuff too." I give him a playful wink back, and he nearly chokes again.

"Graham, did you mean what you said about us being together? Is that what you want?" I ask, but I don't make eye contact with him. I can't make eye contact; I'm too afraid.

He sets down his food, tugs me closer to him. "Yeah, Winry, I meant it. I want to give us a shot. I can't say that I will be great at it all the time, but I will try my best. You have been the only girl that I have ever wanted to try with. So, yeah, we are together...unless you don't want to be."

"No, I want to. I just wanted to be sure, I tend to overthink things."

"What are you thinking, Win?" Graham pulls my hair out of my face and places it behind my ear.

"I don't know, that I pressured you into this." I still can't make eye contact.

"You did not pressure me. If I didn't want to be with you, last night wouldn't have happened. I know I was apprehensive, but," he lifts my chin so I have to look at him, "I want this, Winry."

"Why were you apprehensive?" Doubt starts to fill my brain.

"It's not important, buttercup. What is important is that we are together." He takes one of my hands and tangles his fingers in mine.

"It was what my dad said to you, wasn't it?" He didn't have to tell me my dad said something to him yesterday. I could tell they were in deep conversation during the game, and whatever was said clearly had some effect on him.

"It is no big deal, Winry. It doesn't matter now." He gives my hand a reassuring squeeze.

I know he can see the frustration on my face. I am not really trying to hide it, though. Why won't he tell me what he said? Clearly it was significant enough for him to be hesitant about being with me. I don't want to let it go, but I don't think pushing is a good idea either.

Graham interrupts my derailing train of thought. "Hey, want to hear a joke?"

"You are just trying to distract me like last night." I roll my eyes at his attempt.

"Possibly, but I think I can do better this time."

"All right, let's hear it." I turn to him, giving him my full attention.

"Why did the coffee file a police report?" He asks, grinning goofily.

"I don't know, why, Graham?" I fold my lips in, suppressing my smile.

"It was mugged."

I try to contain my laugh but fail. It isn't because the joke is funny; it's because he is just so cute telling it I can't help but laugh.

"There she is." He gives me that look again that makes me feel all warm and beautiful.

"All right, small improvement from the first one, but you may want to keep trying." I go back to my food, completely forgetting why I was frustrated to begin with.

"I'll tell all the stupid jokes I can just to hear you laugh." My heart flutters at his words, and my body feels like it's vibrating.

We finish up our food, and I slide my legs in his lap. "So, are you liking working for the police department?"

"I like it. I still ride with Owen, which never makes it boring, but he likes to make me write all the tickets to 'give me practice.' The asshole just doesn't want to do them. He sticks me with them and calls it training."

"Hmph, yeah that sounds like Owen. What made you want to move here to be a cop? Why not stay in your hometown?" I ask, munching on the last of the chips.

"Um, well, I'm not very close with my family. My mom can be a little much, and Dad does the bare minimum. So, when Owen called about the opening, I took it. It's only like thirty to forty-five minutes away depending on traffic, so I didn't go far, but far enough that it doesn't feel like my mom is breathing down my neck all the time."

I want to dig deeper about his parents, but I decide to wait and play it safe. "And no siblings, right?" I ask.

"Nope, it's just me. I'm a product of a one-night stand that came with consequences," he shrugs.

"I'm sorry, I'll let you borrow my sisters if you want the sibling experience," I offer.

He laughs it off, but I can tell talking about his family is not a fun topic for him. "I think I'm okay. I don't mind not having siblings. Especially if it includes talking about sex, I'm not sure I would do too well at the sibling bonding."

I let out a giggle. "We may be a little closer than others. I don't imagine all siblings talk about sex. My sisters and I always blame our mom for being so casual about stuff like that. She always walked around naked and encouraged us to be open about our bodies and sex. Not that she would encourage us to have sex, but she didn't want us to not be able to talk about it and didn't make it out to be this bad thing."

"Please tell me you haven't talked about our sex life with your mom. Sisters I can handle, but I don't think I would ever be able to be in the same room with your mom again." Graham looks white as a sheet.

My head falls back in laughter. "No, I haven't talked to her. I imagine my sisters called her this morning though after they found us."

"Oh, God. I'll never be able to go to your parents' house ever." He covers his face with his hands.

"Come on now, you can't tell me that your parent don't know that you have had sex. I mean your mom practically sent Claire to your house for it. Plus, they would find out we are together at some point; they can put two and two together." I place my hand on his shoulder, massaging lightly.

"Okay, I'll give you the Claire situation, which was definitely uncomfortable. Especially because I had my eyes on the hot girl next door." Graham pulls me into his lap.

"Oh really, well I would suggest you do something about that." I give him a pouty but seductive look.

"I intend to."

Chapter 12

Graham

The next two weeks fly by. Winry and I spend every moment we can together. To be honest, I was afraid I would freak out by now, but I can't seem to get enough of her both in and out of bed. It's so refreshing being with her; every time we are together, I learn something new about her that only makes me adore her more. Like how she hates anything remotely scary—movies, haunted houses, doesn't matter, she will not budge. She loves anything chocolate chip, especially cookie dough, and she kicks ass at every game and sport known to man apparently. I haven't beaten her once.

It's one of our Mondays off, so we will have the whole day together. I get off at seven and know she won't be up for a couple of hours, so I go for a run, shower, then head to Crossroads for her favorites.

"Hey, Graham." Ivy greets me as I walk in the door. "Here to get some stuff for Winry?"

"Yeah, double her order, I'll take the same." I slide her my card.

"Man, couples really do start to act like one another over time." She whips up our drinks and grabs two banana chocolate chip muffins. "Here you are. Oh, hey I wanted to ask you if you had any plans for Winry Saturday for her birthday."

"Her birthday? This Saturday?" I must have a puzzled look on my face because Ivy gives me a sympathetic look in return.

"Of course she didn't tell you. Ugh, that girl, I swear. Yes, her birthday is Saturday, but she hates her birthday, so usually she stays in her house the whole day hiding. I was hoping you would be able to talk her into doing something, but I guess not." Ivy's shoulders slump.

"Why does she hate her birthday?" I ask, still confused.

"Because something always goes wrong on her birthday. I'll let her tell you about it. Some are pretty funny, but don't laugh, she will kill you." Ivy sends me off with our breakfast.

I can't believe she didn't tell me it's her birthday this week and she was just going to hide all day in her apartment. No fucking way.

When I get to our apartments, I go to knock on her door. I can hear her talking to someone, I am assuming over the phone. It takes her a minute to answer the door. When she finally answers and I get a good look at her, I know something is wrong. Her chest is blotchy red, and her eyes are puffy like she has been crying.

"Hey, what are you doing here? I figured you would come over after you slept." She is putting on her best fake smile, but I'm not buying it.

"Winry, what's wrong?"

"What? Nothing, I'm fine. Want to come inside?" She turns and walks back to the downstairs bathroom, leaving me standing in her doorway. She is not getting off the hook that easily.

I walk in, closing the door behind me, and set our stuff down on the coffee table. She comes back into the living room but is looking anywhere else, careful not to face me. "Winry, come on. Tell me what's going on."

"Hmm, I am good. I'm just going to go..."

"Winry," I grab her hand before she walks away, turning her to where she finally is looking at me. My other hand finds her cheek. "Talk to me, buttercup."

"I, um—sorry this is hard." A tear escapes down her cheek and I wipe it away. My chest physically hurts right now; seeing her upset is heart-wrenching. "I just had a therapy appointment, I do them through Zoom calls sometimes. I didn't think you would be over until after you slept some. I didn't plan on burdening you with this so soon. Everything is going so well; I don't want to ruin it."

"Hey, look at me. You are not going to ruin this, and you are not a burden." I stare into her eyes and lightly run my thumb over her cheek. "I promise you can tell me anything."

"Oof, okay. Why don't we sit down?" As we sit, I grab her legs, pulling them in in my lap, and place my hand on her thigh. "Well, um, ever since I was a kid, I have had a hard time with anxiety. Everything made me a nervous and stressed constantly, and I never slept…still don't really sleep honestly. I constantly felt like I was responsible for everyone. I felt like I was responsible for my sisters, and when Mom would stay up listening to the police scanner, I would stay up with her. Just knowing she was worried would make me worried. I carried all of their emotions. It just got worse over the years. Don't get me wrong, I love my family, but I felt like I had to hold it together. My sisters and my mom would lean on me, especially when Dad was at work. Every tear they shed I caught. There was one night when I was in high school and Mom and Dad had gotten into an argument. Nothing crazy, but still she cried the whole night while I sat there and wiped her tears, and I have done the same for my sisters many times. I shouldered it all, and I started having issues with depression also."

I rub her thigh, silently encouraging her to go on. "Anxious thoughts mixed with depressed thoughts is a dangerous combination. I started having panic attacks when I moved out. Just being alone with my thoughts was too much. When I was home, it was like I didn't have time for a panic attack because I felt like I needed to be strong for everyone else. Then my brain started telling me I was a burden to my family, that I was broken, and they would be better off without me."

She pauses to take a deep breath. "The only person who I have ever told this to is my dad and therapist, but she told me today I have to stop carrying the weight of it, so here we go. A year ago, on my birthday…I have always hated my birthday—something always goes wrong. Last year, my family forgot about it. I went the whole day without a single call from my family. The voices were just so loud that I started to have a panic attack, the worst one I ever had. I couldn't come out of it, it just felt like I was drowning, and no one was going to help me. I decided the only way to get it to stop was to end it. I know it is crazy, I know my family loves me and I have a great life, but in that moment those negative voices canceled all reason. Right before I did anything, Dad showed up here. He found me curled up in a ball in the bathroom. I told him everything, and he held me until I fell asleep from exhaustion. Overnight I guess Dad made some calls; I know the department has connections to psychiatrists and therapists. So when I got up, he had numbers for me to call for appointments. I promised I would go as long as he promised not to tell anyone ever."

A lump forms in my throat, "Oh, Winry." I pick her up into my lap and grip her tight. She is full on sobbing now and tears threaten my eyes when I think about what could have happened. The idea of her not being here in my arms makes me want to come apart. I remember her dad telling me about her struggles, but I never expected this. Winry is always so happy. I want her to always be happy. I will always do whatever I can to make her happy. I hold her so tightly like I am afraid she will just evaporate into thin air.

After a few minutes, her breath evens out and she wipes the tears from her cheeks. "I'm sorry, that was a lot. I didn't intend on unloading all of that on you today."

"Win, don't you dare apologize, you have nothing to be sorry for. You are so strong; I know reliving that had to be hard. Thank you for trusting me with that." I squeeze her tight again.

"I am better now. I take medicine and go to therapy at least once a month. I still have some hard days, today being one of them. That's why I hadn't told you about my birthday; I don't like to think about it."

I press a kiss to her temple. "If you don't want to do anything for your birthday, baby, we won't. I'll lie in bed all day with you if that's what you want to do."

"No, I want to do something this year, especially with you. Being with you makes me happy. I don't want it to always have bad memories, so let's plan something. Even if it's just to the movies, I don't care."

"Okay, leave it to me, buttercup." She looks at me with a smile, and a few tears escape. I wipe them away, and I have to bite back those three words. It's too soon for those words, right? But I feel them, or I think I feel them. I have never been in love before. I definitely know what it doesn't look like from my parents—hell, they barely told me they loved me themselves. I know this is different from my parents, but I don't want to freak her out, so I hold them in.

"Okay, enough crying, you must be worn out. Why don't we lie down for a while? I could go for a nap myself. Talking about that has made me mentally exhausted," she says as she nestles her head in my neck.

"Okay." I scoop her up, and she lets out a giggle. Oh, that sound, I know for sure I love that sound.

I wake up a few hours later, my body tangled in hers as she plays with my hair.

"Hey, how long have you been up?" I peer up at her.

"Not long. You look so cute when you are asleep. I couldn't bring myself to wake you up." Her hand moves down to scratch my back.

I lay my head down on her chest, listening to the steady beat of her heart. A heartbeat, I never thought it would be such a beautiful sound.

"Hey, my dad messaged that he is grilling some burgers and wanted me to come…would you come with me?" Winry asks sheepishly.

"To your parents' house? Together? Is your dad good with me coming?" I have a feeling he won't love the idea of me being there.

"What, are you afraid of him or something?" Winry jokes.

"No, I'm not afraid of him." I am a little afraid. "I just didn't know if he knew we were together that's all."

Her hands stop playing with my hair. "Graham, are you ever going to tell me what you and Dad talked about?"

"Nope," I lean up giving her a quick kiss. "I'll go with you tonight, Win."

"Okay, you're sure? You don't have to go if you don't want to."

"I'm sure."

I am not sure. Part of me wants to go up and thank him for saving the best thing that has ever happened to me. The other part is afraid he will think I am not good enough for her. Which I know I'm not, but I want him to think I am, because I am trying to be.

I run back over to my place to shower and get ready. Right before I head back over, my phone starts ringing. Great, just what I needed, to feel stressed before dinner.

"Hi, Mom."

"Hi, sweetie. I was calling because it doesn't seem like you know how to make calls. Considering I haven't heard from you since I sent Claire over and you broke her heart." She uses her usual judgmental tone.

Oh great, starting with a guilt trip right off the bat. "Sorry mom, I have been meaning to call, but I have been busy. But that was not okay what you did with Claire. I told you we weren't going to be together."

"Too busy for your mother? Goodness, Graham. I was only doing what's best for you, why can't you see that I just don't want you to be like your father?" It's always the don't-be-your-father speech. Just once, I would love to talk to her and not hear those words.

I take a breath and run my hand over my face. I don't want to fight with her. Especially now. "I understand, you thought you were doing something for me with good intentions, but you didn't listen to me."

"You don't know what you want Graham, your father never knew what he wanted either. So I had no other option but to show you."

I hear a knock at my door; I know it is the person I want. "Actually, Mom, I have started seeing someone here in Aster, and...I think I'm going to marry her." That felt weird to say, but in a good way. It wasn't a scary thought but weird because I never thought I would find someone I did want to marry. Now that I have her, I don't want to let her go.

"What! Marry her? Graham, are you serious? What is going..."

"I've got to go, Mom; I will talk to you later." I open the door and see the girl I love just smiling at me.

"Don't you dare hang up on me." Mom is still rambling in my ear.

"Sorry, but I've got to go, I promise I'll call you later."

"Graham Taylor, so help me..."

Click.

"Hi, buttercup, you ready to go?" I close the door behind me.

"Yes, the real question is are you ready?" Winry nudges me with her elbow.

"You mean to have dinner with not only my boss but my girlfriend's dad?"

"Yup, come on. Don't worry. It will be fine for you. For me, on the other hand, I'm sure my family will bring up every embarrassing moment I have had in my life."

"I can't wait." I kiss her forehead, and we hop in my car.

"So, who was on the phone?" Winry asks, buckling up.

"My mom, she was quick with a guilt trip because I haven't called her. I told her that my new girlfriend was occupying all my free time."

"Graham, you'd better not have. I want her to like me." Winry playfully smacks my arm.

"Oh, she will love you." Just not as much as I do. I take her hand in mine then bring it up to kiss the back of it.

We make it to her parents' house right on time. I hop out and open the car door for Winry. She is so beautiful. She has her hair up in a ponytail and is wearing light jeans and a black fitted tank top. I want so badly to take her back home and kiss her all over, but for right now I will just have to settle for holding her hand.

We don't even make it to the door and her mom is rushing out on the front porch ready to pull us in a hug. "Winry, Graham, I am so glad you guys came."

"Thank you for having me, Mrs. Bennett."

"Oh, please, I'm so happy you are here." Her mom gives me a sincere smile. "Come on in, Dad is almost done with the burgers and your sisters are already here."

Once inside, her sisters jump to give hugs. Apparently, the Bennett family is full of huggers. It's odd to see a family so close when all I have seen is my parents, and they definitely were not the show-your-feelings family.

"So, Graham, has Winry told you about her birthday Saturday? I was hoping you could talk her into doing something. She won't let me do anything anymore." Mrs. Bennett gives Winry a sideways glance.

"Well, the last party you planned everyone got food poisoning from the cake." Waverley defends her sister as she munches from a bag of barbecue chips.

"Um, yeah, she told me. I think we will do something, just not sure yet." I rub her back; I'm sure this topic is still raw for her. I know it is for me, and I just listened.

"Oh good, she needs to celebrate it. I'll admit things have gone wrong in the past, but I have confidence you can break the chain." Her mom gives me an encouraging look.

"Mom, can we talk about something else and not put 24 years of bad birthdays on Graham's plate?" Winry leans into me for a moment; knowing she needs the comfort, I continue to rub her back.

"Oh Winry, they weren't all that bad." Mrs. Bennett counters. I have to bite back a response and remind myself that she doesn't know what happened.

"Okay, Isabel, new topic." Winry's dad comes in with a tray of burgers and sets them down on the kitchen table. He gives Winry a sympathetic smile, but once he sees me, his smile fades.

"Fine, fine," Mrs. Bennett holds her hands in the air. If she only knew what happened last year, she would understand.

"Hey there, moon baby. Come give your old man a hug." He motions for her to come over.

"Hey, Dad, thanks for inviting us." Winry goes in, and he wraps her in a hug.

"Oh, so it's 'us' now?" Chief stares at me. Crap, now my hands are sweating.

"Griffin, be nice." It's Mrs. Bennett's turn to give a stern look.

"What? I can't ask a question?" Winry shoots her dad a warning glare and then makes her way back over to me.

"Oh, come on, Dad, we already told you they were together." Waverley chimes in, not being helpful. My mind immediately panics. Surely, he doesn't know about how her sisters found us that morning.

"Right, must have slipped my mind. Graham," Chief holds out his hand and I take it. He grips my hand a little harder than necessary.

"How are you, Chief?" I stand my ground; he may be intimidating, but I can't let him know that.

"Good, glad all my daughters are here." He claps his hands together, "Well, let's eat."

We all gather at their kitchen table, which is just big enough. I take my seat next to Winry and she places her hand on my thigh. The dinner starts out with the usual small talk about everyone's days. Winry and I gloss over our emotional day. Every time I think about our conversation, my chest hurts and I have to reach out to touch her to make sure she is still here, still breathing.

"So, Graham, how are you liking it here?" Mrs. Bennett asks, pulling me out of my thoughts.

"I like it a lot..."

"Clearly," Chief grumbles under his breath cutting me off.

"Dad," Winry snaps.

"No, that's okay. Yeah, I think it's safe to say Winry has a lot to do with it, but work is good too. I still ride with

Owen, but that's not so bad, makes the nights go by a little faster."

"I can't imagine riding in a car for twelve hours with Owen West. Shoot me now." Waverley sticks out her tongue and acts like she is gagging.

"You two would shoot each other," Wyla adds.

"Anyway, I was…ah fuck," Mrs. Bennett knocks her drink all over the table.

All of the Bennett's burst out into laughter. I try to hold it in, but it escapes a little bit.

"Stop laughing, it is not funny, someone help me." She is scrambling to clean up the drink.

Winry gets up to get some napkins to help her mom. "You know we aren't laughing that you spilt your drink, we are laughing because you said 'fuck' again."

"What? I most certainly did not," Mrs. Bennett says adamantly.

"Yes, you did, Izzy," Chief laughs but takes his wife's hand in his.

Winry comes back to my side. "Mom does this thing where she says 'fuck' but has no memory of it. The first time ever was one Christmas Eve, I was like ten, and a dog ran out in front of her. We missed it but she screamed 'oh fuck.' We were all mortified, and she still claims to this day that she did not say that."

"Winry Ann, stop saying that. I do not say that word." Mrs. Bennett looks offended by Winry's accusation.

"Okay, sure, Mom." Winry gives me a wink as she takes a bite of her burger.

"Winry, remember that time Mom tried to give you bangs and they were so short," Waverley snorts at the memory.

"Oh gosh, how could I forget? Ugh they took forever to grow back." Winry turns to me. "You will never see a picture of me from middle school. I burned them all."

"Oh, come on, I'm sure they weren't that bad," I couldn't imagine Winry looking bad ever.

"Thank you for trying, Graham, but they indeed were that bad. I helped her burn the pictures myself," Mrs. Bennett buries her face in her hands. "I cried just as much as she did the night I cut them."

"What about the time Mom got pulled over for speeding because we were jamming 'Black Betty' by Ram Jam." Wyla says, continuing to throw their mom under the bus.

"Hey, I got out of that ticket, thank you very much." Mrs. Bennett says with pride in her voice.

"Yeah, because you would not stop talking to the cop; the guy had cut you off to tell you we were free to go," Winry adds to the pile.

"Well, we were in a different county, I couldn't use your father to get out of it, so I had to do something," Mrs. Bennett exclaims.

"You literally annoyed him out of it." Waverley laughed.

"My word, girls, are you guys going to talk about any of the good I have done? Graham, do you talk to your mom like these brats?"

"No, ma'am, but in their defense, I think the funniest thing my mom did was make me run laps around the house when I got in trouble, which was often," I chuckle at the memory.

Mrs. Bennett nearly chokes on her water. "When you got in trouble you would have to run around the outside of the house?"

I shrug my shoulders. "Yeah, backfired on her a little, I enjoy running now and it kept me in shape."

"It sure did," Waverley jokes.

"Waverley," Winry gives her a look and throws a chip at her. Waverley just sticks her tongue out in response.

The rest of the dinner goes smoothly for the most part. Chief barely speaks and there is this weird tension between us. I know he had to like me at some point—I mean, he did hire me for a reason. Granted, he probably didn't think I would date his daughter within a month of starting. The girls help their mom clear the table and I notice Chief walk outside on the back porch. I decide to slip out to talk to him.

"Chief, you got a minute?" We have to clear the air for Winry's sake because I don't intend on going anywhere.

He is sitting in one of the rocking chairs with a beer and motions for me to take the one next to him. "What's on your mind, Taylor?"

I take the seat and take a deep breath. "Well, I guess I want to start with a thank you. Winry told me today what happened last year... I don't know what to say other than thank you. Thank you for saving her, sir."

He takes a long pause like he is processing what I just said. "Ah damn it. If she told you about that then she must be serious about you...don't get me wrong, Taylor, I do like you. I wouldn't have hired you if I didn't, but you look at her like I look at their mom. Like she hung the moon, and I'll tell you, Winry did. Waverley and Wyla may be sunshine, but Winry shines the brightest in the moonlight. All I want is for her is to find someone who loves and accepts her. I just thought I was more prepared for it. Turns out I'm not."

"I do love her." I thought saying out loud would feel weird like it did in my head, but saying it out loud made it all make sense.

"Yeah, I know you do. I guess I'd better get on board." He takes a long swig of his beer.

"Hey, what are you two doing out here?" I hear the sliding door and Winry steps out walking to us.

"Oh, nothing. I was just telling Graham about how you used to try to sneak out and go skinny dipping at the beach," Chief says casually.

My head falls back from laughing. I'll add that to the list of things I want to do with her.

Winry's mouth is agape. "Okay, and we are leaving," She grabs my hands pulling me up out of the chair.

"Thanks for having us, Daddy." Winry gives her dad a kiss on the cheek, and we head inside to say our goodbyes. I get hugs from all the Bennett girls and Chief gives me a normal handshake and doesn't look like he wants to punch me.

I open up the passenger door for Winry.

"That wasn't so bad, was it?" She asks as she climbs in.

"No, it was good. Your dad didn't kill me and only minimal embarrassing stories for you." I tug lightly on her ponytail, "Remind me to take you to the beach more often."

"You don't have to take me to the beach to get me naked, just out of my parents' driveway and I'm all yours." Winry teases me with a sexy smirk.

Before work Wednesday, I decide to call my mom back. She has messaged me nonstop asking questions about Winry.

She answers by the second ring. "Finally, you call me back."

"I know, sorry, Mom. How was your day?"

"No, don't try to act normal, like you didn't tell me that you found a girl you want to marry. You'd better not have been lying to me, Graham. I have been waiting for this day. Even though I am a little sad it's not Claire, but happy, nonetheless." She is talking a mile a minute.

"Mom, calm down, I'm not lying to you. Her name is Winry, and I'm serious about her, Mom, so no more Claire talk," I say, annoyed.

"Winry, interesting name. Tell me about her," Mom demands.

"Well for starters she is beautiful, with dark hair and hazel eyes. She is my neighbor and my chief's daughter actually. She runs her own business; it's a bookstore and café called Crossroads. I realize that it is a little quick, but I don't know, I just know she is the one." I normally would never be so candid with my mom, but Winry has brought out a new side of me.

"She runs her own business? Rather ambitious. I mean, have you thought much about how that will affect your family? Both of you having demanding jobs, Graham, is not ideal. Plus, you should really think about a different field too if you want a family."

My good mood immediately soured. "Mom, come on. I am talking to you about a girl I am serious about, and you are ruining it."

"I am most certainly not ruining it. Graham, these are things you have to think about before you decide if you want to marry this girl. I mean it is probably best you move back here too."

I rub my hand over my face and take a deep breath. This is exactly what I was worried about. "And why would I need to move back?"

"Well, I am here for one. I am retired, I could watch the children." She responds like I am stupid or something.

"Mom, you are years ahead of us right now, there is no reason to be talking about this right now. I am not moving back, and I am not making a career change, and I'm not going to have her do those either. I called to talk positively about the girl I am seeing, Mom." I let my aggravation out a little bit.

"Graham, I am just being realistic. But I suppose we can start small; I need to meet her." Mom says bluntly. "It's the Summer Festival this weekend in Rosewood, why don't you bring her for the weekend?"

"That actually isn't a bad idea, but before you ask, we aren't staying at the house. I'll get us our own place." After this conversation I am hesitant to bring Winry to meet my mom, but I do love the summer festival. I want to make memories there with her.

"Why not? There is nothing wrong with my house," she says defensively.

"That's the deal, Mom, take it or leave it." I know once she meets Winry, she will love her, and I hope all of the questions and judgment will cease.

"I'll take it. I can't wait to meet her." I can hear the joy in my mom's voice.

"Okay, we will work something out for this weekend. I'll talk to you later." We say our goodbyes then I send off a group message to Winry's sisters and Ivy.

Me: Does Winry like festivals and carnivals?

Ivy: Yes, she will kick your ass at some carnival games.

Wyla: She sure does. Does this have to do with her birthday?

Me: Yeah, there is an annual summer festival in my home town that always has a bunch of booths set up and a carnival. I thought it would be fun for her birthday. Thoughts?

Waverley: She would love that. Gold star, Graham.

Me: I was planning on us staying the weekend, but y'all could drive up Saturday; I thought it would be good for her to have you guys there too.

Waverley: Even better!

Ivy: I'll be there!

Wyla: Count me in!

I hear a car door open and close. I check the time. It's a little after six, I don't have to be at work till seven, so I decide to quickly throw on my uniform then head over to Winry's.

I knock on her door, "Police, open up."

She opens the door and looks me up and down in my uniform, biting her lower lip. "Oh perfect, the stripper I ordered is here."

"Hi, buttercup." I cup her face and bring her in for a quick kiss.

"Hey, think you could call out tonight and stay here with me? I think we could use these cuffs for something else." She pulls me to her by my belt and looks up at me with sultry eyes.

I groan and harden immediately at the thought of Winry naked and cuffed to the bed. "Oh, don't do that to me. Now I'll be thinking of all the possibilities all night."

Her head falls back laughing, so I take advantage and kiss her neck. If I'm going to have to leave turned on, she will too. I continue to kiss her neck, then slip a hand under her shirt and rub her breast. I can feel her nipples harden beneath the thin fabric of her bra.

"Graham," she says breathlessly.

I pull back, "Tell me, buttercup, are you as wet as I think you are?"

"Wetter. Too bad you have to go to work. I think I will just have to take care of myself." She gives me a wicked smile and my knees wobble.

"Damn it Winry, you win."

"It's too easy," she laughs.

"I did actually come over here to talk to you about our plans this weekend." I create a little distance so I can focus and not start kissing her all over.

"Oh, yeah? What are you thinking?"

"Rosewood is having their annual Summer Festival and Carnival. I thought we could go up for the weekend. And maybe visit my parents. My mom has been begging to meet you, but it's your birthday, so if you don't want to do that, we will do something else." I run my hands through my hair and look down waiting for her answer.

"No that sounds like fun. I want to see where little Graham grew up and meet your parents." She smiles.

"Okay good, there is a little bed and breakfast. I'll get us a room, and I invited your sisters, Ivy, and Owen to come Saturday for the carnival. Again, if you want them to; if not I'll..."

"Graham, it sounds perfect." She interlocks her fingers behind my neck.

"Okay great." I check my watch. "Shit, I've got to go, babe."

She lets out a groan, then pouts. I can't resist anymore; I kiss her and bite her pouty lip.

A male voice huffs out, "Taylor, aren't you supposed to be headed to work and not groping my daughter?"

We turn to see Winry's dad standing at the entryway with his arms crossed, looking entirely unamused.

"Oh, hi, Dad. I forgot you were stopping by." Winry takes a step back, nervously tugging on the hem of her shirt.

"Yeah, I gathered that," he says, still staring.

"Sorry, sir. I'd better get going. I'll talk to you later, Win. Chief," I nod in his direction, "have a good night."

He does his best to remain stone-faced but breaks slightly and claps me on the back on my way out. "Be careful tonight, Taylor."

"Yes, sir." I turn back and give Winry a wink and head to the station.

I arrive without a minute to spare; Owen waits for me at his car outside with his arms crossed. "Cutting it a little close today, aren't we, Taylor?"

"Sorry, I got held up." I say, climbing into the patrol car.

"Held up or tied up?" Owen wiggles his eyebrows at me.

"I wasn't tied up…she was about to be though." The image of her cuffed to her headboard resurfaces and I have to adjust my pants.

Owen busts out laughing, placing a hand over his chest. "Man, you two are really happy, aren't you?"

"Yeah, we are." I still haven't told her that I loved her yet. I have never told a girl I loved her. I'm a little nervous about it; I don't want to freak her out. We haven't been together long, but hey, when you know you know.

"Well buckle up, lover boy, we have full night ahead of us." Owen gives me a shove then puts the car in drive and we get the night started.

We ride around for a couple of hours. The night is pretty slow. Winry messages me halfway in.

Buttercup: I can't stop thinking about you in your uniform.

Me: I can't stop thinking about your handcuff joke.

Buttercup: Who said I was joking? <winky face emoji>

I must let out an audible growl because Owen starts to laugh.

"Quit sexting Winry and tell her I said hi."

"Shut up, we're not sexting...yet." I laugh and Owen smacks my shoulder.

Then a call comes over the scanner, "Requested unit at Bluebird's, possible criminal trespass. A white male in a blue t-shirt refusing to leave the property."

Owen clicks on the radio, "210 enroute."

We arrive at the bar and head straight inside, where there is a man in a blue shirt yelling at the bartender.

"What seems to be the problem here?" Owen asks, cutting off the man yelling at the poor bartender.

The man whips around, and I let out a curse when I realize who it is. Flynn fucking Martin. A little smile is brought to my face when I notice his nose is a little crooked where Winry broke it.

"What the fuck are y'all doing here? Aren't you tired of harassing me? I mean really, don't you have better things to do?" Flynn slurs angrily.

"I cut him off a half hour ago, he started yelling, so we kicked him out. He just keeps coming back after we have told him to leave several times," the bartender, Lacey, fills us in.

"Okay, come on, Flynn let's go. Luckily for you I am good mood, so why don't you let us call you a ride and we can call it a night?" I let Owen do the talking. I don't think I can talk rationally to this guy. Hell, just looking at him reminds me of seeing him on top of Winry—my Winry—and my whole body tightens with anger.

"You know, I don't really feel like going home, maybe I should go see an old ex of mine. Eh, Officer Taylor, what do you think?" Flynn sneers and puffs out his chest.

Keep your cool, Graham.

"I would suggest you take us up on calling you a ride. I don't care where you go, but you can't stay here and you aren't going to Winry's, so pick somewhere, or Aster Creek jail will gladly take you for the night." I keep my tone even; getting me mad is exactly what he wants, and I refuse to give this dipshit any ammunition.

A blonde girl races up and tugs on Flynn's arm. She looks at us with wide eyes. "I'm sorry, he is just drunk. I'll call us a cab; I will make sure he gets home."

"No, Sara, I'm not going anywhere." Flynn yanks his arm back. "What I really want to know Officer Taylor is does she taste as good as I remember? Man, what I would give to taste her again."

I clench my jaw and my firsts. "Flynn, this is your last chance."

Sara comes back up, looking frantic, "Please wait, I called a cab, it should be here soon. Flynn, let's just go back to my place."

"Okay, Winry...oops, I mean Sara. My mistake." Flynn smirks then wraps his arm around Sara, walking out of the bar.

Owen glides past me and pats me on the back. "I am going to make sure they actually get in the cab. Cool off then meet me outside."

I take a moment to calm down. That fucker doesn't deserve to say her name. I'd love nothing more than to shut him up, but that's what he wants, and I sure as shit won't be doing that. I let Lacey know to call us if he comes back then make my way outside to the car. I fall into my seat, finally able to breathe. I run my hands over my face and let out a deep breath.

"I listened to the girl give the address and it wasn't Winry's, but we can swing by her place if you want to check on her," Owen says, pulling out of the Bluebird's parking lot.

"Yeah, if we could." I keep it short because I am still on edge.

I don't think I unclench my jaw the entire drive over, and I definitely don't say anything to Owen. He knows I'm pissed, so he keeps his mouth shut too. We pull into my apartment, and I can see that her lights are still on, so I hop out.

"I'll be right back," I say bluntly, closing the door behind me.

I walk up and I can hear the TV going, so I knock on the door. I hear her yelp inside. A smile immediately tugs at my face. "Winry, it's just me. Open up."

I hear her shuffle to the door and pull it open. She looks so cute. Her hair is in a messy bun, and she is wearing one of my sweatshirts with some pajama shorts. "Hey, what's going on? Is everything okay?" Worry mars her face.

I debate telling her about the run-in with Flynn. Part of me wants to tell her, but the other part of me doesn't want to freak her out. I don't want her being anxious all night, especially since I can't be there with her, but I don't want to keep things from her either. I decide it's best to wait to tell her later, so I just say, "Yeah, everything is fine, I just saw your lights on and wanted to see my little night owl."

A smile brightens her face, and she steps closer, wrapping her arms around my waist. I pull her in tighter and rest my head on the top of hers. I take in a deep breath, and I am met with the smells of peaches and honey. The smell will forever be tied to her; I don't think I could smell or eat either without being turned on.

"Aw, this has to be the cutest thing I have ever seen," Owen hollers as he rolls down his window.

Winry and I both flip him the bird and he bursts out laughing.

"All right, I'd better go. Get some sleep, okay?" I cup her chin, placing my thumb in her dimple.

"Sure thing, Dad." She rolls her eyes playfully, then smirks.

"Don't get sassy with me, buttercup, I'll make sure you pay for it." I tighten my grip on her chin.

"Exactly what I am hoping for, now kiss me like you want to do something about it."

I lean in and kiss her; it's not a gentle kiss, it's hard and demanding. Her lips part, and I explore her mouth with my tongue. She tastes like wine, and my pants start to feel tight.

"In case you two forgot, I am still here," Owen yells, interrupting us. "As much as I enjoy the show, we've got to go."

"Okay, okay. I'll think of you when I break out my vibrator tonight." Winry purrs and gives me a playful push out the door.

"You just love to torture me, don't you?"

"Yeah, I do, now go before I pull you in here and give Owen a real show." She winks.

"So naughty. I'll talk to you tomorrow, buttercup."

"Okay, be safe." She gives me one last quick kiss.

"Always. Good night."

Back in the car with Owen, I wait for the teasing to start. I know he's got jokes ready to go, but I don't care. He can say whatever he wants; it won't affect me. Nothing is going to change how I feel about her.

"Feel better?" Owen asks, backing out of my driveway.

"Yeah, thanks. I don't think I would have been in the right headspace had I not checked on her," I admit.

"You tell her about running into Flynn?" He seems to have the same hesitation in his voice.

"No, I will tell her tomorrow. I didn't want her to worry about it all night and be paranoid." I think I will be worried enough for the both of us.

"I'd say that is a good call. She really has you wrapped around her finger, doesn't she?" Owen smiles.

"Yeah, she does. I'm not going to even bother lying about it." Call me whipped, I don't care.

Owen claps my shoulder. "That's good, I'm happy for you."

"Thanks, man." Feeling more at ease, I focus on the night ahead.

Chapter 13

Winry

I unlock the back door at Crossroads bright and early at six in the morning. Clicking on all the lights, I make my way to the front to get everything opened up. I tidy everything up and get all of our machines up and ready to go. Ivy comes strolling in about a half an hour later.

"Ready for the day, sugar?" I ask as she makes her way back to the kitchen.

"Oh, as ready as I will ever be. Hey, have you talked to Graham?" Ivy hangs up her bag and gets started on our normal pre-shift coffees.

"About this weekend? Yeah, he told me. I am trying to think positively about my birthday and pray this awful curse breaks this year." I cross my fingers and a say a silent prayer.

"No, I meant...never mind." Ivy turns back to making our coffees.

"Oh, come on Ives. Tell me, is there something else about this weekend I should know about?" I walk up to her and nudge her with my elbow a few times. "You know you want to tell me."

"It's not about your birthday, but I am looking forward to it though. No, last night I was at Bluebird's and Flynn was there. He got plastered again. I don't know what is up with him, I mean I never knew him to be such a drinker. Anyway, he got kicked out but wouldn't leave so Lacey had to call the cops. Graham and Owen showed up, and he did his best to get under Graham's skin. Flynn kept talking about you, Graham looked like he wanted to kill him. They didn't arrest him though, his unfortunate new girlfriend managed to get him in a cab."

"No, he hadn't told me, but now this makes sense why he came and saw me last night. He showed up at the apartment in the middle of the night last night. He said he just saw my lights were on and wanted to check on me. I wonder why he didn't just tell me."

Ivy shrugs. "He probably didn't want to freak you out. I mean you would be home all night by yourself, and I know you, you would be worried about Flynn showing up all night. It's sweet though that he came to check on you. I swear, that man is obsessed with you." Ivy hands me my usual latte.

"Yeah, I guess you are right, I definitely would have been on edge. And he is not obsessed with me." I mean yeah, we spend every moment we can together, and I am pretty sure I am falling in love with the guy, but I keep that to myself.

"Um, yes, he is, and you are just as obsessed with him. Don't try to lie to me, Win, I know you. I don't think I have ever seen you this happy. Want a chocolate chip scone? Sorry, I don't have any muffins." Ivy pulls out a tray of scones that we have wrapped from yesterday.

"Yeah, hand it over." I reach out for the chocolate chip goodness and then hop up on the counter.

"Everything is going good, right?" Ivy perks her eyebrows in question.

"Yeah, everything seems to be going great." I keep my answer short. To be honest with myself, I do love him. I just push that thought aside; there is no way he is in love with me. Do I think he likes me? Yes, but love...I don't know if I am good enough for his love.

Ivy cocks out her hip and gives me her listen to me look. "Seems to be? Come on, Win, I can see those gears turning in your head. You can think whatever you want, but we can all see it. He is head over heels for you."

"I think I am for him too. But come on, it's time to open up." I hop down and unlock the door, ready to start the day.

The day seems to go by fairly quickly. A small group of girls come in and grab some coffees. One of them looks oddly familiar, but I can't seem to place her. I continue with my normal daily tasks, wipe down some tables, and help Ivy where she needs. Our door chimes, and in walk Owen and his adorable niece, Annabelle.

Owen's younger sister, Natalie, is a bit of a mess. She had Annabelle at sixteen but never really grew up. I get going out every now and then, but if Annabelle isn't with Owen, she is with her grandma. Annabelle's dad signed away his rights as soon as she was born, so Owen has sort of taken on that father figure role, but with his schedule it can be hard.

"Hey guys, what a treat. What brings you in?" I walk around the counter and give Annabelle a hug.

"Belley here had demanded to come back to her—and I quotc— favorite store in town." Owen ruffles her hair, and she swats his hand away the best she can.

I let out a laugh. It's always so sweet to see Owen with Annabelle; he loves her fiercely and it shows. "Annabelle, you will be going into the fifth grade, right? Maybe next year you will get Waverley as one of your teachers."

"Oh, I really hope so, that would be so cool." Annabelle says ecstatically.

"I hope not, I want you to actually learn something in school." Owen places his hand on her shoulders and gives her a little shake.

I roll my eyes at Owen's joke. "Annabelle, we just got in some new books in the young adult section—why don't you go take a look? See if you can sweet talk your uncle into getting you a couple of books." Annabelle bounces by completely focused on finding a new book.

"Thanks for that, I'll be broke by the end of this."

Annabelle always has her nose in a book. At eleven years old, she is reading at a twelfth-grade level. Sometimes she walks here after school and reads until her grandma can pick her up, and I love seeing her so enthralled by the book she is reading.

"Anytime, now what else can I get you? Coffee?" I ask, walking back behind the counter.

"I'll take a just a black coffee and a decaf mocha frappe for Belley. I'd better wait to pay until she is done because I know I will have to buy some books."

"Coming right up." I whip up their drinks, and in that short amount of time, Annabelle brings four books in hand to Owen and is jumping up and down pleading for him to buy them all. Owen gives me a "see what you did" look and I just laugh.

"Okay, guys, here are your drinks. Annabelle, would you like me to ring up those books for you?" I wink at her, and she giggles. She knows she has got her uncle's number.

I bag up her books and they take their drinks to go. "Thanks, Winry, I'll see you this weekend." Owen says.

"Can't wait. Bye, Annabelle." I say as they start their way out.

"Bye, Winry." She hollers back as they walk out the door.

I go to wave but accidentally knock over our cup of pens. Thankfully the cup doesn't break but I pick them up and when I stand back up there is a familiar blonde standing in front of me.

"Oh, hi. Sorry, I am a little clumsy. How can I help you?" I study her face. Where do I know her from?

"You're Winry, right?" Her tone is bland and unimpressed.

"Um, yeah that's me. I'm sorry, you look familiar; do I know you?"

She scoffs like I have offended her. "I'm Sara, we met at Bluebird's about a month ago. I am Flynn's new girlfriend." She broadens her shoulder and turns up her nose. "I didn't know you worked here."

"Well, I own the place, so yeah, I guess you could say I work here. Is there something I can get for you?" I don't really know how to speak to her. I in no way am intimidated by her; honestly, I feel sorry for her.

"Just for your little cop friend to leave Flynn alone." Sara places her hands on the counter, leaning in. "I mean really, it's a little pathetic."

"He is just doing his job, and Graham is my boyfriend not my little friend." It felt good to correct her.

"Oh, please, honey. He is a little out of your league don't you think?" She looks at me like she feels bad for me, like I am delusional or something.

My patience is wearing thin. "Definitely an upgrade from Flynn, I would have to agree with you there. I mean, he doesn't attack me and sling me across the room or anything."

Sara seems taken aback for a moment by my words but then quickly snaps back. "Don't be childish, that was a misunderstanding, and you know it." Sara puts her hands on her hips in protest.

"A misunderstanding?" My mouth gapes open, my patience is now gone. "He broke into my apartment and gave me a concussion. That is a misunderstanding? Look, if you aren't here to buy something, I think it is best you move on." I nod toward to the door, tempted to tell her to not let it hit her on the way out.

"Oh, snappy little thing, aren't you? I would suggest—"

"I would suggest you find somewhere else to get coffee," Ivy comes up, cutting her off.

"I'm sorry, are you kicking me out?" Sara scoffs.

"Sure am. Your friends can stay or go, don't matter to me, but like Flynn was told last night, you can't stay here. Funny how couples act alike, isn't it?" Ivy snaps.

Sara's jaw drops, and she stares between us for a moment then stomps her foot turning to walk out the door, "Come on guys let's go, this place sucks anyways."

We watch them as the small group files out, I am sure we will get a couple fake bad reviews over this, but oh well. I let out the breath I didn't realize I was holding and turn to Ivy.

"Thank you. That, that was…I don't really know what that was." I fidget with my hair and tuck it behind my ears. My mind starts to replay the night that Flynn broke into my house, the fear I felt when he trapped me up against the door and then threw me and pinned me down.

"Win, why don't you take a break?" Ivy rubs my arm and I nod. A break, I need a break.

The little conversation put me in a serious funk. I am pretty much silent the rest of the day, my smiles are fake, and I am second guessing everything. I mean really, how could what happened be a misunderstanding? And Graham may be out of my league, but he likes me…right?

I start our end-of-day cleaning and lock up the front door as soon as 6 hits. I am so ready to be home, even though I know I will just be stewing in this mood. Thankfully Graham works tonight, so I can wallow in it, and it will be out of my system by this weekend.

"You all done up here?" Ivy asks, walking out of the kitchen.

"Yeah, just finished. You ready to go?" I grab my bag from under the counter.

"Yes, let's get out of here." Ivy hits the lights and we make our way out the back door.

"You going to be okay tonight, Win?" Ivy asks.

"Hmm..." my brain had checked out the moment I walked out the door. "Yeah, I'll be fine. Don't worry about me, I'm good. Promise." I manage some half-ass smile and unlock my car.

"Okay, call me if you want to talk, all right?" Concern crosses Ivy's face.

"I will, love you lots." I blow her a kiss and hop in my car.

The drive home is silent, and I catch myself doing that thing where you have been driving but honestly have no memory of it. You just check out and muscle memory takes over. I snap out of it a couple of times and make it to my place. Graham's car is already gone. Is it odd to be a little relieved? I just don't feel like pushing my mood on anyone else.

Once inside, I immediately climb into some sweats and throw my hair up. I collapse on the couch and run my hands over my face. I flip on the TV then flip it off again.

Come on, Winry. Snap out of this funk.

I hear my phone vibrating, and I am tempted to ignore it, but I look to see who it is first at least. Ivy's name pops up on my screen.

"Hey, Ives. What's up?" I fake sounding perky.

"Hey, why don't you come help us carry in this food, okay?" I can hear her digging around in her car.

"What are you talking about?"

"Just come outside."

She hangs up and I stand up going to my door. Swinging it open, I am met with Ivy and my sisters with food and bags in hand.

"Sleepover!" They all shout together.

"You guys, you didn't have to come over. I am glad you are here, but you didn't have to."

"Quit your yapping and move out of the way." Waverley says, pushing me out of the way.

"Come on, Win. We know Graham is working tonight, and we are not about to let you wallow alone all night. We brought some of your favorites." Wyla shakes the bags in her hands all giddy.

"All right, I'm listening. What you got will determine whether I'll kick you out," I joke knowing good and well that they would never leave.

They set all of the bags down on the coffee table. I already see wine, so that's a plus.

"Well for starters, we got a Mexican buffet. We ordered enchiladas, tacos, burritos, rice, and your own salsa and cheese dip so you can mix them," Ivy says, unloading the food and getting it spread out.

"Then we got bottles of your favorite wine, and it's not the same as yours but we got a pack of cookie dough." Wyla takes the wine and cookie dough and pumps it into the air.

"I'll get the plates and silverware." Waverley jumps up and heads into my kitchen.

"Thanks guys, for all of this." A lump forms in my throat, but I swallow it down and let out my first genuine smile in hours. Waverley comes back and we all take a plate and dive in.

"So, do you want to talk about what happened earlier or something else?" Wyla asks, scooping out some rice.

"Ugh, I don't know. She bothered me. Not in the 'she is Flynn's new girlfriend' way but in an 'I'm the problem' way. She called the night he broke in a misunderstanding...in what world was that a misunderstanding?" Anger starts to bubble up, but at least I am feeling something other than the doom and gloom I was before.

"She was just trying to get under your skin, Win. Last night at Bluebird's she was a mess, and to piss Graham off, Flynn kept talking about you and even called her Winry. I am sure she is just jealous." Ivy mumbles the last part as she takes a bite of her taco.

"Last night? What happened last night?" Waverley looks back and forth between me and Ivy looking for more information.

"Flynn got kicked out of Bluebird's but wouldn't leave so Lacey called the police. Graham and Owen showed up and Flynn kept poking at Graham about me. They didn't arrest him, just made him take a cab elsewhere," I say filling her and Wyla in.

"Graham looked absolutely feral. Gah, it was so hot," Ivy fans herself with her hands.

"Hey, watch it," I tease. "He's mine."

"First, we would never, but even if we tried to seduce him, we would all fail. He only has eyes for you, Win." Waverley stabs a piece of chicken with her fork and plops it in her mouth.

"See, I told you," Ivy echoes. "Forget what Sara said, Winry."

"You're right, you're right. Sorry guys, let's move on to better topics," I say, dusting my hands of the conversation.

"Are y'all planning something special for the anniversary of opening Crossroads?" Wyla asks in between bites.

"I think we should do something. Ives, what do you think?" I ask.

"I'm down for whatever," Ivy shrugs. "You are the planner girl."

"Well, I think we could do like an open house party. Have some samples of our treats and little coffee shots out, and do some door prizes like gift cards, some of our blind date books, and maybe some like coffee mugs. Mom has one of those machines so she could put our name on them." I ramble off my ideas. "I say we do it the first Saturday in September, which would give us plenty of time."

"Yeah, that sounds like a great idea. See, this is why you are the planner. I'll let you throw all that together and I'll make little shots of our favorite drinks and then maybe just have our daily brew set out with some sugar and creamer."

"Oh, Ivy, make those fruit pizza cookies, but make them like bite sized samples. I love those cookies. Oh, oh, and those chocolate chip brownie tarts. Man, what I wouldn't give for one of those right now," Waverley says licking her lips.

Ivy nods, "Yeah, those will be good, and easy to make a bunch of."

"I'll handle all the decorations and marketing for it, and Abigal can assist us where we need it. Oh, I'm so excited, I can't believe we have been open for almost a year." Pride radiates through me.

"I know, it's crazy, it feels like y'all just opened it. I mean that's a big accomplishment; a lot of people don't have the growth you guys have had in a year. Oh, hold on let's have a toast," Wyla picks up her glass. "To Crossroads and the beautiful women who own it."

We all lift our glasses and clink them together. "Cheers!" We chorus together and laugh.

"Ugh, I am stuffed," Waverley leans back on the love seat and rubs her belly.

"Me too," I collapse back also, copying Waverley.

"Let's take our wine on the back porch," Wyla stands, grabbing her glass and bottle.

"Oh, yes," I follow suit and head out the back door with my glass and bottle.

Outside, Blackjack is curled up in the little cat bed I have laid out for him. "Hey there, bud." I say, giving him a little pet. He meows and swats me away. "Okay, ungrateful, I'll leave you alone."

Ivy and I sit on the couch while Wyla and Waverley sit in the hanging chairs. We are at least one bottle deep each, and our buzz is kicking in. I finish my glass and Ivy pours me another.

"This is just what I needed, guys. Thank you," I reach out and grab Ivy's hand and give it a squeeze and start to laugh for no reason.

"Oh, here we go, Winry's drunk," Waverley laughed with me. I may be a giggler when I get a few drinks in me—sue me.

"Shut up, at least I am a happy drunk." I laugh again. My phone starts ringing on the small side table. "Ivy, can you hand me that?"

"Sure thing." Ivy leans over grabbing my phone. "It's lover boy." Ivy hands me my phone and does a little dance with her eyebrows which makes me laugh again.

"Gimme that." I take a deep breath, trying to calm my giggles. I try and fail. "Hey, you." I say in between laughs.

Ivy hits my leg, "Put him on speaker." So I do.

"Hey buttercup, what's so funny?" Graham lets out a light chuckle at my laughing fit.

"She's drunk, Graham." Waverly yells. "I hope you like a giggle box drunk because that is what you got."

Graham really laughs at that, "Babe, are you drunk?"

"Just a little...it's their fault. They brought a bunch of wine," I say defensively.

"And how much of it have you drank, buttercup?"

"I don't remember," I lie and laugh.

"She is halfway through her second bottle, Graham," Ivy answers for me.

"Whose side are you on?" I give Ivy a little shove.

"Hey, Win, want to hear a joke about paper?" Graham asks.

"Always."

"Never mind, it's tear-able."

My head falls back and I belly laugh, "That one is the best so far babe."

"I think that's because you're drunk, Win, but I'll take it either way. Hey, I got to get off here; be sure and drink some water, okay?"

"Okay, I'll see you tomorrow," I have a strong need to say I love you but instead I say, "Be safe tonight."

"Always."

I hang up the phone and I am wearing a cheesy smile on my face, feeling all warm and fuzzy inside, and not from the alcohol. We stay out on the porch chatting and gossiping for about an hour.

"All right, like daddy Graham said, let's drink some water. We, unfortunately, still have to work tomorrow." Ivy takes my wine glass, and we head back inside.

"Let's move the coffee table and make a sister pile tonight," Wyla says as she gets four bottles of water out of the fridge.

"Yes, and I need some more chips and salsa." I grab the bag of chips and cup of already mixed dip.

"I don't understand how you mix it like that. Cheese dip is perfectly fine on its own," Waverley scrunches her nose as I scoop up another big bite.

"I'll get the pile started. Can someone help me move the table?" Wyla steps toward the living room and Ivy follows.

"Come on, Wav, just try some." I hold out a chip for her, which I know she will not take, but I know it will push her buttons. She hates it when people try to get her to eat new foods.

"Ew, no way. Winry, get that away from me," she shrills.

I laugh, relishing that I got the reaction I wanted.

"Okay, you two. Why don't y'all come in here and help?" Wyla nearly has the pile ready, but she knows that left without something to do, Waverley and I will pick and poke at each other.

I grab some more blankets and pillows from upstairs, and after that, our heap of comfiness is complete. We climb under the blankets and cuddle together.

"I don't know about you guys, but I am beat," Wyla snuggles her blanket, already close to falling asleep.

"At least you and Wav don't have to work tomorrow. Ivy and I will be waking you guys up with us bright and early at 6."

"Um, yeah, no thanks," Wyla puts her head under the pillow.

"Hey, I don't want to hear it from you either," Ivy gives me a little kick. "Someone is leaving early to go on a romantic weekend with her boyfriend. I'll be stuck there from 7 to 6," Ivy groans.

"Mm, I can already feel the wine headache kicking in." I pinch the bridge of my nose, trying to relieve some of the pressure.

"Well, that is what happens when you drink two bottles," Waverley teases.

"Ugh, sorry, Ives, I will be useless tomorrow," I shut my eyes, already feeling the pull of sleep.

"I was already prepared for that. Abigal said she would come in after her 8 a.m. class to help us." I feel Ivy shuffling to get comfortable.

"Ivy, you are the best," I say while I stifle a yawn. "I love you guys."

"We love you too," Wyla whispers.

Chapter 14

Winry

My alarm pounds at 6 in the morning, and we collectively groan.

"Ah, turn it off," Waverley mumbles.

I roll over and scrounge for my phone. My head feels like it is going to explode with each blare of the alarm. I finally find it under the pile of pillows and shut it off.

"Ivy," I give her a little shake, "we've got to get ready."

"Mm, five more minutes," She replies rolling away from me.

I begrudgingly climb out of the pile and head upstairs to shower and get ready. The hot water helps my headache a little, but I grab some medicine out of the cabinet and take it. I really hate being hungover, and I need to shake this if I am going to enjoy tonight with Graham.

Back downstairs, everyone is up moving around slowly. Ivy has changed her clothes but now sits on the couch with her eyes closed on the verge of falling back asleep. Waverley and Wyla are finishing folding the last blanket.

"Coffee, I need coffee." Waverley collapses next to Ivy.

"Why don't y'all come with us to help open up? I'll pay you with coffee," Ivy says.

"Deal," Wav and Wyla respond together.

We all head over to Crossroads; I unlock the back, and we all wince when I hit the lights.

"I'll get started on our coffees. Everyone want their usual?" Ivy asks.

"Yes," we mutter in response.

"Thanks, Ives. Wav and Wyla, why don't y'all hit the lights up front and turn on some music. Nothing provocative, and not too loud." I rub my temples with my fingers. "I'll help Ivy turn everything on back here, then I'll be up there to count the register."

"Aye, aye, captain," Waverley gives me a salute and they head up to the front.

It takes us the whole half hour to get everything on and ready to go because we are moving at snail's pace. I unlock the front door right at 7 and Ivy passes out our coffees.

"Oh, come to momma," Waverley takes the cup and takes a big gulp with no regard for how hot it is. "Ah, it's a good burn."

We all chuckle lightly and sip our coffee. The front door chimes and we all wince again.

"No, no, turn that off," Wyla cries.

I turn slowly to greet our customers because I think if I move too fast my head will explode. I scrounge up my best fake smile, but then it turns genuine when I am met with chestnut eyes.

"Morning, buttercup. How are you feeling?" Graham is still in his uniform, and even after being up all night working, he still looks perfect.

"Mm, better now." I round the counter and let him wrap me in a hug. "What are you doing here?"

"Just wanted to see my girl before I crashed. You're getting off early, right?"

"Yeah, I'll leave here around 3 and I just need to pack then we can go. What are our plans for tonight?" I bite down on my lower lip. Thinking about a full weekend with Graham has me feeling better by the second.

"Well, you know, it occurred to me that I have been a terrible boyfriend and haven't taken you on a proper date. So, tonight I thought would be perfect to wine and dine you," he leans in closer and whispers, "but if you keep looking at me like that, we will never leave my bed."

I swear I purr in response and give my best fuck me eyes.

"Get a room, guys," Waverley jokes, pulling us out of our intense gaze.

"You don't have to tell me twice," Graham picks me up and carries me to the door and I squeak out a laugh.

"Hey, I still need her," Ivy hollers.

Graham places me down, "Damn, so close." He gives me a little kiss on my nose.

"Go get some sleep, babe, I'll be over soon."

"You'd better." He gives me a quick kiss, then waves bye to Ivy and my sisters.

"Bye, Graham," they sing.

Walking back behind the counter, I have a smile plastered to my face and my headache is forgotten.

"My boyfriend is just so dreamy. I love him so much," Waverley mocks.

I stick out my tongue at her, "Leave me be, I'm happy."

"Yes, nauseatingly so," Waverley imitates throwing up.

I roll my eyes at her dramatics.

"All right, we'd better go." Wyla hops off the counter. "Last night was so fun, love you guys."

I hug them both, "Love you, thank you for cheering me up last night."

"Of course, bye Ivy," Wyla waves.

"All right, let's get this day moving." Ivy and I high five and get to work.

Abigal comes in right before the lunch rush starts. We get into our perfect rhythm, picking up where the other needs it. Before I know it, 3 hits, so I turn the front over to Abigal and head back to my place. I will myself to go home first and pack instead of climbing into bed with Graham.

Once upstairs I stare at my duffle bag. Packing is the worst. How am I supposed to know what I am going to want to wear all weekend? I let out a huff then throw in a dress for tonight, jeans for Saturday and Sunday and a couple of tops so I have some options. I grab my makeup bag and my pre-packed travel toiletries bag.

I change into some ripped mom jeans and the Corona beer shirt I wore the first day we met. I shoot Graham a message letting him know that I am ready when he is. My phone starts to buzz in my hand, but it's not Graham.

"Hey, Dad, what's up?" I answer.

"Hey, moon baby." I smile at Dad's endearment. "I needed to talk to you about something, you got a minute?"

"Uh, yeah. Is everything okay?" My mind always jumps to the worst.

"Yeah, well it will be, but they let me know that they are going to subpoena you to court with Flynn. We charged him with aggravated burglary for breaking in and aggravated assault since he gave you a concussion. He is trying to say that you let him in and that everything was consensual until you broke his nose."

"What? Dad, he pushed me up against the wall…" Panic is radiating through me.

"Win, honey, it will be okay. You will just have to go and corroborate your story with what you told Graham when it happened. He and Owen will be subpoenaed too. Has there been anything else that has happened with him that would help support your side?"

"Yeah, actually the night we broke up Flynn and I got into an argument and Owen and Graham broke it up before anything bad happened. I don't know if they will have a record of it because they didn't arrest him. Also, Wednesday night, Owen and Graham got called because Flynn had gotten drunk and wouldn't leave Bluebird's. They didn't arrest him that night either, but there should at least be a record that they were called. Ivy was there and said Flynn kept talking about me." I start twirling my hair nervously.

"Okay that's good, honey. I'll talk to Graham and Owen, and we will get it taken care of. Don't stress about it, okay?" I can hear the concern in my dad's voice. I know he is worried how this will affect me, especially with it being one year since the night.

There is a knock at my door, and then Graham walks in. I wave and mouth hi at him.

"Okay, Dad, I promise I won't. I got to go though." Graham puts his hands on my hips pulling me into him.

"I take it Graham just got there, so now I'm chopped liver, huh?" Dad grumbles.

"Oh, come on, don't be a baby." I let out a laugh when Graham nuzzles my neck with kisses.

"Yeah, yeah. I'll talk to you later. Have a fun birthday weekend, sweetie, love you."

"Thanks, Dad, love you too." I click off with him, and Graham stops attacking me with kisses.

"Hey, buttercup. Sorry, I couldn't help myself." Graham tucks a side of my hair behind my ear. "What was your dad saying?"

"He was filling me in about the whole Flynn court thing."

"Yeah, I got my subpoena last night. Listen, I wanted to tell you about the other night." Graham runs his hand through his hair. It's his tell that he is nervous.

"About Bluebird's? Ivy told me yesterday, she was there, heard it all."

I see the panic in his eyes that he has done something wrong. "I swear I was going to tell you, I just didn't—"

"Want me to worry, Graham it's okay. Really, I understand. Now come on, I don't want to talk about anything to do with that whole mess. I want to enjoy this weekend with you." I interlock my fingers behind his neck and lean my body into his. I stare into his chestnut eyes; they fill me with such warmth and comfort.

I'm tempted again to tell him that I love him, but the fear of putting my feelings out there like that holds them back. It almost feels like he is sitting on saying something too, but we just stare into each other's eyes instead.

He breaks our stare first. "You ready to go, buttercup?"

"With you? Always."

We load up in his car and hit the road for Rosewood. The drive isn't long, and we pull up to this adorable cottage-style bed and breakfast. It has rose bushes galore in every color and green vines growing up the side cobblestone wall.

"Oh, Graham, this place is so cute." It looked like that little place that you read about in fantasy books where the enemies to lovers are forced to share a bed.

"I thought you would like it. It's run by some friends of mine from high school. They said they would be here too this weekend." He pulls into the parking lot and puts the car in park.

"I can't wait to hear all about you in high school." I unfasten my seat belt and hop out of the car, eager to get this weekend started.

"Sorry, buttercup, I have plans for tonight and they don't include reliving my high school memories." He winks at me and grabs our bags. We make our way up the little stone pathway. There is a fancy wood sign with the name "Rosemary's Bed and Breakfast" by the entryway.

The inside is just as adorable as the outside, with warm greens met with oak wood beams and accents. The theme is very cottage garden inspired with flowers and plants at every corner.

"Oh, you're here. Jace, honey, they are here." A woman with strawberry-blonde hair bounces up and down with a huge smile on her face.

"Hey, Mary, long time no see." Graham says, putting down our bags.

"I'm so happy y'all came, sorry, I'm a hugger." Mary comes up wrapping Graham and me in a group hug.

I chuckle at her tight grip. "Don't worry about it. I'm a hugger myself. I'm Winry."

"Oh, I know. Graham talked about you nonstop on the phone when he booked for this weekend."

"Gee, way to be cool, Mary." A man rounds the corner with a little strawberry-blonde girl wrapped around him. He walks up to Mary and gives her a kiss on the cheek.

"Win, this is Jace, Mary, and their little girl, Sage. As you guys already know, this is Winry." Graham places his hand on my lower back.

"Hi, I'm so happy to meet you guys. This place is beautiful."

"Thank you. We are so happy to meet you; I don't think we have ever met any girl that Graham has seen before." Mary gives me another hug.

"Sorry, she is just a little excited." Jace pulls his wife back and hands over Sage, who is being shy. "We are glad you are here." He goes up to Graham and does the basic man hug with the pat on the back. "Y'all probably want to get unpacked. We have plenty of time to catch up later."

"Graham said you run your own bookstore, so I reserved the library room for you two. Jace will show you where it's at," Mary beams.

"That sounds perfect. Thank you." I like her already.

Graham and Jace grab the bags, and we follow him up the stairs. He unlocks the first door on the right and hands the keys over to Graham. "Here we are. If y'all need anything, just text me or Mare."

"Thanks, man," Graham responds because I am too busy gawking at this room. Each wall has some form of shelf with books on it, and the long wall is completely full of books.

"You like it, buttercup?" Graham closes and locks the door behind us.

"It's perfect." I spin around to face him. He is giving me that look again, like I am the most beautiful thing in the room. "Graham..."

"Yeah?"

"I love you."

"What?" His eyes grow wide, and I swear he is holding his breath.

I start to panic internally. Crap, what if he doesn't love me back, what if this totally freaks him out?

No, no what-ifs. Be confident, Win.

"I love you; you don't have to say it back if you aren't there yet. But I love you."

Graham moves, closing the distance between us. He crashes his lips to mine in a passionate kiss that I feel deep in my core. "I love you." He moves his hand to the back of my thighs, picking me up, and I lock my legs around him. "You are my everything, Winry Bennett."

Happy tears threaten my eyes, but I draw them back and kiss him ferociously. He loves me, I repeat in my head. He carries me over to the base of our bed and lays me down. His kiss explores down my neck and collarbone, while my hands pull up his shirt and scratch his muscular back. He breaks away for a moment, and I take advantage, pulling his shirt over his head. My hands move up and down his torso, mapping out each and every curve of muscle. He pulls me to the edge of the bed and presses his erection against my center. I stifle a moan at the contact.

"Nuh uh, buttercup. Don't you dare be quiet, I want everyone to hear how much I love you." He unbuttons my jeans and pulls them down. I am not usually one for underwear, but this time I put on my sexy red lace panties. I pull my shirt over my head to show off the matching bra.

"This looks amazing on you, but I think it will look so much better on the floor over there. Raise your hips for me, baby." I lift them, and he slides the small lace fabric down my legs. He drops to his knees, "Now I'm going to fuck you with my tongue until you until you come, and that bra had better be gone too by the time I'm done."

With the first stoke of his tongue, my back arches and my body writhes with pleasure. I don't know how I manage the brain capacity, but I get my bra off and one of his hands reaches up, squeezing my breast and rubbing my already hard nipple.

"Graham, I..." some gibberish leaves my mouth, completely incomprehensible.

"What was that, buttercup? Want me to stop?" He teases.

I raise up on my elbows meeting his wicked smile. "Don't you dare."

My hand grips his hair and I pull him back down. He growls and completely loses all restraint. He wraps his arms around my legs, locking them in place and devours me. With each pass of his tongue, I get closer until I finally succumb to my orgasm. I let out a string of curses and my hand tightens its grip on his hair, and my hips involuntarily move, thrusting out every bit of pleasure.

Graham kisses up my body, pausing to give my boobs attention. "Fuck, Graham."

"We will, buttercup." He breaks apart and undoes his jeans, pulling them down. I sit up and pull his underwear down myself. My hand wraps around his shaft, doing slow strokes.

"I need you inside of me now." I go to pull him on top of me.

He pauses me, "I should get a condom."

"You don't have to; I mean I am good if you are. I'm on the pill and I have never been with anyone without a condom, but to be sure I got tested after Flynn said he had been cheating on me."

"You sure? I am good too; I just want you to be sure." He cups my face.

"Yes, Graham. I want to feel you, every part of you. Don't hold back."

He closes his eyes and lets out a low groan. In a second, his strong hands pick me up and toss me up to the top of the bed, and he climbs on top of me. Our kiss is full of love and need. Graham grabs my legs and brings them up over his shoulders and pounds into me. I have never felt fuller in my life, never felt more complete and loved than I do in this moment.

"You take me so well, buttercup. Like you were made for me."

"Graham," I moan louder than I mean to.

"Louder, Winry." He leans forward slightly, deepening the angle and my eyes roll to the back of my head.

"Oh, God. More, more," I plead.

"That's my girl." Each thrust is harder, and I can feel him getting closer. "Fuck, Winry." His fists fall, bracing himself on each side of me, and he lets out a low growl and I can feel his orgasm take him over. My legs fall off his shoulders, and he gives out the last few strokes of his climax.

We stare into each other's eyes, heart pounding, trying to catch our breath. Graham brushes the hair away from my sweaty face. "I love you."

"I love you too, Graham."

He rolls to the side but keeps my body flush with his. He lightly strokes my hair, and I am tempted to drift off to sleep in his arms.

"Mm, as much as I want to stay here naked with you, our reservations are in a half hour, and I am determined to take you on a real date." He places a quick kiss on my nose.

"Half an hour? Damn, I need to clean up." I try to get up, but he grabs my arm, pulling me back down. "Graham, I've got to hurry."

"I'll let you go, just let me clean up the mess I caused first. Let me get a towel and I'll be right back."

"Okay." My head falls back on the comfy pillows, and I take in this moment of pure bliss.

A warm towel comes down my center. I lean up and watch Graham clean me. Why must everything this man does be so erotic?

"There we go, now you're free to go." He rolls my body slightly to the side and gives it a playful smack.

I saunter to the bathroom, my knees still a little wobbly. When I get in there, I am in awe yet again. There is a big walk-in tile shower with a waterfall-style showerhead in the center; we will definitely be showering together later.

I turn to the mirror. Thankfully, I don't look as bad as I thought I would. I grab my makeup bag and touch it up. My hair still has its loose curls from this morning, so I just add some dry shampoo to cover the sweat and give it a little volume. I throw on my dress; it's not usually my first choice, but it fits in with the theme of this bed and breakfast perfectly. It's a light green floral sundress with a sweetheart neckline and a slit up the left side. I add some jewelry and slide on my nude heels.

I head back into the room where Graham is also sliding on his shoes. He has on a nice pair of black dress pants and a white button-up shirt with just the right amount of button undone, and his black sports jacket is on the bed next to him.

"Wow, don't you look handsome?" I stroll over to him, and he stands up off the bed.

"'Wow yourself." He takes my hand and twirls me around. "You look gorgeous, buttercup."

"Thank you," I grin.

"Come on, let's go."

I grab my purse, and we head down the stairs. We can hear laughter coming from the living room, so we poke our heads in before we leave. A family who I assume is also staying here is in the middle of playing a game with Jace, Mary, and Sage.

Mary spots us first and her eyes spark with joy. She bounces off the couch, marching toward us. "Oh, look at you two, all dressed up. Where are you taking her, Graham?"

"Don't ruin their fun, Mary, let him surprise her," Jace walks up, nudging her.

"I am just so excited that Graham has a girlfriend. I have waited years for this," Mary pouts at her husband then at Graham.

"Why don't we have some beers by the fireplace when we get back?" Graham says, leaning in and giving Mary a quick kiss on the cheek. "I promise I'll let you tell her all the stories of us in high school."

"Deal," she clasps her hands together and bounces up and down. Jace pulls her into him and mouths "sorry" to us over her head.

Graham takes my hand, and we walk out to his car. "So, where are you taking me?" I ask as he opens the door for me.

"Like Jace said, let it be a surprise," he winks.

We pull out of the parking lot. Graham has one hand on the steering wheel and the other on my thigh. It only takes about ten minutes to pull into this fancy restaurant called Rivulet that sits right beside the river. Graham gets out and opens my door for me. He holds out his hand, so I take it.

"You look so beautiful, Win."

"I feel it, you make me feel beautiful." I squeeze his hand.

The corners of his mouth turn up, and he places a quick kiss on my nose. "Good, because you are."

We head into the restaurant and give the hostess our name. She escorts us through the dining area out to the balcony that looks over the water. We thank her and take our seats.

"This is so nice; I love the view," I wink at him, careful to not specify whether the view I am talking about is the water or him. It's a little bit of both, really.

"Tell me about it," he winks back at me. Our waiter comes up with the menus, and Graham orders us a bottle of Riesling.

"So, what's our plan for this weekend?" I ask while skimming the menu.

"Well, tomorrow for your birthday, we have the festival and carnival. Your sisters, Ivy, and Owen will be here around 3. I figured I would hold you captive in bed for a little while first. Then Sunday we have brunch with my mom."

"What about your dad? Are we meeting him?" The waiter comes back with the wine and pours us both a glass.

"I sent him a text that we would be in town, and he said cool, so no." Graham takes a drink of the wine. "He is more the call me-when-you're-dying kind of dad."

"Oh, I'm sorry. Does that bother you?" I feel bad. I wouldn't know what to do without my dad.

"Not really. It's the way he has always been. He's not a bad guy, just not one to show any emotion or affection either. Now, my mom on the other hand has not left me alone since I told her about you. I think she messages me five questions a day. It was much to her dismay that she won't see us till Sunday."

I chuckle. "I'm excited to meet her; think she will like me?" I ask, reaching for my glass. I'd be lying if I said I'm not nervous about meeting her.

"She'll love you, just be prepared: She can be a little overbearing. She may ask you to convince me to have us move in with her or ask you about how many children you want right away." Graham's lips curve up in a smile, and he laughs.

"Why are you laughing? Are you a giggle drunk too?" I tease him.

"No, it's nothing," he waves me off.

"Oh, no way, buddy. Tell me what you made you laugh," I play footsie with him, trying to pester him into telling me.

"It's nothing, Win. I guess I just thought it was funny that I never really thought about introducing any girl to my mom before. Now, there's you, and I think about a lot of things."

My cheeks turn pink, and I try to use my wine glass to hide my cheesy smile. "Yeah, like what?"

"I guess you will just have to wait to find out," he smirks at me, and our waiter comes up and takes our orders. I was so wrapped up in him that I really hadn't even looked at the menu. I pick out the first thing that sounds good and go with that.

We fall into casual conversation, our food comes, and we devour it. Every bite was so delicious that we fell silent, leaving only the sound of our forks against the plates. The waiter comes back and asks us about dessert, but I couldn't eat another bite. Graham pays the bill, and we head back to the bed and breakfast.

"That was wonderful, Graham, thank you." I interlock my fingers with his as we walk up the little path leading up to Rosemary's.

Graham wraps his arm around my shoulder, pulling me in, and kisses the top of my head. "Anything for you, buttercup. Now I will have to apologize to you though." We pause halfway up the path.

"Why?" My anxiety skyrockets.

"I can already see Mary peering out the window at us; she's dying to get ahold of you. Promise me you will still love me after she tells you all of my embarrassing high school stories." He places his forehead to mine.

"I promise," I smile.

"Good, let's go."

And with a quick kiss, we head inside.

Chapter 15

Graham

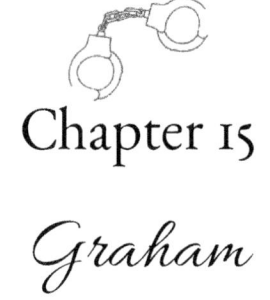

My head has been spinning ever since Winry's confession. She loves me, and obviously I love her, but she actually loves me too. Every time I look at her, I want to tell her again and then kiss her senseless. I'm pretty sure I have been turned on ever since she said those words. I want nothing more than to go back into our room, but right now I am being cockblocked by my best friends from high school. We don't even make it halfway to the door and I spot Mary peeping from the window.

"Oh, yay, you're back. Sage is in bed and Jace just went out to light the fire. Perfect timing," Mary beams. She has always been this way; she has never met a stranger, and she is not about to start with Winry.

"Huh, it's almost like someone was watching us from the window," I raise my eyebrows at her.

"I most certainly don't know what you are talking about. Winry, would you like a beer?" Mary turns her nose up to me. "Graham can have one after he stops being a baby."

Winry laughs, "Yes, I would love one. What do you have?"

"Bud Light, Michelob, Corona, and Coors."

"I'll take a Corona with a lime if you've got them."

"Me too." Mary shoots me a look, so I give her my best smile. "Please."

"That's better. Why don't y'all head on back? I'll meet you out there with the drinks."

"Thanks, Mare." We mosey through the living room out to the back patio, where Jace has the fire going. I take off my jacket and offer it to Winry; she drapes it over her shoulders.

"Thank you." Her eyes twinkle under the night sky.

"Hey, y'all have a good time?" Jace hollers as he turns on the electric fire pit.

"Yeah, we did." I take a seat and pull Winry in my lap.

"Did he take you to Rivulet, Winry?" Jace asks, taking the seat next to us.

"Yes, it was so good. I think I ate every bite." Winry lays her head on my shoulder, snuggling closer.

"Yeah, it has great food for sure. I met Mary there my junior year of high school. Her parents actually own the place." Jace takes a swig of his beer.

"You'd better not tell the story yet." Mary comes out with the beers in hand and passes them out. "I want to be the one to tell it."

"No way, Jace tells it so much better than you do," I poke at her.

"He so does not. Graham, you know that he embellishes the story." Mary plops down in Jace's lap.

"But Jace's side is more fun. You've got to hear this story, Win."

"Fine, Jace you tell it." Mary swats at Jace, who is staring at her like he could just eat her.

"Okay, so Mary and her family had just moved here and opened up Rivulet. Mary was just a freshman, so I hadn't seen her at school before, but for our junior prom we all decided to go eat at Rivulet before. I honestly could not tell you my date's name..."

"It was Courtney Jones," Mary adds quickly.

Jace rolls his eyes. "Anyway, we went there for dinner. Graham here went solo because a date was 'too much work,' but he came in our group. So, we put on our tuxes and the girls got all fancy. The one thing I do remember about Courtney was she was a grade-A bitch, and poor Mary was stuck being our waitress. I remember thinking she was the cutest thing in her little uniform. She made doe eyes to me all night." Jace squeezes her and she giggles.

"I did not, and I remember thinking you looked like a douche bag," Mary laughs.

"I was a little bit; every teen boy is. Well, something came out wrong and Courtney lost it, I could see the steam coming out of Mare's ears. She got so mad that she dumped Courtney's plate of pasta all over her dress."

"Oh no," Winry covers her mouth to stifle her laugh.

"I did not do it on purpose. I went to grab the plate and she tried pulling it back and when I let it go, she yanked it all over her," Mary protests and crosses her arms.

"Sure, honey, it was an accident. But really, she was just upset that she wasn't the one with me, so she sabotaged my date, and I had to go stag with Graham." Jace punches my shoulder.

"It was awful," Mary buries her face in her hands. "I had to work for months to pay her back for that dress.

"After prom, I saw Mary in the hallway. So, naturally I chased her down and the rest is history." Jace kisses Mary's cheek.

"How was it when you two met? I know you are neighbors, but how did this happen?" Mare asks pointing between us.

Winry and I look at each other. "You tell it," Winry says and wiggles slightly in my lap, which my dick responds to immediately.

"Same way," I shrug. "Winry saw me with another girl and decided she wanted me for herself, so she sent her away."

Winry hits my chest, "Graham, that is not what happened."

"Okay, okay. So, Claire showed up at my house at the crack of dawn wanting to 'see my place and talk.' I had been up all night, so I was exhausted, and I was just trying to get her to leave," I recall the day I met Winry.

"Oh, Claire. That girl sure is persistent, isn't she?" Mare interrupts and rolls her eyes. I never formally introduced Claire to Jace and Mary, but they knew of her since it's a small town and Claire was always very vocal about how we were "dating."

"She was, but Winry pulled in and pretended to get stuff out of her car so she could eavesdrop on us."

"I was not eavesdropping…" Winry cuts me off.

"If you weren't, then how did you know my name was Graham, and how did you know I wanted her to leave?" I raise my eyebrows at her.

"Busted," Jace's and Mary's heads fall back in laughter.

"Like I said, eavesdropping. So, she decided to act like her AC was broken and that I needed to come over and fix it. Don't ask me how I understood what she was trying to do, but I finally pieced it together and headed over to her place until Claire left."

"Oh, my word, that is awesome. Good thinking, Winry," Mary leans forward, holding out her beer for a toast. "To winning over our men."

They clink their drinks and laugh. We stay out by the fireplace for the next couple of hours. Mary tells Winry all the stupid things that Jace and I did. Including the time we got busted for rolling people's houses with toilet paper. It took us the whole next week to clean them all up.

"I think we are going to turn in," Jace says as he stands up, taking Mary with him, and she laughs.

"Us too," Winry hops off my lap and pulls me up. Jace turns off the fire pit and we all head back inside.

"Oh, Winry," Mary grabs her hand. "Graham said tomorrow is your birthday and that you love banana chocolate chip muffins. They may not be as good as your friend's, but I found a recipe to make for breakfast."

"That is so sweet, thank you," Winry pulls her in for a hug.

"Good night, guys," Jace calls over his shoulder, walking into their room.

"Good night," we say together.

"That was nice, I really like them," Winry says as we enter our room.

"I'm glad, buttercup. I liked seeing you with them." I shut our door and turn at the perfect time to see Winry already naked. She has one of my t-shirts in her hand and starts to put it on. I rush over and take it away from her and toss it back in the bag.

"Hey, gimme that." She looks so cute and sexy with nothing on. While I know she would look cute and sexy with just my shirt too, I'm going to save that for later.

"Not a chance, buttercup." I toss her on the bed, and she giggles. "I love you and I'm not done showing you how much yet."

―ele―

I wake up with Winry's naked body tangled in mine. Her lips are still plump from the millions of hard kisses, her hair is a mess from me pulling at it all night, and from this angle I can see a hickey on her right hip. I lie here just watching her breathing in and out. She looks so peaceful, and her cool skin feels amazing against mine.

I check the clock on the nightstand; it's a little after nine. As much as I hate the thought of leaving, I untangle myself and throw on a t-shirt and a pair of shorts and sneak downstairs.

Unlike us, everyone else seems to be up and ready for their day. I follow the sweet smell of coffee and muffins to the kitchen. Sage is sitting at the kitchen table with her notebook and crayons.

"Morning, Sagie, what are you drawing?" I peer over her shoulder. It looks like a flower field; Sage is almost four, so it's a bit of a mess but not too bad either.

Sage puts down her crayon and holds up her picture for me to see better. "Flowers, Mommy loves flowers. Does your friend like flowers too?"

"She does, her favorite are daisies."

"I can draw those; I will draw her a picture." Sage turns to a blank page and starts on a picture for Winry.

"She will love it, Sage. That is very sweet of you." I ruffle her hair and turn in search of what I originally came down here for.

"Mare saved you two some muffins. Here, she hid them because she didn't want the other guests to eat them all." Jace walks over to a random cabinet and pulls out a plate of two big banana chocolate chip muffins. "Here are those, and coffee is in the pot over there." Jace points and has this goofy smile on his face.

"Stop it. Why are you looking at me like that?" I give him a puzzled look.

"Nothing, it is just weird seeing you all in love and crap." Jace goes over to another cabinet and pulls out two mugs.

"I don't want to hear it. I had to watch you be all in love and crap with Mary since high school. It's your turn to watch." I pour the coffee and add the creamer, plus sugar in Win's because she likes it sweet.

Jace laughs. "Hey, don't get me wrong, I'm happy for you. Just never thought I would see the day that Graham Taylor, Mr. Relationships Are Too Much Work, be crazy about a girl. Don't fuck it up," Jace pats me on the back.

"Daddy, that is a bad word," Sage scolds him. "I'm going to tell mommy."

"Don't be a snitch. How about I give you a cookie and we forget this whole thing happened?" Jace bribes her and she agrees.

I grab the coffee mugs by the handle with one hand and the plate of muffins in the other one, carefully not to spill or drop either. Winry is curled up in a blanket, still asleep. I set the stuff down on the nightstand and sit by her on the bed.

"Morning, buttercup." I gently caress her face, and her eyes flutter open. "Happy birthday, baby."

"Thank you." Her lips curve up in a sleepy smile.

"I brought up breakfast, coffee and muffins." I brush her hair out of her face.

Winry sits up and pulls the covers up to her bare chest. I hand her cup of coffee and she takes a sip. "Mm, you really do love me."

"Yeah, I do." I look at her sitting naked sipping coffee, and if I died right now it would be with a smile on my face.

We have our breakfast in bed, then hop in the shower together; some touching does occur, but she started it. It takes us a good hour and a half to get out of our room and go downstairs.

"Well, look who it is." Mary and Sage are sitting in the living room with some puzzles out in front of them.

"Hey Mare, Sage. What are you two doing?" I take the seat next to Sage and Win sits next to Mary.

"We are playing puzzles. Want to play?" Sage scoots a matching puzzle in front of me.

"Sure thing, Sagie. Thank you." I glance up to meet Winry looking at me with a wide grin.

"Sage, it's Miss Winry's birthday, can you tell her happy birthday?" Mary says sweetly to her daughter.

Sage looks at Winry for a moment and tells her happy birthday but comes out more like happy bird-day.

"Happy birthday, Winry. I am so happy you are here." Mary pulls her into her millionth hug.

"Thank you, I'm happy to be here too." Win and I make eye contact and she smirks at me.

"What do y'all have planned today?" Mary asks.

"Well, we are about to head out to the festival, then some friends from Aster Creek are meeting us at the carnival later." I place a piece of the puzzle Sage gave me in its place.

"Why don't you guys joins us?" Winry turns, asking Mary.

"Thank you, Winry. We would love to; we were planning on taking Sage later anyway. I am sure we will have to do some kiddy stuff first though, but we will catch up with you when we can." Mary's smile is a mile wide. "Now, you two go and enjoy your day. Unless you want to be stuck playing kid games for the next few hours."

"Okay, see you later Mare. Come on, buttercup." I pull her up off the couch.

Winry waves bye to Mary and Sage, and we head into town. It's a little hot but the perfect day for the festival otherwise. It is unusual to have such a sunny day during the festival weekend. I remember years of rainy parades and closed carnival rides growing up. I glance over at Winry; she has her hand out the window and her hair is flying like crazy from the wind, but she just seems to be taking in the breeze.

I grab her hand and bring it up to place a kiss on the back of her hand. She smiles and pulls my hand over to her and kisses the back of my hand. This woman, I swear I am obsessed with her. I'd do anything for her and follow her blindly anywhere.

My mind wanders back to the hard conversation we had earlier this week. My chest aches at the thought that she could not be here today. I promise myself here and now that I will love her wholly—with every fiber of my being I will. On her dark days, I will be there to wipe her tears and hold her tight. On days when she doesn't feel beautiful, I will remind her. When she doesn't feel enough, I will lift her up. I'll kiss her every fucking day and tell her I love her while I smack her ass.

We ride in comfortable silence, just listening to music. I pull into the first parking spot I see because it is always so congested in town that parking is a nightmare.

I walk over and open her door, "You ready, buttercup?"

"Always." I hold her hand, leading her toward the center of town, where there are food trucks and booths set up. The carnival is set up just a few blocks over at a park with a big field connected.

We run into several people I know since it is small town. I introduce Winry as my girlfriend, and everyone has the same surprised reaction. I just laugh. I know I don't know how I managed to win her over either.

We finally make it to the center, and Winry is beaming. "Where do you want to start?" I ask her.

"Let's do the booths then get some food." She pulls me, taking the lead into the booths that are practically stacked on top of each other. We browse every single one, at least twice to make sure she didn't miss anything. She buys a few things, some jewelry and clothes. I buy her a necklace with a G initial on it because I am cheesy like that now. We finish up at the booths and take her stuff back to the car.

This time we go straight to the food trucks. Winry chooses the taco truck, so I tell her to get me some steak tacos, and I head over the station that has the giant cups of sweet tea.

"Two sweet teas, please." I hand the man my cash and take the teas. I hear a familiar female voice say my name and I turn to see Claire standing behind me.

"Oh, hi, Claire. How are you?" I don't know whether I should act like the last time we were together I didn't break up with her, and it wasn't awkward as hell.

"Good, what are you doing here?" She asks. She seems all right, so I relax a little but not too much. I haven't mentioned Winry yet.

"I—well, I brought Winry here for her birthday." And it's awkward again. "We are together now," I say a little sheepishly, not because I am ashamed of it, but it seems wrong to flaunt it.

"I knew it, I knew you liked her," Claire rolls her eyes and lets out a huff. "Well, I hope you are happy, Graham, despite that it isn't with me."

"Thanks, I am. I hope the same for you. Again, I am sorry about how we ended things. I did like Winry and I shouldn't have handled it the way I did that dinner."

"I appreciate that. I am going to get going, but it was good to get some closure," she shrugs and gives a lopsided smile.

"Right, yeah it was. See you around." We part ways and I find Winry digging into our tacos. "Hey, save some for me," I tease her.

"No way, these are too good. We will definitely need more." She wipes her lips with a napkin and takes one of the teas. "Was the line long? You were gone for a while."

"No, um, I actually ran into Claire. I told her I was sorry about how everything went down that dinner. I was just too smitten with my neighbor." I pull her in by her chin and kiss her.

We part and she has a big grin on her face. "Was she okay? I'm sure that had to be weird."

"It was a little, but it was good too. She said she got some closure." I grab a taco and take a big bite.

"Good, I'm glad. My parents called while you were gone, to wish me happy birthday. They said to tell you hi."

"Really? Your dad said to tell me hi?" I laugh.

"Well, Mom did, but Dad was there too." She returns a laugh and continues to destroy her taco.

I feel my phone vibrate in my pocket. I check it and Wyla has texted.

Wyla: Decided to head over early. Owen is driving us, much to Waverley's dismay. Don't worry, I have already given talks about not ruining Win's day. Text you when we get there.

I shoot the thumbs up emoji back to her and slide my phone back in my pocket. "Wyla said they are headed this way early, should be here soon."

"Oh, great. Thank you for putting this together, Graham." She playfully nudges me.

"Of course, buttercup, nothing I would rather be doing." I thread my fingers through her dark hair.

"Really? Nothing?" She tilts her eyes at me.

"Okay, maybe one other thing." I lean in and kiss her like we aren't surrounded by hundreds of other people.

"Ahem." We pull apart and there stands my mom wearing her typical judgmental tone and arms crossed. "Graham Taylor, what is it you think you are doing? You are in public."

Winry looks at me a bit flustered and confused, which turns to mortified when I say, "Hi, mom. What are you doing here?"

"Well, it's the summer festival, why wouldn't I be here?" Her tone has shifted from judgmental to "you idiot." "Plus, when I saw how brazen you were acting, I had to say something."

I'm taken back a little; surely this isn't how she wants to act right now, it was just a kiss. "Mom—"

"You're right, sorry, Ms. Taylor. I'm Winry, it's nice to meet you," Winry cuts me off and stands to shake her hand.

"Alice Taylor, but Ms. Taylor works fine." Mom does accept her hand but barely spares Winry a glance. "Graham, are you going to stand to greet your mother?"

I'm tempted to tell her no until she changes her attitude, but I can see the pleading on Winry's face. She wants this to go well, so I'd better not make it worse. I stand and give Mom a quick hug.

"Better. Are you having a nice time?" She directs the question to me.

"Yes, we are. Remember I told you it was Winry's birthday today? We were about to head to the carnival to meet some friends." I wrap my arm around Win's shoulder, pulling her closer to me. I give mom my best 'cut it out' look.

"Well, I'd best leave y'all to it. I will see you tomorrow for brunch." She finally turns to look at Winry, "Do try to keep the PDA to a minimum. Happy birthday." Mom smiles like she wasn't just extremely rude and walks away.

"Um, that didn't go well," Winry says flatly.

No, it sure didn't. Why was my mom acting that way? I figured she would be over the moon that I finally found a girl that makes me happy.

"I'm sorry, Winry, I don't know why she was being that way." The smile that has been plastered to Win's face all day is now gone. No, no. Not today. I place my hands on top of her shoulders. "Hey, please don't let this ruin your day, buttercup. I don't know what was wrong with her but I am not about to let this ruin your birthday."

She gives me a lopsided smile, "You're right, tomorrow will go better."

"Yes, it will." I will make fucking sure of it. "Come on, let's walk over to the carnival. I'll even let you win at some games," I tease.

"Whatever you need to tell yourself, babe." Winry playfully shoves me. There's my girl.

I hold her hand in mine and study her as we walk. She is quiet but doesn't seem outright upset. I wish I could read her mind. Or if I am wishing for things, I would wish my mother didn't just act like she did.

"Win, you all right?"

"Hmm..." She jerks her head to me like I just pulled her out of a deep thought. "Yeah, I'm good. Sorry, I got pulled into a daze." A fake smile crosses her face.

I stop on the sidewalk and other people move around us. I don't know what to do next really. It doesn't feel like telling her not to worry about it will work. I mean, it bothered me when her dad talked to me at the cookout, so I would imagine that how my mom acted will affect her too. Thankfully, my saving grace messages me that they are here. Nothing cheers Winry up like her sisters do.

"Hey, Wyla just messaged that they are parking. I told them we would meet them by the entrance."

A real smile crosses her face this time. "Great, let's go."

I spot Owen and the girls at the entrance first, but when the girls spot us, it's a mixture of girlie screams, jumping, and hugging.

"Happy birthday," the girls chorus together.

"Thank you, I'm so glad you guys are here," Winry says and goes in for another group hug. Owen and I just stand back and watch them.

"All right, don't suffocate her." I pull Winry out of their death grip hug. "What do you want to do first, Win? Play some games or ride some rides?"

"Rides first, then funnel cake, then I kick your ass in some games."

"Sounds like a plan." I kiss her nose. "Let's go."

We buy our wristbands and head for the first ride we see. There's not a lot of them, just your usual teacups, Ferris wheel, and stuff. We ride rides for the next two hours. We did have to take a break halfway in because somehow Waverley and Owen got paired in the same teacup. Naturally, he spun theirs too fast, making her sick.

Next, we chow down some funnel cakes. Jace, Mary, and Sage catch up with us as we finish. Mary joins in their girl group immediately, like she has always been there. We start on the games next, and the girls kill all of us. It's brutal. I don't think Jace, Owen, or I won a single game.

I stand back watching Winry kick Owen's ass at a ring toss game. Her smile is full, and her head falls back in laughter. It's the best thing in the world. I am completely enthralled by her.

Winry makes the last ring and pumps her arms in the air in victory, while Owen hangs his head. Winry comes bouncing over to me. "Did you see me? I kicked his ass."

"I sure did, buttercup," I place my hands on her shoulders and plant a kiss to her nose.

"She cheats," Owen walks over the group.

"No, you just suck," Waverley jabs.

"Enjoy walking back to Aster, Wav," Owen winks at her, and she sicks out her tongue.

"We are probably going to head out," Jace says while holding a nearly asleep Sage in his arms.

"Yeah, if it's okay, could we too? Someone has to keep Crossroads open," Ivy jokes and gives Winry a nudge with her elbow.

"Hey, sorry not sorry," Winry gives her a little kick back.

We all say our goodbyes, and the girls give each other a bunch of hugs. We decide to call it a night ourselves and head for the car.

"Have you had a good birthday, Win?" I ask as we walk.

"Yes, I did. Thank you, Graham. It really means a lot to me." She holds my hand and squeezes.

"I plan on planning your birthday for the foreseeable future, buttercup. They are only going to get better." I mean it, I plan on being here for all of her birthdays. I bring her hand up and kiss the back of it.

Chapter 16

Winry

We are driving to meet Graham's mom at the restaurant. I have felt sick with worry all morning. I was able to forget about the incident with his mom yesterday for a little while, but this morning all my worry and doubt came rushing back, and it's making me nauseated.

Yesterday was a trainwreck of a meeting. Graham has apologized nonstop and assures me that this morning will go better. I'm not sure whether he means I'll be better, or she will. I don't want to dwell on that thought. He says he loves me, but what if his mom doesn't? What happens then? He doesn't act like they are close, but I can't imagine her not liking me will go over all that well. Again, I don't know who for, me or her.

We arrive and I take a deep breath, in and out. Graham takes my hand and squeezes.

"No need to be nervous, baby, what happened yesterday will not be happening today." He gives me an encouraging smile.

"Phew, okay. Let's go." I hop out of the car and look down at my outfit. I really wish I thought more about this. I have on some light wash mom jeans, a white button up, and white converse. I dressed it up some with some fun daisy earrings and the G necklace Graham bought me yesterday. I check my hair and makeup in the mirror. At least I did semi-good on that end.

"Winry, hey." I look up at him and he cups my face. "I love you."

A quick wave of relief floods me for a moment. "I love you too." I smile and he squishes my face, placing a kiss on my nose.

"Come on, buttercup." He tangles his hand in mine and leads me to the restaurant.

Deep breaths. In. Out.

We enter the restaurant; it has a country farmhouse style décor that matches the exterior vibe. I follow him through the dining room toward the back, where we spot his mom. She is sitting at the table with her nose in her phone.

"Hey, mom," Graham says pulling her from her phone.

"Oh hi," she stands and gives Graham a big hug. She turns to me; her face turns unreadable. "Winry, right? How are you?"

"I'm good, thank you. I have really enjoyed getting to see Rosewood with Graham." I give my best smile, but she doesn't return one.

"That's nice, dear. Let's sit," she says flatly.

Graham pulls out my chair; I give him a thank you smile, and he takes the seat next to me.

"So, how was the carnival?" Ms. Taylor asks, looking at her menu.

"Great, we rode all the rides and Winry kicked butt at the games," Graham rubs my back.

"It was a good birthday…" I start, but our waiter comes up to take our drink order.

"Two waters with lemon for us," Graham orders for us.

"And two sweet teas, please." Ms. Taylor tells the waiter.

"Are you super thirsty? Why the extra drink?" Graham asks her.

"Oh, I invited someone to join us." She goes back to her menu, like she doesn't need to say anything else. I look over at Graham, who seems to be getting annoyed.

He reaches over and taps on her menu to draw her attention back to him. "Who did you invite, Mom?"

She looks irritated that he is even asking. Unease settles in my stomach; I don't have a good feeling about this.

Her face softens as she looks past Graham. "Oh, there she is," she stands and waves someone over.

Graham and I turn to see who it is, and fuck me, it's Claire. Why did she invite her? And damn it, why does she look so cute and put together? She is wearing a pink babydoll sundress that is modest and revealing at the same time. Her blonde hair is perfectly curled, and her makeup puts mine to shame.

Claire comes up to the table and looks just as blindsided as we do. Her eyes dart between me and Graham. "Um, Alice, I thought it was just going to be us."

"Mom, what is going on?" Graham clenches his jaw, and Claire and I just make awkward eye contact. She looks uncomfortable; I know Graham talked to her yesterday, but he said they got closure. Why is she here now?

"What? I ran into her yesterday after I saw you two and invited her to brunch. I didn't think you would care. You two are still friends, and Winry doesn't mind, do you Winry?" Ms. Taylor turns to me. Her tone indicates a challenge.

"We are leaving," Graham grabs my hand and goes to stand.

"No, Graham, I'll leave," Claire offers instead.

"No, no one is leaving, quit being dramatic, Graham. Honestly, now Winry, do you mind if Claire joins us?" She asks again in that challenging tone. Daring me to say no.

I look between him, his mom, and Claire. Well, if this isn't a lose-lose situation I don't know what is.

Deep breath. In. Out.

"Come on, Win. Let's go." Graham takes my hand to pull me away, but I stop him.

"No, Graham, it's fine. It's just brunch, right?" I give Claire a lopsided smile. I feel a little bad for her too, being pulled into another scheme. I don't know if saying no would have been better for both of us, but we shall see.

"Yes, just brunch," Claire says, sitting down across from me and next to Ms. Taylor.

Graham is still standing, studying me to make sure I am good. I completely avoid his gaze and stare down at the table. If I look at him, he will immediately know that I am indeed not good.

"Graham, sit down, she said she's fine," Ms. Taylor snaps.

He takes his seat begrudgingly. The waiter comes back with our drinks, and I know even he can feel the tension.

"I think we are ready to order," Ms. Taylor tells him.

I wasn't ready, and I'm sure she knows that. They all order and I pick the first thing I see, yet again. My appetite is completely lost anyway.

"So, Claire was telling me about her new promotion. Tell me again, what is it you will be doing?" Ms. Taylor asks. She is absolutely beaming at Claire right now.

Claire looks a little uneasy but tells us about her new promotion and how she will be able to do all of her job at home, make more money, do her own schedule, and blah, blah, blah. I try to remind myself that she was manipulated too, but it's hard to hold it together when the mother of your boyfriend is actively trying to get him back with the girl across from you.

"That sounds really great, Claire, congratulations." I say trying to sound like I have been listening.

"Thank you, Winry. How is your store doing?" She seems genuine in her question, so I relax a bit, thankful things have turned to me for a bit. I want Graham's mom to get to know me.

"It's doing great, we actually are coming up on our first anniversary. The first weekend in September we are doing an open house anniversary party." I say, feeling good with how the conversation has shifted. "We are going to have a bunch of samples and door prizes to give away."

"Oh, that's great, Win, you hadn't mentioned that yet." Graham smiles for the first time since it all went south.

"Why hadn't you mentioned it to him?" Ms. Taylor snaps. "Any reason?"

"Mom. Cut it out," Graham warns her.

"It's okay. I had just discussed this with my partner the other day. The open house is a new development; it must have slipped my mind with all of our other plans." I reach for Graham's hand under the table, needing it to steady both me and him.

"Well, I think that sounds great, Winry. It's really awesome that you have been open for a whole year," Claire tries to smooth over the palpable tension.

"Oh, I have a wonderful idea," Ms. Taylor jumps in her seat. "Graham, why don't you bring Claire with you to the opening thing? I mean, Winry will be working, and this way you can have someone to be with and you can show Claire around the town. I know she wanted to see it the last time she came to visit. Such a shame that didn't get to happen." She places a hand on Claire's shoulder, giving her a sympathetic look.

I'm pretty sure my jaw hits the floor, is she seriously suggesting they go on a date right in front of me.

"I don't know about that, Alice. The event sounds fun, Winry, but..."

"Oh, no buts. You just said it sounded fun; Graham can take you," she says it so nonchalantly like we should all love this plan.

"Okay, that's it. Mom, can I talk to you outside?" Graham doesn't wait for an answer he just gets up and walks toward the door.

"Mercy. Excuse me," she gets up and follows him out with a huff.

It's silent for a moment. Claire and I just stare anywhere but at each other.

When the tension almost becomes unbearable, Claire speaks first. "Winry, I'm sorry. I really had no idea that you two would be here. I ran into her after I had talked with Graham, and she just invited me to brunch with her. If I would have known, I never would have come."

"It's okay, Claire, I believe you. I can't say I saw this coming either, but we ran into her yesterday and she didn't seem too fond of me anyway. I had hoped today would go better, but I guess not." I stare back down; I feel so rejected. She never even wanted to give me a chance.

"If it's any consolation, it won't matter what Alice thinks about you. I mean clearly, not for this to come off wrong, but she loves me, and he doesn't want to be with me. He wants to be with you. I could tell from that awful dinner we had at his apartment." Claire looks just as hurt as I do.

"This really sucks, doesn't it?" I let out a sigh.

"It sure does," Claire sips her tea, and we go back to silence.

Graham and his mom come back, and the tension only gets thicker. Our waiter brings out our food as soon as they take their seats, but honestly, I don't think anyone is hungry. Except for Ms. Taylor, who dives in immediately, completely unfazed by the mess she has caused.

I stare at my breakfast sandwich. It makes me want to be sick, but I take a small bite anyway. I can feel Graham's eyes on me, trying to read me. I may fall apart if I look at him.

"So, Winry. Tell me a little about yourself," Ms. Taylor says blandly and takes another bite of her eggs.

Tell her about myself? What is this, my first day in a college class where I have to introduce myself?

Deep breath. In. Out.

If this is how she wants to be, so be it. "Well, I am the oldest of three girls. I own and run my own bookstore and café with my lifelong friend, Ivy. My favorite color is green, I love reading, writing, and your son."

Graham places his hand on my thigh and squeezes.

"Don't we all?" she says, looking at Graham. I think she truly believes that she has done nothing wrong here.

The rest of brunch goes by at a snail's pace. This has to be the most horrible meal I have ever been a part of. We only speak a handful of words the rest of brunch. Graham's mom makes no effort to get to know me or even let me get to know her.

Finally, our bill comes, and Graham pays it right away. "Come on, Winry. Let's go home," he holds his hand out for mine and I take it. "Claire, I am sorry you got dragged into this. Mom..." He spares her a glance and pauses like he may say something else but doesn't. He pulls me away from the table.

Ms. Taylor stands to protest, but I can feel the anger radiating off of him, so I follow him quietly. We make it to his car, and he opens the door for me. I slide in; he shuts my door and rounds the other side. It's not until he sits down does he let out a breath.

"Winry—" He starts but I cut him off.

"Let's just go home. Please." I don't want to talk about it right now.

I need this car ride to process what just happened, because I am having a hard time fully grasping the fact that she really just tried to push him back with Claire right in front of me. I mean, what was she thinking? That he would just run back into her arms?

"Okay, buttercup," he puts the car in drive, and we head back to Aster Creek.

Chapter 17

Graham

I don't know what just happened, I truly don't. In fact, I don't even believe what just happened. Why, why did my mom do that? Claire seemed to be one of her victims in this horrid scheme. She had just gotten the closure she wanted, just to be sucked back in.

And poor Winry, my heart breaks a little every time I look over at her. Winry just sits silently in my car, staring out the window. She's upset, I understand, hell I'm upset. I don't know what to say, I don't know what to do. How can I fix this? What can I do to make it better? I spend the whole drive trying to figure it out, but all I do know is that I can't lose her over this. I refuse.

We pull into my driveway and just sit in the car for a moment.

"Win, will you come inside please?" I'll beg her if I have to, I don't want to just leave her upset.

"Sure," she croaks out. She opens her door and gets out without looking at me.

I get out of the car and unlock the front door. I pull it open and gesture for her to go first. She has been avoiding eye contact since this whole mess started.

"I am just going to go to the bathroom really quick," she mumbles.

I let her go, and my phone vibrates for the thousandth time. Mom has called and texted nonstop since we left, but I haven't answered a single one.

I pace in my living room, too anxious to be still. I hear the bathroom door open and shut. I turn and we finally make eye contact. Her eyes are bloodshot, and her chest is starting to turn blotchy. I walk over to her and encase her in my arms.

"Winry, I am so sorry. I truly am. That was not okay, what she did today was horrible." A tear escapes down her face and I catch it with my thumb. "Please don't cry, baby. What happened doesn't change anything for me, okay?"

"She didn't even give me a chance, Graham. Why? What did I do?" She takes a step back, breaking out of my arms, and wipes another tear.

"Nothing, Win. You didn't deserve this; I don't know why it happened. I wish I could go back and not even go this morning. Please don't let this taint our whole weekend. Like I said, what happened doesn't have any effect on how I feel about you." I capture her face in my hands. Her big hazel eyes look up at me, tears pool at the bottom.

"Okay." I can tell she is doing everything she can not to let all of the tears out.

"Hey, want to hear a joke?" I say, pulling her into a hug, and she nods her head.

I reach for my phone in my pocket and pull out my notes. I may have written down several jokes to have handy. "What kind of shoes does a thief wear?"

"I don't know, what?" She whispers and nuzzles her head deeper in my chest.

"Sneakers."

She muffles a laugh. "That was a good one."

I rub her back, "I've got some more if you need another."

"That's okay, save them for next time." She tightens her arms around me.

Next time. That's the best thing I have heard all morning. "What do you want the rest of the day, buttercup? I'll do whatever you want."

She takes a deep breath, "Ugh, I want to take a nap and forget this day happened."

"Okay, come on." We go upstairs and I give her a t-shirt to wear, and we climb in the bed. She cuddles up next to me and I kiss the top of her head. She drifts off pretty quickly and I follow shortly after.

Winry goes back to her place the next morning. After our nap, we stayed up half of the night just hanging out. She cheered up some, but she was still off when she left this morning.

I check my phone. I have twenty-eight texts and fifteen missed calls and counting, all from my mom. I'm uninterested in her excuses. I don't even bother reading the texts. I know they will just add fuel to the fire. I shut off my phone and decide to go for a run to clear my head.

I run through town, pushing myself to go past my usual five miles. I need to work out some of this anger. At the end of the day, she is my mom and I know I will need to talk to her, but right now I'm likely to say something I will regret.

I make it back to the apartment; I am tempted to knock on Winry's door but decide to give her some space. Plus, after seven miles in the middle of July heat, I am drenched in sweat. I hop in the shower, hating that I am alone in here.

I get out and it's not even time for lunch yet. I work tonight, so I know I will be kicking myself if I don't at least get some sleep before my shift. My schedule went to shit this weekend, but I don't care. It was all worth it, watching

Winry be so happy, up until yesterday that is. I collapse on the bed and force myself asleep.

I sleep for a few hours but am drawn from my sleep by someone knocking at my door. It can't be Winry, usually she just comes in. I throw on some sweats and a t-shirt and go downstairs.

Another knock comes. "I'm coming," I holler. The thought that it's my mom crosses my mind and I'm a little hesitant to open. But the last person I suspect stands on the other side. "Dad? What are you doing here?"

"Hello to you too. Can I come in, or do you just want to stand in the doorway?" He asks, looking over my shoulder like he is looking for something.

"Uh, yeah. Sorry, I just was not expecting you to be here. To be honest I didn't think you even knew where I lived." I step aside, letting him in. He walks in and takes a seat on the couch.

"Well, your mom sent me here to, and I quote, 'talk some sense into you.'" He rolls his eyes. "Come on, sit down. I got an earful from your mom, why don't you tell me what really happened?"

"You came here because mom asked you?" Why are my parents acting so weird.

"Asked? No, more like demanded and would not stop messaging and calling me. She promised she would leave me alone if I came and talked to you. You got any beer?" He stands and walks to the fridge.

"Top shelf. None for me, I work tonight." I take a seat at the opposite end of the couch.

He grabs a beer and sits back down. "Listen, if you just call your mom back that would save me a lot of trouble. Otherwise, I'm going to need to finish this beer before we talk."

"Sorry, don't plan on doing that. I'll talk to her eventually, but right now the answer is no." I don't mean to be harsh, but she has to understand that what she did can't go without consequences.

"All this over a girl, huh?" He takes a big swig of his beer.

"Not just any girl, Dad. She's important to me, and Mom treated her horribly." I don't know why we are even talking about this. I don't think my dad has ever butted into one of my and Mom's disagreements.

"You going to marry her?" he asks with another swig.

"Yeah, I am. I know how you feel about marriage, but I love her and I'm going to marry her," I say adamantly.

I prep myself for a lecture about how marriage is awful, but instead he just shrugs, "Can I meet her?"

"You want to meet Winry? Why?" Am I in the twilight zone or something?

"You say you love her, so I want to meet her. I promise I will be good. No ex-girlfriends, no judgment." He takes his finger and makes a cross over his heart.

"Um, okay, I'll see if she can come over. I'll be back." I stand and study him for a minute.

"I swear I will be nice. Now go." He drains the last of his beer, and I walk out the door.

I knock on Winry's door and wait a few seconds for her to open up. "Graham, hey." I can tell she is not her usual happy self, and it hurts my soul.

"Hey, buttercup. I know this is crazy last minute and I get if you don't want to, but," I run my hand through my hair and rock on my feet, "my dad is here. He wants to meet you."

"I don't know…" I can see the fear in her eyes.

"I know, Win, but he swears he is here to get to know you. I don't know, he has never done this before, so if you don't want to you don't have to." My palms are sweaty, I am nervous for her to say yes and to say no. I don't know how my dad will act with her, so I am just as apprehensive.

I can see the anxiety all over her face. "Okay. Just give me a second to change."

"You don't have to change, Winry. You look beautiful." I pull her into my arms and kiss her like I wanted to when she opened the door. "Come on, I promise he does not care what you are wearing."

"Okay." She holds my hand, and we saunter back over to my place.

My dad sits in the same spot but stands up when we walk in. "Dad, this is Winry. Win, this is my dad."

"Hi, Mr. Taylor, it's nice to meet you," she holds out her hand for a shake.

FEEL IT ALL

My dad does something I rarely see him do: he smiles, a big smile too. "Hi, please call me Sam," he shakes her hand.

Winry and I take the couch and my dad moves to the recliner.

"So, Winry. How did someone so pretty end up with my son?" he chuckles.

She laughs back. "We had hung out a few times as just friends, but I don't know, we just kind of had this chemistry. He makes me laugh, treats me right, and he isn't too bad on the eyes either," she grins at me, and it feels good to see her smiling.

"Glad to know he isn't like his parents. His mom and I didn't exactly show him the best relationship. How is your family? Did they mess you up like we did Graham?" Dad asks.

"Oh, a little bit, but in a different way. My parents are still together and obnoxiously in love. I'm the oldest of three girls and—"

"Three girls? Man, bless your dad's heart," he says, shaking his head.

Winry's head falls back in laughter, "Yeah, we get that a lot. So much so that we always joke about it when one of us does something stupid, we say, 'Bless your dad's heart.'"

"Winry's dad is actually the Chief of Police here in Aster Creek," I add.

This time, my dad's head falls back in laughter. "Oh boy, you really went all out and said 'I'll date my neighbor and boss's daughter,' didn't you?"

"Yeah, what was I thinking?" I tease and scoot closer to her.

She gives me a little slap to the arm. "My dad gave him a bit of a hard time at first, but ultimately, Graham won him over too. I don't know if you know this, but he can be pretty charming when he wants to be."

"Well, he learned from the best," Dad points and winks at me. "You're welcome."

I roll my eyes and we all talk for the next hour and a half about anything and everything. We talked about our jobs and how Dad is planning on retiring soon. We talked childhood stories and how I was chased by ducks as a kid, which is where my fear stems from. Dad was actually being very pleasant and really tried to get to know Winry. He asked her questions and listened when she answered.

A little before 6, Winry had to leave for dinner with her family. "I'd better head out, but it was lovely meeting you, Sam." She gets up from the couch, and before I can even get up, my dad is up and giving her a hug.

"It was so good meeting you too. Listen, I'm sorry how things went down with Alice, but give her time, okay?" He lets her go, and I walk her out to her car.

"Well, that was…nice." Winry says, turning to me.

"Yeah, it was." I push her hair behind her ears. "I think he likes you more than me. I think he has maybe hugged me twice in my whole life."

"Poor Graham. Don't worry, honey, I'll give you all the hugs you want." She wraps her arms around my waist and squeezes.

"Don't patronize me, buttercup," I return her squeeze even harder making her giggle.

"I've got to go," she relaxes in my arms.

"Okay," I pop a quick kiss on her nose. "I love you."

She beams up at me. "I love you too." I open her car door, and she climbs in and backs out of the drive.

Back inside, my dad is in the living room holding one of the pictures Winry had printed off and framed that I have on my side table.

"She's great, Graham. I'm sorry your mom didn't give her a chance. I mean it only took me a minute of seeing you two together to know that you are in love with each other. I am sure your mom saw the same and maybe that scared her." He sets the picture back down. "Neither of us really had that. Don't get me wrong, I love your mom, but I don't think we were in love. Don't think I ever have been."

"It still doesn't give her an excuse to treat her so badly," I cross my arms; I get what he is saying, but still.

"No, I know. I'll talk to her, maybe call her tomorrow?" He walks over and places his hand on my shoulder. "Look, we both just want you to be happy. I can see that Winry does that. Your mom is just afraid of what that could mean."

"I'll call her," I agree.

"Good, now I'll get out of here so you can get ready for work. It was good to see you," he says and walks to the front door.

I walk over with him, "Yeah, it was good. Thanks for today, Dad."

"Yeah, yeah. Now go on and get ready for work. I'll talk to you later." He waves as he walks out the door.

I get ready for my shift and head over to the station. Owen meets me at our usual spot, and we get the night started. We have a couple of tickets, a call or two. Around 9 or so, my phone buzzes and I pick it up hoping it's Winry, but "Chief" flashes back at me.

"Hold on, Chief is calling me," I tell Owen then pick up. "Hello, sir."

"Hey, are you and Owen in the middle of anything right now?" He asks, his tone neutral like always.

"Not at the moment, what can we do for you?" I ask.

"Meet me back at the station," he orders. "I want to talk to you both about the Flynn court date."

"Yes, sir. We should be there in about five minutes." I motion for Owen to turn around and mouth station to him.

"10-4," he replies then hangs up.

"He wants to talk to us about the Flynn situation." I tuck my phone back in my pocket.

"Fine with me. How did the rest of the weekend go by the way?" Owen turns the car around to head back to the station.

"It all went to shit Sunday at brunch with my mom...and Claire." I let out a sigh. "My mom practically set me and Claire up on a date right in front of Winry."

"Oh, that's rough. I bet Win was crushed."

"She was. I was pissed, but Win and I are still good, and that's all the matters to me." I shuffle in my seat, already irritated at the thought of yesterday's events.

"Well good, I'd hate to ride about with your mopey ass if she ever dumped you," he pushes me with one arm.

"Not happening, now quit pushing me and focus on the road."

"Yeah, yeah. Don't get your panties in a twist," Owen waves me off.

We meet chief in his office, and he motions for us to take a seat. "So, Winry told me you guys have had a few run-ins with Flynn before and I want to make sure we get all of our ducks in a row for this. I think we can all agree we want Winry involved as little as possible." He looks at me at the last part.

"Yes, sir," I agree.

"Okay, so walk me through what happened," he gives us his full attention.

I start with the first night, how I noticed them arguing in the parking lot at Bluebird's. He dissects every piece, and we move on to the night he broke in. That part was torture, just talking about it made me pissed all over again. I hate talking about this guy, and I hate that he is putting Winry through this. Then we talk about the run-in we had at Bluebird's. Owen tells Chief how Flynn was baiting me about Winry the whole time.

"And you didn't arrest him that night either?" Chief raises an eyebrow.

"No, it was my call," Owen says. "I wanted to give him an opportunity to go somewhere else."

"I don't know if that will work for us or against us. On one hand it shows that you two aren't out to get him, like he claims. But it could go in his favor that he isn't extreme enough to do what he did to Winry," he crosses his arms and leans back in his chair. "Dispatch has the call from the bartender recorded. I'll get a copy and maybe she mentions him being aggressive or something in the bar."

"I hate that he is bringing her back into this," I grumble.

"I do too, and he knows she is an easy way to get under your skin, Taylor. So, no matter how much he pushes, do not push back. In or out of uniform, I don't care, don't let him get to you. Same goes for you, Owen. I want this court date to be smooth sailing," Chief orders.

"Yes, sir," Owen and I respond in unison.

"Good, now you guys are good to go back out," Chief taps on his desk and stands up.

Owen and I push to our feet and turn toward the door. "Actually, Graham, I need to talk to you for a second," Chief says as we were about to walk out.

"Good luck, buddy, I'll be in the car," Owen claps me on the back and walks out.

Chief rounds his desk to the front and leans back on it, crossing his arms. "I just wanted to thank you for taking Winry out for her birthday. She seemed so happy tonight at dinner and I believe it has a lot to do with you two together."

"No need to thank me, nothing I would have rather done this weekend. I'm just glad to hear that she is happy, that's all I want," I say candidly.

"I know, I know...damn it, I'm her father, I'm supposed to be hating you, not thanking you," he pushes off his deck and holds out his hand.

I step forward and shake his hand. "Thank you for giving me a chance." I don't know how I would fare if her family didn't like me. I know that has to be Winry's concern about my mom, but now that I have her, I don't think I will ever be able to let her go.

"All right, now go. Y'all be safe tonight."

"Yes, sir," I nod and head out.

Chapter 18

Winry

Sweat pours down my back; why must southern summers been so humid and hot? Why I chose to workout outside in the middle of August, I'll never know. It's just eight in the morning on a Monday, but damn, I'm dying. In my pre-heatstroke state, an idea comes to me. So I send a quick text to Graham.

Me: Hey, babe, call me when you get up. <kissy emoji>

He usually sleeps till about three so until then I hop in the shower then head to meet my sisters at Aster Creek Middle School. We are helping Waverley put the finishing touches on her classroom before she has her "meet your teacher" day. Waverley has been a bit of a drill sergeant these past two weeks. Our whole family and Graham have been roped into putting her room together.

I pull in the parking lot and call Waverley to meet me at the front door. She has been here since the crack of dawn.

She called me at 7 this morning already asking me to bring her a hot glue gun and more sharpies when I come.

"Hey, hey, hot stuff," Waverley holds the door open for me.

"Hey, hey. I brought your stuff," I shake the bag of goodies in my hand.

"Ugh, praise. You are a lifesaver," she takes the bag from me, and I follow her to her room.

Waverley's classroom reflects her personality so well. It's full of vibrant colors and it gives off this fun-while-learning vibe. Waverley will just teach English and reading for sixth grade, so she has a whole corner dedicated to reading books and another for writing.

"Look who I found," Waverley says to Wyla as we enter her room.

"The favorite sister is now here. Ready to help…and get the hell out here," I mumble, and Wyla laughs.

"Shut up, Win. I have to get this room ready and I need y'all's help." Waverley digs out the sharpies and plugs in the hot glue gun.

"Yeah, yeah. Tell us what to do, Wav," I grumble.

"Okay, Winry, you start putting the books out on those shelves, and Wyla, help me finish these posters," Waverley commands.

"Aye, aye, captain," I give her a salute and start organizing the books.

"So I think I have decided on what I want to do," Wyla says while working on the poster in front of her.

Waverley and I look at each other and back at Wyla. "Are you going to tell us?" I ask.

"I think I'm going to be a vet tech. I fixed my schedule so I will start in the program next week. I love working with the people and the animals at the shelter. I think I would be good at it."

"Hell yeah, you would," Waverley confirms, and I nod.

"We are so happy you have found something you enjoy, Wyla." I walk over and give her a hug.

"Me too, me too," Waverley jumps in the hug, and we squeeze each other.

"Okay, squeezing me too hard guys," Wyla wiggles out of the hug.

"We just love you," I go up to her and pinch her cheeks like she's a little baby.

Wyla rolls her eyes, "You don't have to suffocate me though."

"Yeah, but then where is the fun?" Waverley shrugs. "But enough lollygagging, get back to work."

We go back to our designated jobs and work in silence for a bit, but it doesn't last long. "Win, I saw the post for y'all's open house party. It looked so good, how is the planning coming?" Wyla asks.

"Good, we have gotten a lot of questions about it at the store. We pooled together three hundred dollars' worth of gift cards. Mom made some mugs with our logo, and I made two surprise book bundles for door prizes."

"What do they have to do to win?" Waverley asks. "Because I want one of those book bundles. You always pick out the best books."

"Well, we are doing it by tens. So the first ten people get a twenty-dollar gift card. Then the twentieth and thirtieth people get a mug and a twenty-five-dollar gift card. Then the fortieth and fiftieth people gets a book bundle, a twenty-five-dollar gift card, and a mug. Then we have all of the free samples too." I stack my last book and walk over to where they are finishing their posters.

"And it's the first Saturday in September, right?" Wyla takes a seat in one of the kiddie chairs.

"Yes, the day after my court date with Flynn." I nearly vomit at the thought.

"Gross, I hate him," Waverley says shortly.

"I hate him and the fact that he is dragging you into court," Wyla retorts.

"Me too," I dread the idea of going into that courtroom knowing that he will be there. At least I know Graham will be there with me, but I fear the outcome. I know what happened. I know that Flynn knows what truly happened, but the thought that he could convince someone else that it was all consensual, that I was the one to freak out...the thought makes me sick.

"Everything will be fine, Winry. Between Graham and Dad, nothing bad is going to happen," Wyla places her hand on my shoulder.

"I just more worry about the outcome. I know he won't be able to physically hurt me at the court date, but what if they do decide that it was my fault? What if he tries to charge me for breaking his nose or sues me?" I twist my hair in my hands, panic vibrating through me.

"That's not going to happen, Win. He broke into your home and attacked you. You were just defending yourself." Waverley finishes the last poster and hangs it on the wall.

"I know, I know. It just makes me feel uneasy. I just want to get it over with and put this whole mess behind me." I run my hands through my hair.

"I get it. Sorry, another sore topic, but have things gotten better with Graham's mom?" Wyla asks sheepishly.

"Ugh, no. He did talk to her a little bit about two weeks ago. I don't think it went all too well." My good mood is starting to sour.

"How come?" Waverley pulls up a sit next to us.

"Well, Graham wouldn't tell me what they talked about. When I asked, he told me that it didn't matter either way, his feelings for me would never change." My shoulders slump.

"Aw, man. Well, it sucks, but at the same time, that man loves you so much. If it doesn't matter to him, don't let it bother you," Waverley stands and pulls me out of my chair, giving me a hug.

"I agree," Wyla wraps her arms around us for our second sister group hug.

We stay there for about a minute, but I break away when my phone starts to ring.

"It's Graham," I say to them. "Hey, babe."

"Hey, buttercup. What are you doing?" His 'I just woke up' voice is so sexy.

"Oh, just helping Wav finish up her classroom. We are finishing up now. Do you have any plans today?"

"Only to hang out with you. Why, you have something in mind?" Sleepiness still riddles his voice.

"Yeah, I do. I'll be back home soon to get ready. Just put on some swimming trunks and pack a small day bag of clean clothes. I'll pack the rest."

"Okay, buttercup. See you soon, drive safe."

"Always." I hang up.

"Well that was quick, I figured you would be arguing over who loves each other more for a least a few minutes," Waverley laughs.

"No, Graham, I love you more," Wyla mocks imitating my voice.

"No, I love you more, Winry," Waverley plays along.

"Ha, ha, very funny," I roll my eyes. "Well, now that this is done, I am heading out. And yes, I'm going to hang out with Graham."

"I'm shocked, aren't you Wyla?" Waverley jokes.

"Totally, I mean you guys never see each other."

"Oh, I almost forgot, I have something for you two." I pretend to look through my bag, then pull out my hand with the middle finger raised, and they burst out laughing.

Chapter 19

Graham

I hang up with Winry and roll out of the bed. Whatever she has planned had better involve her being in a swimsuit too. The idea already has me excited, both mentally and physically. I take a quick shower, washing last night's shift off me. It felt like the longest night ever and we weren't slow either.

It started with serving a bunch of civil papers that the station has been behind on. Then a car wreck, thankfully with just minor injuries, but it shook the family up pretty good. After we got everyone all cleared, we let the little boy sit in our patrol car and play with the siren to help make him feel better. We had several traffic stops, but most we just let off with a warning, and we finished up the night by going through some paperwork to refresh for upcoming court cases, one being Winry's. It's about two weeks away, and I have been reviewing it every chance I get.

Out of the shower, I have to search for a little while to find some swimming trunks. I don't swim often, so I really have only two pairs, and where I put them is beyond me.

After I find a pair, I throw some clean clothes and shoes in a duffle bag. I grab my phone and see I have another message from my mom with another attempt to get me to talk to her. I called her the morning after Dad came over, and it did not go well. He did call and talk to her about it like he said he would, but she hasn't budged on giving Winry a chance.

I can't even get a good reason from her either. All I managed to get is that she is just not the one my mom wants for me. I informed her that it didn't matter who she wanted for me, it was who I wanted, who made me happy. That meant very little to her, so we haven't spoken much since then.

I did my best to make Winry feel better about the whole situation, but I know it still bothers her and I hate it. Meeting my dad did repair some of the damage, considering he loved her, but the damage from mom is still there.

A knock comes at my door about five minutes later and Winry beams at me when I answer the door. She looks perfect with her hair pulled back in a clip, a white knit swimsuit cover-up and a black bikini underneath.

"Hey, handsome, want to go on a date with me?" She grabs my hand, pulling me toward her.

I breathe in her peach and honey scent and smile. "With you? Most definitely. Especially if it involves you ditching this thing." I tug at her cover-up and pull her in for a kiss.

"Well, come on then. I got my bags in my car. You got yours?"

I hold up my bag and close my door, following her to her car. "Where are you taking me that it requires a change of clothes?"

"You'll see, now hop in." She winks at me, and we get in her car.

We drive for about twenty minutes and the ocean comes into view. We pull into the parking lot with a sign that reads "public beach access," and over to the side is a restaurant with a huge deck coming out by the water.

"We are here," Winry says giddily. We get out of her car and the salty air hits my face. I go the back, where Win has the trunk popped. It looks like she packed her whole house.

"Goodness, Win. Did you leave anything in your apartment?" I laugh.

"Shut up and help me. I packed us a little picnic, but I figured we could do dinner at the restaurant here. Now here, take this bag." We unload her car and head down toward the beach.

"Right here looks good." Winry sets down her bag and digs out a big picnic blanket and lays it down. We weigh it down with the other bags and picnic basket then take a seat.

Winry starts to dig through the basket, pulling out some fancy board with meats, cheeses, olives, and cracker all plastic wrapped. Then she pulls out some wine tumblers, a bottle of champagne, and some fruit.

"Goodness, I thought you said a small picnic," I tease her.

"Hush you, or else I won't share." She gives me a little shove and carefully pops the bottle of champagne. She pours us each a glass, and she puts some raspberries in hers. "Cheers, to many more spontaneous dates with you."

I smile at her, and we clink our glasses. I take a look around at the beach. It's a beautiful day, not a cloud in the sky. The water is clear blue, and I'm dying to dive in. The beach isn't overly crowded thankfully, and there is a volleyball net over to the side.

"So, how was your day?" I ask and take a bite of a strawberry.

"Good, I worked out this morning, helped Wav finish up her classroom…oh, and Wyla finally decided that she wants to be a vet tech," Winry beams.

"That's awesome, she will be great at that." I hold out a strawberry for her to take a bite of.

"Mm, those strawberries are so good. How was your night?" she asks, grabbing another.

"Busy and long, just a bunch of tedious stuff, except a minor car wreck. A little boy and his family got into a fender bender. Everyone was fine, but it scared him, so we let him play in the patrol car for a bit."

"Aw, sweet." She fidgets on the blanket for a second. "What do you think about kids? Would you want them one day?"

Originally, I never had thought about kids and didn't really see them in my future, but now..."With you? Yeah, I do. Only with you though. I want little Winrys running around and having me wrapped around their fingers just like you do." I grab her chin, placing my thumb in her little dimple.

Her smile grows wide, and she leans in, giving me a sweet kiss. "I want it all with you, Graham."

"I'll give it to you, buttercup." I deepen the kiss, tempted to climb on top of her right here on the beach.

"Hmm, you want to go cool off in the water?" she asks, breaking apart.

"Yeah, probably a good idea," I laugh.

Winry stands and reaches a hand to pull me up. I stand and take off my t-shirt. Winry pulls off her cover-up and her curves in that bikini do not help my growing situation at all. Her body is something else; I swear I'll never tire of it.

She takes the clip out of her hair and lets it blow in the salty breeze. A big gust of wind comes, and she holds out her hands and tilts her head back taking it in. "Ugh, I love that."

"I love you," I wrap my hands around her waist and give her another kiss.

"I love you too," she says, our foreheads still touching, and I try my best not to go back in. "Hey, I'll race you," she shoves away from me and runs toward the water.

Oh, she'll pay for that. I chase after her and capture her in my arms right before she reaches the water. I pick her up and throw her over my shoulder. She giggles and smacks my ass. All right, that's it. Once the water gets deep enough, I dive into the water, taking her under.

I bring her back up, and she wipes her face. "You are so going to get it," she splashes me then tackles me back under the water.

We come back up again. "Okay, truce," I grab her and she wraps her legs around my waist and her arms around my neck.

"I knew you couldn't handle me," she teases.

"Now that's where you are wrong buttercup. I can handle this just fine," I press my erection against her, letting her know exactly what I mean.

She lets out a little moan and moves her hips, tempting me even more. "You'd better stop that."

"But it feels good," she pouts out her bottom lip and I bite it in warning.

She lets out a little yelp and untangles herself from me, with a wicked smile on her face. I miss her touch immediately, but I know it's best she isn't wrapped around me anymore. We stay out in the water for about twenty minutes, just floating, talking, and touching a little. I can't help it, and neither can she.

We head up back to the blanket, and I check out her ass the whole way. She tosses me a towel, and we dry off. Winry wraps back up the meat and cheese board and pours another glass of champagne. We sip and sunbathe for a bit. What I enjoy the most being around her is how easy it is. We can do anything, and it all feels natural.

"Hey, a group is starting a volleyball game, want to go join?" I ask her.

"Hell yeah."

We head over and join different teams because "she can beat me at anything."

"Game on, buttercup." I pat her butt and send her to the other side.

"Ladies first," one of the guys tosses her the ball for her to serve. Naturally, she breaks out a serve like she has played for years.

We go back and forth for a while, but ultimately Winry's team pulls out the win. They share a round of high fives. We start round two, and this time my team manages to win.

"What happened, buttercup? Losing your touch?" I taunt.

"Don't get too cocky, babe. We will see who wins this time," she winks at me.

"Here, Winry, you start us off again." A guy named Andrew tosses her the ball. He has been blatantly staring at her the entire game. I know he knows that I see it, but who doesn't pay him any attention is Winry. Her mind is solely in the game and beating me. I love every second of it.

She hits another killer serve and we struggle to recover it. My team pulls it together the first half but fall apart in the second. We are one point away from losing and Winry is back up to serve. She hits it over with ease and we volley it back and forth for a while, but ultimately Winry hits the spike to win the game.

She jumps up and down in joy, her team gives her a round of high fives then she bounces over to me. "I'm sorry, babe, better luck next time," she taunts.

"Come here, you little sassy pants," I pull her into me and give annoying kisses to her neck and tickle her.

"Ah, let me go," she giggles.

"Say you're sorry," I continue.

"Okay, okay, I'm sorry," she says breathlessly.

I stop and let her go. We walk back to our blanket again. I check the time on my phone and find a few more messages from my mom that I ignore. It's a little after 6, and the beach is starting to clear a bit.

"You ready to go eat?" I ask her.

"Yes, let's rinse off and take this stuff to the car and we can change clothes in the car."

"Sounds like a plan," we clean up and dust everything off.

At the showers, my erection comes back watching Winry rinse off under the water. She is so sexy, especially in these moments when she isn't trying to be. When it's my turn, I am thankful that the water is cold, not that it helps much.

We dry off and I let her change in the back seat first. I know if I am in there, things will turn steamy quick. She comes out and does a little twirl, showing off her dress. It's a little white flowy sundress that ties behind her neck, so it shows off her sun-kissed back. Her hair is pulled back again in her clip with a few strands down in the front.

"You are quite possibly the most adorable thing I have ever seen." I take her hand and twirl her around again. I give her a quick kiss then grab my bag to change in the back of the cramped car. I throw on a pair of jeans and a white short-sleeve button up.

"Looks like we match," she giggles as I climb out.

"We sure do, I like it. You ready?" I hold out my hand for hers.

"Let's do it."

We head to the restaurant, Flounders, and Winry asks for a table on the back deck. It overlooks the water, and there is a stage where a band is starting to set up.

"They have live music?" I ask.

"Yup, every night. They even have an open spot for dancing," she winks.

We take our seats, and the waitress comes over immediately to take our drink orders, and I watch Winry as she studies the menu. Her cheeks and nose are a little pink from the sun, and freckles sprinkle her shoulders.

I am helplessly in love with this woman.

She looks up at me, and I swear there is a twinkle in her eyes, but then she quickly shifts her eyes away. "I, um, I wrote you something," she mumbles.

"You did?" Warmth spreads through my chest. I have been wanting to read some of the stuff she writes, but I haven't wanted to push her either. "Can I read it?" I ask.

"Yeah, I...uh, sorry I haven't shared my writing with anyone before, so I'm nervous." She slides a letter over to me. "I wrote this poem the other day, I was just thinking of you, and it sort of just came to me. I wanted you to have it, but I have been too chicken to give it to you."

"I'm sure it's great, Winry." I open the envelope and pull out the poem:

When I pray for love.
Let the sound of your voice always make me smile.

Bless the opening of my eyes to see that the grass I am standing on is always greener.

May the touch of your hand make my heart beat a little stronger.

Allow me to see love isn't always easy but forever worth it.

Be my love for I am forever yours.

"Wow, Winry. This, this is so amazing. You wrote this?" I stare at the poem, reading it again.

"Yeah, it's not much. I liked it though," she shrugs.

"Winry, I love it. Thank you for trusting me with this," I take her hand in mine and interlock our fingers. "I mean it, it's amazing, just like you."

"Thank you, I'm glad you like it." Her cheeks turn even more pink from blushing, and her lips turn up into a smile.

The waitress comes back over and takes our order. We fall into normal conversations, and the band starts to play some cover songs. It doesn't take long for our food to come out and for us to clean our plates. An afternoon at the beach can really make you hungry.

Winry sways in her seat to the music. "Care to dance, buttercup?"

"Really?" Her eyes light up.

"Yeah, come on." I take her to the front and join some of the other couples on the dance floor. I spin her around then pull her close to me. I hold one hand then place the other hand on her lower back, and we sway to the music.

"Not too bad." Her smile is infectious.

"Hey, I can dance. You may beat me in every sport, but I'm not too bad on my feet." I twirl her around so now her back is to my chest. I hold her there for a moment then spin her out and pull her back in.

Her head tilts back with a giggle. "I could stay like this forever. Here in your arms."

"Good, because I don't intend on letting you go." I kiss her nose and dance with her as the sun sets.

Chapter 20

Winry

My alarm blares, pulling me out of a deep sleep. I shut off my alarm and I roll over to wrap up in Graham's warm body. He draws lazy circles on my back, and I snuggle deeper into his chest.

"Good morning, buttercup," Graham whispers. "It's time for you to get up."

"No, I don't want to," I grumble, keeping my eyes glued shut.

"Come on, baby, you are going to be late for work." He is still lightly rubbing my back, which is only lulling me back to sleep.

"What are they going to do, fire me?" I tighten my grip on him, refusing to get up.

"Winry," he nudges me softly. "I don't want you to leave either, but I also know you will blame me if you're late. Come on, I'll get up with you."

"Ugh, okay...but you have stay shirtless. If I'm getting up, I want something to look at."

Graham chuckles, "Okay baby."

We roll out of the bed, and I head into the bathroom to get ready. I forgo a shower and just wash my face and dry shampoo my hair and throw it in a clip. I throw on some light makeup and put on a pair of biker shorts and an oversized graphic tee with the Crossroads logo on it. We are going for the semi-put-together but also comfy look.

Graham keeps his promise, remaining shirtless the entire time he watches me get ready. He catches me checking him out several times, reminding me to focus on getting ready. When I can't seem to keep my hands to myself, he goes downstairs to fill my water tumbler and grabs me a breakfast granola bar.

Finally ready, I mosey down the stairs and find Graham lying back on the couch with his arm draped over his face. I climb on top of him and lay my head on his chest.

His arm comes around, encasing me, and he takes a deep breath. "I changed my mind, let's go back to bed."

"Hmm, that does sound nice. Unfortunately, I do have to go. At least you get to go back to bed." I listen to the steady thump of his heartbeat and wish I could climb back in the bed.

"It's not the same without you," he mopes.

"I know, I hate it too." I force myself up and he groans at my absence. I put on my Converse and grab my bag.

Graham runs upstairs and throws on his clothes to walk me out.

The sun is just starting to rise, so there is a pinkish-orange hue in the sky. There is a slight chill in the air, but I know in just a couple of hours the heat will be here.

Graham opens my door and puts my water in the cupholder and my bag in the passenger seat. "Okay, buttercup. You are ready to go." He cups my face and pulls me in for a kiss.

"Mm, I love you," I say just above a whisper.

"I love you too," he leans in for another kiss that I can't bear to end. He breaks away first, "You're going to be late."

"It's your fault," I tease.

"I knew it. Get out of here," he laughs and gives my ass a little smack as I get in the car. "Have a good day."

"Talk to you later," I say and pull my door closed. I back out of the driveway and head to Crossroads.

I pull into work ten minutes later and get everything up and ready. Ivy comes in late on Thursdays, so Abigal and I will be in charge of making all the coffee drinks for a few hours. When we first opened, I spent weeks learning the machines and recipes. Abigal went through the same training when we hired her, but it still isn't the same as Ivy's.

"Good morning," Abigal exclaims as she walks in the back door.

"Good morning, you ready for the day?" I ask, finishing the last of the morning opening tasks.

"Oh yeah, ready for people to compare my coffee to Ivy's," she laughs and puts her bag on the hook.

"Tell me about it." I check the time and head to the front to unlock the door.

The first few hours fly by; we are super busy but thankfully it is all paced out, so we never have a big wait time. Ivy comes in in the middle of the lunch rush and has to jump into her day immediately. Finally, we get a break around 3 in the afternoon.

"Man, that was wild," Ivy says and lays her head on the counter.

"Seriously, but on the bright side, we told everyone about the anniversary open house. I hope most of them will come back," I beam.

"Phew, yeah, I can't believe that is next Saturday," Abigal wipes down the tables up front.

"I know it, I think we have everything ready for it. I went ahead and bought all of the decorations and have all of the prizes. We have a shipment of all of the supplies Ivy needs to make all the samples coming in two days before. So, all we have to do is put it all together," I exclaim.

"Awesome, it is going to be so great. Look at us," Ivy holds out her hands for us to high five her.

The rest of the day goes by quickly. We don't get busy like we were that morning, but the afternoon crowd is steady nonetheless. Since I opened everything up, Ivy and Abigal handle the closing list. I sneak out right at 6 and head straight home, hoping Graham didn't leave early for work.

I pull in the driveway and thankfully his car is still in his driveway. I head straight over; Graham gave me a key, so I unlock the door and walk in. "Babe?"

I hear the shower running so I sneak upstairs, taking off my clothes on the way.

Steam fills the bathroom, and I pull open the shower door and see Graham in all his naked glory. He spots me and smiles when he notices I am also naked.

"Well, isn't this a pleasant surprise?" His eyes trail up and down my body.

"I thought you could use some company," I say and press my body against his.

"Mm, you were right," his hands go around my waist and down to cup my ass.

I stand on my toes and pull him down, crashing his lips to mine. My hands move from his face, down his torso, then down to his already hard cock. Before I can even do a third stroke, he twists me around.

He pulls me flush with him and whispers in my ear, "Brace yourself on the wall, buttercup, this is going to be fast and hard."

I place my hands on the tile wall, leaning forward. I part my legs a bit, giving him enough room to slide in with ease. I press back into him, taking him deeper.

"Hmm, that's my girl. Always ready and eager." He grabs the back of my neck and pulls out slowly then slams back in.

"Again," I moan, begging for more.

He tightens his grip on the back of my neck and begins pounding into me, abandoning all restraint.

I steady myself against the wall, and when I start to feel myself getting closer I buck back against him, intensifying each thrust.

"Fuck, Graham. I can't hold it any longer," I pant.

"Let go, baby." His other hand reaches around my front, playing with my clit, and I fall over the edge with his name on my lips, and he falls after me with my name on his.

My eyes roll to the back of my head, and I see stars. My arms give out on me, and I press my cheek on the cool tile as we each ride out the last strokes of our orgasm.

"Damn, Win," he pulls out of me and turns me around to face him. "You are everything to me."

My heart swells in my chest, and I can feel the rush of happy tears threaten to fall. My hands find his face and give him a kiss full of love and passion. How can one person make me feel so alive? With him I feel so confident, so beautiful, and adored unconditionally.

We stay in the shower for a moment, just letting the hot water run over us. I want to stay here forever, but unfortunately we have to get out and he has to go into work. I don't know how he did it this morning. The need to hold him here with me is so strong.

I watch him as he puts on his uniform. He looks so sexy in it. I just want to handcuff him to the bed and keep him here.

"What are you thinking about? You have this mischievous look on your face," he chuckles.

"Just plotting to find a way to keep you here with me tonight." I bite my lower lip and think of all the fun possibilities.

"Don't you get any ideas, buttercup," he finishes the last button on his top and then puts on his bulletproof vest.

"Ugh, but you just look so good. I can't help it, it's your fault, really. I mean no one should look this good in a uniform." I tug on his belt, bringing him closer. "I think I will have to make a citizen's arrest."

"I wish, but I'm running late. This time I get to blame you." He taps my nose and I snicker.

"Blame yourself. No one should look this good." I look him up and down and give him a wicked smile letting him know I'm thinking something dirty.

"You're going to be the death of me." Graham kisses my forehead, and we head downstairs. He grabs his phone and keys, and we walk out together. It takes a good five minutes for us to say our goodbyes, but I finally let him go and he heads off to work.

Once in my apartment, I get a quick dinner started and plop down on my couch with some spaghetti and turn on the TV. Halfway into my dinner, there is a knock at my door. I check my phone. No one has texted saying they are stopping by.

Another knock comes. I head to the door, a little apprehensive. I check the peephole, and the very last person I suspected is on the other side.

Chapter 21

Winry

Graham's mother faces me. I don't even know what to say to her.

"Hi, Ms. Taylor...Graham isn't here, he's at work." I say, cautious of my tone. I don't want to make our relationship worse, but I definitely won't be bubbly for her.

"I know, I'm here to see you. Can I come in?" she says, her tone equally bland.

What the hell is going on right now, is she here to try to make amends? "Um, sure." I step aside and let her in. "Would you like to sit?" I gesture to the couches.

"Yes, let's sit. I have something I want to talk to you about." She takes her seat. She turns her nose up at the sight of my food on the coffee table. She is holding in a back handed comment, I can tell.

I pick up my plate and take it to the kitchen then come back, taking a seat on the other side of the couch. Awkward tension fills the air and I don't really know what to say.

"So, there was something you wanted to talk to me about?" I am getting more anxious by the second.

"Yes, I am here to talk to you about you and my son. I want you to break up with him," she commands, leaving no room for questioning.

My mouth gapes; I'm in complete shock. I don't even know how to form words right now. Each time I think I have a good response, I change my mind because she seriously couldn't have just said that.

"I can see you are trying to wrap your head around what I just said, so I will repeat myself. I want you to break up with Graham."

"Why?" is all I can manage to say.

"I know you both think you are happy and 'in love' but I know this won't work in the long run. I mean this is just lust. You are a new shiny toy that has his attention for now, but you aren't wife material, dear." She says it so plainly like I should already know this.

"I'm sorry, but you don't even know me," I respond flatly.

"I know enough. I didn't get a good feeling the first time I saw you two together, and my gut is never wrong. Between how you acted at the brunch and that Graham's dad tried to talk me into giving you another chance—honestly, the fact that he liked you only confirms that this is not a match—I can tell."

I think I just blink back at her.

"And he has barely spoken to me since the festival. Do you really want to be the reason he doesn't even talk to his own mother?" she tilts her head to me in question.

"Sorry, I need a minute to process this," I stand and pace in the living room. Surely this is all just a dream or something. Am I hallucinating?

"Honestly, it will happen eventually. Graham will come to realize that he is better suited for someone else…"

"You mean Claire," I interrupt bluntly.

"Yes, Claire for example. Who has a steady job, and one that gives her good flexibility with kids. She lives in Rosewood, which is Graham's real home. Not to mention she knows not to show inappropriate affection in public," she rolls her eyes. "I want Graham to marry someone who can give him everything he deserves. That is not you."

"What about Graham? What about what he wants? What if I am the one he wants?" I ask, frantic and still pacing in the living room.

"He doesn't know what he wants," she waves me off.

I scoff. "I can't believe this is happening right now. Let's just say I don't break up with him, would you ever give me a chance?" I pause pacing and hold in a breath waiting for her answer.

"Oh dear, you are going to do it. You won't let yourself be the driving wedge between him and his mom. If you want to play hypotheticals, then we can. No, I don't think I would change my mind, I would simply wait for this to run its course." She shrugs and lets out a huff like I am annoying her.

"I think you need to leave," I say, somehow mustering up some backbone.

"Are you kicking me out?" she looks shocked, like she hasn't been insulting me in my own home.

"Yes, yes, I am. I need you to leave." I walk to the door and hold it open.

"All right then." Ms. Taylor stands and walks toward the door. "Give what I said some genuine thought. I know you will come up with the right answer."

Again, I just blink at her with my mouth gaping open. I watch her get in her car and pull out of the driveway before I shut the door. The tears come immediately after it closes.

I slide down the wall and pull my knees to my chest. What the actual fuck just happened? I mean, did that seriously just happen? Why did it happen? I never did anything to her. I am in love with her son and make him happy...right? I don't understand.

Everything in the room feels like it is starting to spin. My breathing is starting to get uneven, and my mind is going a mile a minute. My mind is screaming, actually. "You aren't good enough. You are a burden to everyone. You are an unlovable mess. You are broken."

Breathe, Winry. Breathe.

But I can't. The tears are falling, and my brain is too loud. I can't focus on steadying my breath and I don't want to because she's right. I'm not what Graham needs, and how could he be with someone his mom hates? I know I couldn't be with someone my parents hate. She's right, he will end it eventually; I might as well cut it off myself.

I'm in a shit mood today at work. I barely say two words. Ivy has asked me once what is wrong, but I ignored her. She hasn't asked again yet, thankfully. I am barely keeping it together as is.

My panic attack felt like it lasted throughout the night, and I am still feeling the effects. Graham did try to call me at one point, but I let it ring. I couldn't answer. I wanted to so badly but couldn't. How am I supposed to end things with him? I can feel my heart breaking already.

"Why don't you go home, Winry? The day is pretty much over, I can cover the last two hours," Ivy gives me a sideways smile.

"No, Ives I don't want to leave you high and dry. I'm sorry, I am being a shitty friend and partner today." I feel the tears threaten my eyes, so I look away quickly and try to rein them back in.

"Look, something is wrong. I know there is, so you have two options. You can either stay here and tell me, or you can go home and tell me another day." She puts her hands on her hips and raises her eyebrows.

"Oof, okay, I'm going to go home. I'm just not ready to talk about it. Thanks, Ivy." I can't even manage a half smile. I just grab my stuff and drive home in silence.

I pull in my driveway and just the sight of Graham's car in the driveway makes me want to cry. I sneak in my apartment, careful to not shut a door too loudly. I know he will be over later when I originally was supposed to be getting off. Until then, I plan on wallowing and drowning in my sorrows.

I drift off on the couch for about an hour and wake up to the sound of my door opening and closing. I turn slowly, already knowing who just walked in.

"Hey Win, you okay? I was going to see you at work, but I noticed your car was in the driveway." His voice is soft and full of concern. If he only knew how poorly this conversation is about to go.

"Um, yeah. Listen, we need to talk," I say as I sit up. Gosh, even moving hurts. My mental pain has turned physical.

"Winry, what's wrong?" He takes the same seat on the couch as his mom had last night, and I feel like I am going to throw up.

"Graham, this isn't working." The words barely make it out before the tears roll down my face.

"What? What are you talking about?" Confusion mars his face. His gorgeous face that I love.

I wipe some tears and choke back the lump in my throat. "This. Us. It isn't working."

"Winry, this doesn't make any sense. Yesterday...yesterday everything was good. What has happened in the last twenty-four hours that has made you think that this isn't working?"

My heart is shattering, but I have to keep going. "I'm sorry, Graham. I just can't do this anymore."

"Do what anymore? Talk to me, what is really wrong? Because I'm not buying this bullshit." He moves closer, reaching for me, so I stand up quickly taking a few steps away, tears streaming down my face.

"Please, just trust me, okay? This is for the best," I choke out.

"No, that's not a good enough answer. Try again." He stares at me, waiting for an answer I can't give him.

"Graham..." I shut my eyes trying to find the right words. "Please."

"And I am what? Just supposed let you go, let you walk away from this? Winry, come on. I love you, please don't do this." He stands up and places his hands on my shoulder.

"I can't do this, Graham, I just can't. You deserve someone better, someone who isn't broken." I need this to end, I don't think my heart can take much more.

"You are not broken. I refuse to let you talk about yourself like that," he cups my face and wipes away some tears.

"You deserve someone your family likes and who can be what you need her to be. I'm not her, Graham." I grab his wrists, pulling them down from my face, and take another step back.

"Winry, please. Don't do this," his voice cracks a little, and I have the need to be sick again.

"I'm sorry," I cry.

"When you feel like telling me what really is going on, you know where to find me," he turns around and slams the door on his way out.

My heart shatters into a million pieces.

When I can finally move again, each step feels like agony. I send a text to Wyla to come pick me up. I need to be anywhere but here, so I pack a bag for a few days. I just need three days, right? Three days of extreme pain, then it will be better. I hope.

Chapter 22

Graham

This has probably been the most miserable weekend of my entire life. I still can't wrap my head around what happened. How the fuck did we go from fucking in the shower to breaking up? Something isn't right, and I don't know what happened or how to fix it.

She left shortly after and hasn't been home all weekend. I am assuming she is either at Waverley's or her parents' house. I have grabbed my keys more than once to go find her and beg for her to come back to me, but I ultimately put them back down. I want to fight for this, but I don't want to force her either. I just pray a few days to clear her head is what she needs.

I pull on my uniform and drive to the station. Tonight is going to be a long night, and I am dreading it. My head isn't in the right space, and I have got to get it together quickly. But damn it, I miss her. All weekend I played our breakup over and over in my head, and I still don't understand.

I find Owen inside the station talking to a couple of the other night shift officers. He spots me and waves me over.

"Wow, you look like shit," Owen pats me on the back. "Are you feeling all right?"

"Just fine, I'm going to wait on you outside." I grumble and turn around without saying another word.

Outside, I take a deep breath in and exhale out. I close my eyes and try to calm down. I'm so frustrated and angry. I just want to know what happened.

"You know, sometimes it helps to let it all out, Taylor."

Startled, I jump a little and open my eyes to see Chief Bennett in front of me.

"Sorry, sir, I just needed a minute."

"I understand. Listen, get your head on right before you guys go out tonight. I don't want any of my officers getting hurt or making wrong choices." His tone is stern but not harsh either. I can't tell if he hates me now or not.

"Yes, sir." He nods and starts to walk away, but unable to control myself, I stop him. "Chief, I know this is probably super unprofessional, but I just need to know if she is okay."

He halts and turns back to me. He lets out a sigh. "As her dad, I shouldn't say anything, but I will tell you that physically, she is safe. Otherwise, I should probably keep it to myself that she is doing terrible. And if you tell her I told you any of this I will deny it...but maybe you should talk to your mom and ask about her little visit here Thursday night. You might find out something interesting."

"Thank you, sir" is all I can say before he turns around and walks away.

My mind starts to race. My mom? Her visit? What does that have to do with me and Winry? I had already told her what happened with my mom didn't change how I felt about her. But Chief said something about a visit Thursday. She didn't come see me Thursday...

My train of thought is interrupted by Owen. "Dude, are you all right?"

"No, but hopefully I will be."

I decide it's best to talk to my mom in person, so I head up to Rosewood Wednesday afternoon. I don't call her to let her know I am coming. I don't want to give her the time to get Claire involved again. I don't really know what to expect out of this meeting. Chief just said she came into town Thursday, and I know she didn't see me, so something must have happened with Winry.

I pull into her house. Normally you are supposed to feel happy about coming back to the house you grew up in, but right now I'm indifferent. How am I even supposed to navigate this? She is my mom, but if she is the reason Winry broke up with me, I don't know what to do.

I contemplate all of the possible outcomes of this meeting, and I don't like a single one of them. If my mom had nothing to do with Winry breaking up with me, then I'm back to square one. If she is the reason, then how do I move forward? How do I convince Winry to come back when my mom won't treat her with respect? How do I convince my mom to give Winry a chance when she has her mind so dead set on not liking her.

With a sigh and a quick inner pep talk, I get out of the car and go knock on the door. Mom answers the door and smiles when she sees me. "Oh, Graham, this is a pleasant surprise. Come in, come in. I just made some chocolate chip cookies."

My heart hurts a little, reminded by how much Winry loves anything chocolate chip. "None for me, I'm not very hungry."

"Come on, just one cookie." She walks into the kitchen and comes out with a plate of cookies. "It will make you feel better."

"Feel better? How do you know I am upset?"

"I just know. A mother knows things, Graham," she brushes me off but takes the plate back to the kitchen. She is careful to not make eye contact with me, so I haven't been able to read her very well.

She comes back into the living room, and we sit down. "So, what brings you here? I have missed you."

"Yeah, I am sorry for icing you out for so long, but you have to understand where I was coming from."

"I understand it caught you a little off guard. I shouldn't have ambushed you, but you need to understand that I was only doing what is best for you," she says defensively, crossing her legs and arms.

"That's the thing, Mom, you were doing what you thought was best, but that doesn't mean it was the best for me. Winry is important to me, and you knew that." I try to keep my tone calm and neutral.

"You're right, let's not argue about the past. What brings you back home?" She pats me on the leg and smiles brightly.

"I just wanted to talk to you about something," I shuffle in my seat and say a silent prayer this doesn't go south too fast.

"What is it, honey?"

I take a deep breath and hope for the best. "Did you come down to Aster Creek last Thursday?"

Something unreadable crosses her face briefly; it flashed so quickly I almost missed it. "Um, I might have been in town. It's a free country, Graham, I can go to Aster if I want to," she deflects.

"Why were you there? You didn't see me, what were you doing there?" A pit forms in the bottom of my stomach.

"Are you warm? It's a little hot in here, don't you think? Do you want a drink?" She stands up, completely ignoring my questions.

"Mom, what did you do? Please tell me," I stop her before she can make it too far.

She huffs and comes back to her chair. "Nothing that wasn't for the best, Graham."

"What does that mean? I am going to need you to tell me what is going on," I demand, starting to get a little irritated.

"Ugh, don't be mad, but I might have gone over to Winry's. We had a little chat, after which she kicked me out of the house, by the way," she rolls her eyes. "I may have mentioned to her that it would be better for you if she ended things. I just told her what she already knew, honey."

I rub my hands over my face in utter disbelief. "Oh, my gosh. You, you are the reason she broke up with me."

"She did?" her face perks up. "Well listen I know it seems hard now, but…"

"Don't say it's for the best. I can't believe you did this, that you actually did this to her and to me. I mean, did you even think about me at all?" I stand up, no longer able to sit still.

"Graham Taylor, everything I do is for you. That is the whole reason I did it. She is not what you need and…" She starts with her excuses, but I can't hear them anymore.

"Please stop. You cannot honestly sit there and tell me that you did this for me. If you did anything for me, it would have been to actually try to get to know her. Are you that obsessed with the idea of me being with Claire?" I pace back and forth, my mind racing, connecting all the dots. Winry said I deserved someone better, someone my family liked. It was all because of her.

"Claire is the better choice for you, Graham," she says adamantly.

"No, she isn't. The better choice is the person who makes me happy, the person I am in love with and is in love with me. Even Dad could see that we loved each other."

"Pfft, and that is supposed to help your case? Your dad doesn't know what love is," she waves her hand in the air like I just said something stupid.

"Neither do you, Mom. I...I'm leaving," I put my hands up in surrender.

"Graham, don't leave. You will see one day that this is what was supposed to happen." She finally stands up and places her hand on my shoulder like she is trying to comfort me.

"No, one day you will understand that you are the reason we no longer have a relationship," I take a step back, not wanting to be touched right now.

"Don't say that. I will always be your mother. She is just some girl you are infatuated with." She looks shocked by my words, but what did she expect? Me to be happy about this?

"Infatuated? Mom, listen to me, and really listen. I love Winry. I will get her back, and if you ever want us to have a relationship again you will respect that and open your eyes to see how happy she makes me."

"Graham..."

"I don't want to hear anything else unless it's 'I'm sorry.'" I wait a minute, and when she doesn't say anything, I walk out the door.

I sit in my car unsure of what to do next. All I know for sure is that I have to get her back.

I stand outside her door. I have called her repeatedly trying to figure out where she is, but there's been no answer. I knock, and after a minute I knock again. Her car is here, but it has been all week and she hasn't. I knock one more time, but no answer. I try calling her again, but no answer. I get back in my car and head to Crossroads.

I walk in, scanning the place looking for her, but I don't see her.

"Graham, hey," Ivy comes around the corner. "How are you doing?"

"I could be better. Is Winry here?" I ask with hope that she is just in the back.

"No, sorry. Her sisters took her out of town for a couple of days," she gives me a lopsided smile.

Damn it.

"Do you know when she will be back? I really need to talk to her." I try not to sound too panicked.

"She should be back Friday, for that court date for the Flynn incident."

"Okay, great. Thank you, Ivy." I just have to wait until Friday, but then I am getting her back.

Chapter 23

Winry

We pull back into Waverley's place late Thursday night. My sisters took me to Savannah, Georgia, for the past few days to take my mind off the breakup, but it did little to no good. I mostly sat and moped on the beach the whole time. I still can't bear to go to my apartment, and I am dreading tomorrow. I feel like when I see him I will just burst into tears.

I borrow some nice clothes from Waverley for my court date. I stand in the mirror looking at myself. I look like a train wreck. My eyes have been puffy for days, and I am mentally exhausted.

"Everything will be okay, Win. Wyla and I will be there the whole time." Waverley comes in behind me and wraps me in a hug.

Tears threaten again, but I pull them back and let out a deep breath. "Okay, let's get this over with."

We all pile into Wyla's car and head to the courthouse. Dad told me to be there an hour earlier than the court time. I don't know why though. We get out of the car and my parents are waiting for us with a man who I am assuming is the lawyer he has told me he was getting.

"Hey, Winry," my dad pulls me into a hug. "This is Nathan Williams; he is the city's lawyer and yours for today."

"Hi," I hold out my hand. "Thank you for helping."

He shakes my hand. "It's no problem, really. This shouldn't be too bad. I got a call from Mr. Martin's lawyer last night. They want to try to mediate before court."

"Is that a good thing or a bad thing?" I look between my dad and Mr. Williams.

"I don't know yet, but it gives us an opportunity to settle it outside of a trial." Mr. Williams replies.

"A trial?" My face pales and I feel nauseous.

"I don't think it will come to that, Winry, but let's head in." My dad holds out his arm to escort me inside. We follow Mr. Williams to a side room with a table and some chairs.

I scan the room and thankfully Graham is nowhere to be seen, but Flynn and his lawyer sit on one side of the table.

Breath. In. Out.

"Good afternoon, gentlemen," Mr. Williams says as we take our seats.

I must look like I am about to fall apart because my dad holds my hand under the table. Mom, Wyla, and Waverley had to wait outside, but I insisted Dad come in with me. I give him a thankful smile and squeeze his hand.

"Let's get to the point, shall we? We would like the aggravated burglary dropped completely and the aggravated assault down to assault in the third degree," Flynn's lawyer says bluntly.

"Goodness, Charles. Well, we are not dropping all of the charges down that much, so let's go ahead and establish that now," my lawyer counters.

"I don't think you want to take this to court; your client did break my client's nose," Charles stares at me and I feel like sinking in my chair.

"Yours broke into her home, attacked her, and gave her a concussion. So, I think you don't want to take this to trial. Look, we would be willing to drop the aggravated burglary. If he pleads guilty to aggravated assault, we will do a reduced sentence and allow him good faith to turn himself in the following weekend."

Charles looks like he is contemplating the offer and Flynn looks pissed. He has been staring daggers at me the entire time. "How about assault in the second degree, no jail time and he will pay the full fine?"

"No, at least a year sentence," Mr. Williams retorts.

Charles leans over and whispers something to Flynn. He doesn't look happy but nods. "Six-month sentence, a year of probation, and pays the full fine. That's our final offer or else we will take this to trial."

Mr. Williams looks at me then my dad. Dad nods and I do too, unsure but trusting him that this is the right choice.

"Okay, but he turns himself in tomorrow before midnight, and the restraining order stays in place for the full probation," Mr. William lays out our final terms.

"Deal," both lawyers stand and shake hands.

Flynn just sits there, his face now unreadable, but he is still staring. Charles pats Flynn on the back and they exit the room.

I let out a deep breath, relaxing for a moment.

Mr. Williams turns to me and places his hand on my shoulder. "Okay, we will enter the plea. You should be fine to go, Winry."

"Great, thank you." I give him a fake smile because I still can't bring myself to make a real one.

Mr. Williams stands and leaves the room, leaving me and Dad in the room.

"Win, are you okay?" Dad asks, still holding my hand.

"Yeah, I think so. What time is it?" I wonder if I can sneak out of here and not run into Graham.

"It's a minute before 9, court should be starting. He should already be in the room if that's what you are really asking." Dad gives me a sympathetic smile.

"Good, I want to get out of here." Thankfully only Mom, Wav, and Wyla are left outside. We give out rounds of hugs and get the hell out of there.

"Waverley, can I stay at your place one more day?" I ask as we get in her car.

"Yeah, of course. Do you want to swing by your place now and get some stuff?" Waverley starts the car and pulls out of the parking lot.

"Yeah, best do it now, since I know he isn't home." Tomorrow after the open house I will go back home and face this, but I just need one more day.

I pull into Crossroads bright and early at 5:30. Last night, I was finally able to get some sleep. Not that I am feeling great today, but I am feeling slightly rested.

I unlock the back door and start unloading my car with all of the decorations and prizes. I do one load and leave the back door propped open so I can make multiple trips. I set down my first load in the front and start pulling out some of the decorations. I turn around to get round two, and my blood runs cold.

"Hello Winry," Flynn stands in front of me, sipping on a bottle of vodka.

"Flynn. What are you doing here? You can't be here."

"I know, I'm supposed to be turning myself in today. And you know what? I don't feel like doing that. I have officially lost my job, I am having to do jail time, and I have to pay a $2,500 fine, and it's all because of you," he slurs angrily.

I am frozen, completely frozen. What do I do? Ivy won't be here for another hour. I look around for anything I could use to defend myself, but there is nothing close by besides balloons and tablecloths.

Okay remain calm. "Flynn, please, if you just leave no one has to know about this, okay? We can just let it go."

"That doesn't fix any of the damage you have done, Winry. I think it's time you learned that your decisions also have consequences." He stalks toward me and I try to back up but trip over one of the boxes on the floor.

Flynn picks me up and throws me like a rag doll toward the front counter. The blow knocks the breath out of me, and before I can recover, Flynn backhands me across the face. I cry out in pain and try to yell for help, but it won't matter. No one is out in town yet.

"Shut up, bitch," he picks me up again, and this time I have a shot so I take it and kick him in the balls. He drops me and falls to his knees. I take off to the front door, but Flynn recovers faster than I anticipated and grabs me by my hair, pulling me backward.

He spins me around and punches me in the jaw. "You are going to pay for that."

I spit a mixture of spit and blood in his face like he did to me last time. The anger on his face grows. He lands one more punch and everything fades to black.

Chapter 24

Graham

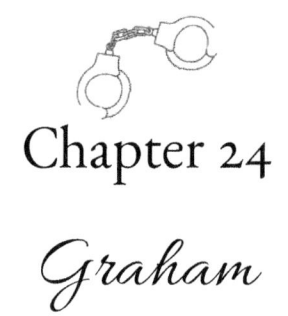

Court starts and ends with no sign of Winry. I lose all hope of seeing her when they submit a plea for her case. Fucking six months for that prick. He deserves more, but I know Winry wouldn't want to go to a trial.

Back home, I go back to her apartment knocking and hoping for an answer, but no luck. I hang my head in defeat. I just need to talk to her. I need two minutes to convince her to take me back and forget everything my mom said to her.

I am tempted to drive around looking for her, but I know today was probably hard. So I kick myself the whole way back to my apartment. I work tonight, so I force myself to get some sleep. It's shitty sleep, but it's sleep.

I wake up a couple of hours later, my mood just as sour as it was before. I head to the station and go through the motions of the night. Owen has been quiet, knowing I am not in the mood to talk, so we make it through the shift in silence.

Back again in my apartment, I have about had it. I am going to find her and talk to her. I can't take it any longer. I grab my keys but put them down, deciding I need to take a shower first and change.

It's probably the quickest shower of my life, but when I get out, I have five missed calls from chief and three missed calls from Ivy. A pit forms in my stomach. I hit the button to call Chief back.

"Graham, finally," he answers his voice in a panic.

"Sir, what's going on?"

"Please, please tell me that Winry is with you," he begs.

I take a seat on my bed knowing I won't be able to stand for this. "No, sir, she is not with me. What's going on? Is she okay?"

"Damn it. Okay. Get down to Crossroads now," he hangs up.

My heart is in my stomach. I grab my keys and race to Crossroads.

When I get there, there are a few cop cars and tape blocking off the small crowd that has formed.

I barely have my car in park when I jump out and race inside. The place is a mess, and there is some blood on the floor. I just stare at it unable to move. I know it has to be Winry's and I think I am going to be sick.

"Graham," Ivy comes up in tears. "I don't know what happened. She was supposed to be here this morning, and I was running late. When I got here, the place was trashed and she wasn't here." The panic in her voice is thick and she is shaking.

I want to tell her it's going to be okay, but I can't. "Where is her dad?"

She wipes the tears from her face. "Next door, he is trying to check their cameras to see if they can get an idea of what happened."

"Okay, I will be back. Are you going to be okay?"

"Yeah, I think so," she nods, and I head over next door. "Chief," I holler as I enter the building.

"Back here," he yells.

I run to the back office of the floral shop and find Chief combing through surveillance videos. "Find anything yet?"

"Unfortunately. Here." He restarts some footage. I lean over, watching intently. For a moment nothing happens, but then the door opens, and I see Flynn carrying out a limp Winry. He tosses her in his truck and they drive off.

Words can't even describe the fear I feel right now. Honestly, it's a miracle I am still standing.

"The time stamp is six hundred hours. He has had her for over an hour, taking her God knows where." Chief stands, running his hands over his face. "Damn it, this is all my fault. I agreed to letting him turn himself in instead of taking him over immediately after court."

"I...I need some air." I walk out without another word. Once outside I just fall to the concrete and put my face in my hands. I can't believe it, he took her. He knocked her out and took her.

"Graham, what's going on?" Waverley and Wyla run up. "What happened?"

I stand up, and I don't know if I can say the words out loud. I open my mouth, but nothing comes out.

"Girls," chief comes outside, clearly distraught. He holds out his arms and captures them both in a tight hug.

"Dad, what is going on? Is Winry here?" Wyla asks confused.

"No, uh, why don't we go back to the station? Your mom is on the way there now." Chief turns to me, "You too."

All I can do is nod.

Back at the station, I sit silently in the conference room, anger and fear coursing through my veins. I want to hit something and feel anything other than this.

"Okay, what is going on? You are scaring me, where is Winry?" Waverley asks and bites at her nails.

Still I can't speak. I can hardly look at anyone. Chief walks in the room with Winry's mom and Ivy.

Chief takes a deep breath. "Okay, I don't know how to say this...but Flynn attacked Winry this morning at Crossroads. We have him on camera carrying her out of the store and putting her in his truck."

Hearing it again feels like a punch to the gut. Waverley and Wyla start to panic, and Mrs. Bennett and Ivy are in tears.

"What happens now, Griffin?" Mrs. Bennett wipes the tears from her face.

"Well, we start looking. We are going through all of his credit card transactions and have a BOLO out on his truck. Girls, is there any place Winry mentioned him taking her while they dated?"

"No, they never really did anything together," Wyla croaks.

"I have her location on her phone!" Waverley exclaims.

"I'm sorry, honey, we found her phone on the counter at Crossroads. I know this hard, but we just have to be patient. I have everyone on this. I called the neighboring counties too. Please, girls, I know you want to go look for your sister, but he is dangerous. I don't want you in trouble either."

The girls all just look at each other, plotting what to do next.

"Girls, promise me you won't go out looking on your own," he gives them a stern look then turns to me. "And you, you need to go home and get some sleep. You were working all last night, and you will be out tonight."

"Like hell I am..." I protest, but he holds up his hand to stop me.

"It wasn't up for discussion. Go home. All of you." He points to us all with a look that says he is not messing around, but there is no way I can just go home and sleep.

To be honest, I don't know what to do next. There is no way that Chief is going to give me any of the information they find right now. I can't just go home and wait though.

"Graham," Wyla and Waverley stop me before I get in the car. "You aren't going home, right?"

"Not a chance in hell, but you two are not coming with me. Your dad would literally kill me."

"But..." Waverley starts.

"No, no fucking way. I am not putting you two in danger also."

"Fine, but just promise us you will find her," tears drop from Wyla's face.

"That I can promise." I get in my car and head to Owen's. I am going to need all the help I can get.

Chapter 25

Winry

My head is pounding, and my entire body aches. What happened? Where am I? I blink my eyes open, the light burning with each blink. At first, everything is fuzzy, but from what I can make out I am lying down on someone's couch.

My vision starts to clear and I am definitely on a couch, but I still have no idea where I am. I try to sit up and realize my hands are tied together with some cable ties. I look around I don't see anyone, but to the right I can see the beach outside from the windows.

I do my best to stand, but my knees wobble and fall back on the couch. I feel dizzy, and there is a lingering metallic taste in my mouth. It suddenly all comes rushing back to me. Crossroads, Flynn, then darkness.

Shit. Shit. Shit.

Where am I? Where is Flynn? I try standing again, slower this time, and make it to my feet. I have to get out of here.

I spot the front door. Damn, why is it so far away? Okay, I can do this. One step at a time. Right foot first, then left. With each step, pain radiates through my body, and my anxiety is astronomical.

I make it to the front door and turn the knob.

"Well, look who is up." Flynn comes up behind me and pounds his hand against the door, keeping me from opening it. "It was really cute watching you try to sneak out."

"Flynn, please let mc go." I close my eyes and pray a silent prayer.

"Not happening. You and I are going to go on our first little trip together today." He smiles at me and picks me up, carrying me back to the couch. "We just have to hang out here until our flight's ready, and we are off to the Dominican."

"Flynn, please don't do this. Just leave me here. You can get out of here. You don't need me." I'm not below begging at this point.

"That may be true, but I want to take you." He brushes the hair from my face, and I flinch.

"I won't go quietly. What are you going to do, knock me out again and stuff me in your carry on?"

"Don't be ridiculous. You honestly think we are flying commercial? That's cute. I made some calls and paid a shit ton of money, but we have our own private plane, and I don't know if you remember, but I have my pilot's license. Our runway will be clear for takeoff in a couple of hours. So why don't you take another nap?"

"Flynn, don't—" and then it's lights out again.

Chapter 26

Graham

Owen and I both change back into uniforms. On the way, I called my dad and had him run literally everything he can to find out as much as possible about Flynn. I'm sure Chief is doing the same thing, but he wouldn't tell me anything since I am not supposed to be out looking for her right now.

"I called one of the guys on shift today. They don't have much yet. He hasn't used any of his cards, and none of the other counties have seen his truck," Owen says.

"Damn it. I haven't heard anything concrete from my dad yet either." I hit the steering wheel. "Where could he have taken her?"

"I don't know, man, but we will find her."

We drive around for a while just looking. Owen keeps in touch with his buddy on shift today. They finally got a warrant to go in his house but there was no sign of Winry. Driving around is starting to feel pointless. He took her more than three hours ago; they could be out of the state by now.

My phone starts to buzz, and my heart starts to race. It's Ivy. I answer and put her on speaker.

"Hey, have you heard anything?" I ask, getting straight to the point.

"Yes and no. I haven't heard anything from her or her sisters, but I did happen to run into Flynn's recent girlfriend, Sara. It took some threatening, but she told me that Flynn's parents own a beach house out in the Northshore area. She couldn't remember the exact address but said it was on Seaside Drive and it's all white with blue shutters on the windows."

"That's great. Thank you, Ivy. We will go check it out and let you know." I hang up.

"I know that area. Pull over and switch with me, and then you can call this in," Owen says.

I want to argue that we don't have time to stop, but I know it will be faster for him to drive since he is familiar with the area. I pull over and we switch. I dial Chief and get ready for an ass chewing.

"Taylor, why are you calling me?" he barks.

"I got a call from Ivy, she said found out that Flynn's parents have a beach house out in Northshore. We have the street name and a description of the house. Owen and I are headed that way to check it out."

"You and Owen… ugh, I should have known you wouldn't listen to me. I will work on getting the address and a warrant for it. You and Owen drive the area in the meantime, see if you see anything. Be smart. We don't want him to get away with this, so don't anything unless you have probable cause."

"Yes sir." We hang up.

Northshore is only about twenty minutes south of Aster Creek, so we are there in no time at all. Chief calls back with a definite address, but we still don't have a warrant yet, so Owen and I just have to sit outside and wait. I feel like I am about to lose my mind waiting.

I stare at this house, and in my gut I know that Winry is in there, but all I can do is sit and wait while he is doing God knows what to her. I can't sit still. I am constantly fidgeting in my seat and bouncing my knee.

"Everything is going to be all right, Graham. She's going to be all right," Owen reassures me.

I let out a deep breath. "I really just can't sit here any—"

"Graham, shut up," Owen grabs my shoulder. "Someone is pulling in."

My head whips back to the house, where a silver car pulls in, and what do you know? Out walks Flynn to meet them.

"Well, there you go. Tired of being still? There is our probable cause right there." Owen pats my shoulder. "Let's see what this car is doing then move in."

Flynn talks to the person in the car for a few minutes; it looks like they hand him something, but we don't know what. Finally, he goes back inside.

"You ready to move?" I ask Owen.

"Fuck yeah, come on." We draw our weapons and head over to the house.

We decide to split. I go in the front and Owen goes around the back. I turn the knob silently, and praise the lord, it opens. I keep my head on a swivel looking for both Winry and Flynn.

I round the corner into the living room, and I was wrong when I said my worst nightmare was finding Flynn on top of her a couple of months ago. This is my worst nightmare.

"Look who joined the party." Flynn holds a beat up Winry and is pointing a gun to her head.

"Flynn, let her go." I aim my gun at him, but there is no way I will shoot with Winry in the way, and he knows that.

"No, sorry. I won't be doing that."

Winry looks like she is fading in and out. Her cheeks are swollen and bruised, and her lip is busted. "Winry, stay with me, baby. Everything is going to be okay."

"Graham..." she whimpers, and my heart explodes.

"Oh, I hate to disappoint, but we are leaving now, and Winry is coming with me," Flynn tightens his grip around her neck and she winces.

Out of the corner of my eye, I can see Owen at the back window, but thankfully Flynn hasn't noticed him yet. Owen motions for me to keep him talking and disappears back around the house.

"Flynn, let's talk about this."

"No, I'll talk, and you will listen. I am taking Winry with me, and you will never see her again. She will forever be mine to do whatever I please with, and there's nothing you can do about it." He looks at her like she is his prize.

"Please, please, just let her go. I will let you get on your plane to wherever you want, but please let her go." I need to keep him talking, I can't let them leave this house.

"Ha. You seriously expect me to believe that you are just going to let me go. I can see it in your eyes that you are dying to pull the trigger. Matter of fact, why don't you go ahead and drop your weapon. Come on."

Flynn motions for me to drop it, and when I don't, he pushes the barrel of his gun to Winry's head. Tears stream down her face. "Flynn, please don't do this."

"Shut up. Drop it now," he demands.

"Okay, okay." I hold up my hands, taking my weapon off him. Flynn smiles and takes his gun off Winry and points it at me.

"Flynn, no, please!" Winry cries and struggles against him.

Owen finally sneaks in. How he got in I don't know or care.

"Flynn let her go and put your hands up slowly." Owen has his gun pointed to the back of his head.

Defeat and anger cross his face, and he is contemplating all of his options. Time stands fucking still, and I hold my breath until he finally lets go of Winry and she races into my arms. I want to embrace her fully, but I can't, not yet. Flynn may have his hands in the air, but we haven't disarmed him yet.

I hold Winry tight with one hand and keep the other one steady on Flynn while Owen disarms and cuffs him. As soon as the cuffs are on, I holster my gun and wrap my arms around Winry.

Sirens wail in the distance. "I'm going to get him in a car." I nod and Owen walks him out.

"Here let me cut those ties." I pull out my pocketknife and cut her hands free.

"Graham, I'm so sorry," Winry cries.

"Hey, listen to me. You have nothing to be sorry for, baby." Tears threaten my eyes just looking at the pain in hers.

"Yes, I do," she sniffles.

"Let's talk about it later, okay?" I pull her back in my arms. "Right now, I just want to hold you." I kiss the top of her head.

"Okay." Her grip tightens around my waist as her tears fall.

We stay there for a moment, but it doesn't last long because Chief runs in hollering for Winry.

"Dad." She leaves my arms to run into his.

"Oh, my sweet girl. You're safe."

Chief and I both hover over her while she gets checked by the paramedics. She has another concussion, severe bruising on her face, and a minor cut to her bottom lip.

"Okay, guys, she is free to go." The paramedic says, putting the last bit of ointment on her cut.

"Okay, let's get you home. Your mom and sisters are waiting for you at your apartment," Chief says as he helps Winry get down from the ambulance.

"Okay, but I need to talk to Graham before we go." Winry looks over at me.

"Sure, sweetie. Graham, you and Owen can have the night off tonight. Winry, I will be in my truck over there when you are ready."

"Thank you, sir."

"No," he shakes my hand, then actually pulls me into a hug. "Thank you."

He turns back to Winry, just to look at her again, and I understand. I have had to look at her the whole time just to remind myself that she is here.

She walks up to me sheepishly. "Graham, um, would you come over when you get done here?"

"Yeah, I can do that."

"Okay…okay, good." She comes in for a hug that I never want to let go of. "Thank you for finding me," her throat croaks.

"I would have never stopped looking for you, buttercup."

She breaks our hug, and a few tears stream down her face. I gently wipe them from her face, careful of her bruises.

"I'll see you later?"

"Yeah, I just have to drop Owen off at his house, then I'll come over."

"Okay."

It feels like so many words go unsaid, and I want to beg her to say them, but instead I let her go.

Chapter 27

Winry

We pull into my apartment, and I don't even make it out of Dad's truck before my mom and sisters rush out the door.

My sisters tackle me first. My body aches, but I don't mind too much.

"Girls, easy now," Dad says, noticing their death grip.

"Okay, it's my turn now, let her go." Mom peels off my sisters and wraps me in a gentle hug. "My baby, are you all right?"

"I will be." My body is in pain, and if I think about what happened too long, I am afraid I will fall apart. So I am focusing on Graham and getting him back.

When I wasn't knocked out, all I thought about was him. The fear that I would never see him again hurt worse than the beatings. I don't want to be without him anymore or lose him ever again.

"What do you need, honey? Anything you want: food, water? Anything," mom says as we go inside.

"The paramedics said I could take some pain medicine, then I would like to take a shower." Then I would like to get Graham back, but I don't say that part out loud.

"All right, honey. Do you feel okay to stand in the shower? Maybe one of us should sit in the bathroom in case you fall." Mom rambles as I get the medicine out of the cabinet.

"Mom, I will be fine. I know it looks bad, but I can stand in the shower." I pop some in my mouth and get a drink of water.

Mom stares at me with tears in her eyes. "Winry, I'm so sorry he did this to you."

My mind flashes back to just an hour ago, and I feel nauseated. Tears are threating to fall all over again. "Mom, please don't cry. If you start crying, I'll cry, and I really don't think I'll stop if I start."

"You're right, I'm sorry." She fans her face, trying to dry her tears. "Go take your shower."

I give her a fake smile, trying to show that I am somewhat okay. I'm here at least.

Upstairs, I turn on the shower and do what I have been avoiding: look in the mirror. I look how I feel: bruised and beat up. My cheeks are a dark reddish-purple, and the cut to my lip hurts like a bitch. I push off the sink, unable to look anymore, and hop in the shower.

I can feel myself starting to slip mentally, so I force myself to think of better things. I think of things like when Graham and I said "I love you" to each other. When I beat him at every carnival game. When we danced under the sunset at the beach. When he tells me jokes to make me feel better. When he looks at me like I am the most beautiful girl in the world.

My near panic attack subsides, and I finish up in the shower. I brush my hair and throw on some pajama shorts, a crew sweatshirt, and some fuzzy socks.

My family falls silent when I come back down. "You guys don't have to coddle me, you can still talk, just maybe about something other than today." I grab a blanket and lie down on the couch. Exhaustion hits me hard; getting hit in the head several times takes its toll.

There is a soft knock at the door, and my heart beats a little faster, hopeful it's who I think it is. Waverley jumps up to answer.

"Hey. Winry, Graham is here," Waverley marvels at the both of us.

"Let him in," I tell her and sit up on the couch.

When he walks in, it's as if everything else fades away. For no sleep in twenty-four hours, he looks damn good. He has showered and changed out of his uniform into some gray sweatpants and a white t-shirt that fits in all of the right places.

"Hey," I say breathlessly.

"Hey," the corners of his mouth turn up a bit.

"Okay, well, I need to head down to the station. Girls, why don't y'all head home and you can check on Winry tomorrow?" Dad says, trying to be subtle.

"Okay," Wyla and Wav grumble as they stand to give hugs.

"You too, Isabel," Dad touches her back, nudging her to stand up.

"But..." Mom mumbles.

"She'll be fine." Dad turns to me, "You'll call us if you need us, right?"

"I promise." I reach over and squeeze Mom's hand. I know she just wants to make sure I am okay.

"Oof, okay." She fans her face again, drying her tears.

Everyone gets a hug, including Graham. What can I say? We are a family of huggers. Once they are out the door, it's just me and Graham.

"Want to come sit with me?" I ask, and nerves shoot through my body.

"Yeah, how are you feeling?"

"As good as I can feel, I guess." A small beat of silence passes.

Cut straight to it, Winry.

"Graham, I'm so sorry. I never wanted to break up with you, but I got scared and stupid."

"You mean my mom forced you into it," he corrects me.

I study him for a minute. "How did you find out about that?"

I wasn't planning on telling him what his mom had done because I didn't want to further damage their relationship.

"Doesn't matter. I know you felt like you didn't have any other option. I understand why you did it, and if it is still too hard for you, I will respect that." He scoots closer and tucks my hair behind my ear. "I love you so much, but I'll never put my happiness above yours."

I can't hold it in any longer. Tears escape down my face. "You make me happy. I never want to be without you again. I want you to tell me all of your dumb jokes, and I want to beat you in every game possible. I want you to call me buttercup, and I want to stay up late with you on your nights off."

"Come here," he pulls me in his lap, and I rest my head on his shoulder. "And I want you to write me endless poems and make tons of chocolate chip cookie dough. I want to dance with you under every sunset and lift you up anytime you are feeling down. I want it all, Winry." He kisses my forehead. "I was so afraid I was going to lose you today."

I nuzzle deeper into his neck, "I'm here, you found me."

I relax for the first time in what feels like forever in his arms, feeling safe and at home.

Epilogue

Graham - 6 months later

"Come on, Winry, we are going to be late," I stand at the bottom of our stairs waiting on her. Two months after we got back together, we decided to move into her place. We stayed together ninety-nine percent of the time anyway, so it felt pointless for us to both be paying rent.

"Hold on, I'm almost done," she yells.

I pace anxiously in her living room, checking my coat pocket for the thousandth time.

"Okay, I'm ready." Winry walks down the stairs, and I can't help but be in awe of her. She has on a long-sleeve fitted tan dress that complements her curves in all of the right places. Her hair is halfway pulled up with her usual loose curls. What's most beautiful though is the smile she is wearing.

"You look gorgeous, Win," I cup her face and give her a tender kiss.

"Mm, you don't look too bad yourself. I think you should wear suits more often." She pulls me down by my tie and gives me a kiss that has me debating all my plans.

"Quit, you little temptress, we are late already. Come on." I take her hand and pull her to the car.

"I'm so excited to see Mary this weekend. I'm so happy they're having another baby." Winry slides in the car. As far as Winry knows, the party tonight is for Mary and her pregnancy, but I have other plans for tonight.

"I know, another girl too. Bless Jace's heart," I tease her.

She shakes her head. "You know you want to be a girl dad too."

"Hell yeah, I do. I need all the little Winrys." I reach over, tickling her.

She laughs and swats my hand away. "Come on, we're late, remember?"

"All right, all right. Buckle up, buttercup."

"Yes, sir." She gives a flirty wink, and I can't help but lean over for another kiss.

We head up to Rosewood, and I get more anxious by the mile. By the time we get to Rosemary's, I'm nervous sweating.

"Let's take our bags up to the room first, then I think the party is outside," I say, parking the car, and we hop out.

"It's the perfect night to have a party. Look how incredible the stars look." She looks up to the sky, but I can't draw my eyes away from her.

My plan was to do this in the room where we said 'I love you' but I can't wait anymore. I drop the bags. "Hey, come with me."

"What are we doing? I thought we were late," she laughs as I practically pull her to the rose garden.

When I get to the perfect spot, I take her hands in mine. "Winry, when I first saw you, I was immediately enthralled by you. You are just as beautiful on the outside as you are on the inside."

"Graham, what..." her smile is both anxious and excited.

"Let me finish, buttercup. I have never met someone so strong, so capable. You are my moon and all the stars. You are everything I never knew I needed, and now I intend to never let you go." I reach in my pocket pulling out the ring and get down on one knee. Her breath hitches, and she clasps her hands together. "Winry Bennett, will you make me the happiest man in the world and be my wife?"

"Yes, yes." A few happy tears slide down her face. She bends down, placing her hands on my face, and kisses me.

I stand up and pick her up while still kissing her deeply. "I love you," I whisper in between kisses.

"I love you too."

I set her back down. "Want to put this on?" I hold up her ring.

"Hell yeah," she holds out her left hand, and I place the ring on her finger.

"I've got one more surprise for you. Come on." I escort her through the house to the back yard.

"Congratulations," everyone yells when we walk out the door. All of our family and friends are here, and the back patio is lit up with candles and lights.

"Oh, my gosh. Graham, did you do all of this?" More happy tears fall, and I wipe them away.

"I had a little help," I smirk.

"Congratulations, sweetie," her mom comes up and wraps her in her arms.

"Thank you, everything looks so beautiful," Winry sniffles.

"It was all Graham's idea. We just helped." Her dad comes up with tears in his eyes. "I'm so happy for you, moon baby."

"Thank you, Daddy." She hugs him next, then is pulled away by her sisters.

"You did good, son." My dad walks up and pats me on the back.

"I think so too," I watch as Winry shows off her ring; her sister, Ivy, and Mary all huddle around it.

"I'm sorry your mom didn't come." Dad gives me a half smile.

I exhale, "It's okay, I have everything I need here."

I did start talking to my mom again after she apologized to both me and Winry. I invited her to come tonight, but said she didn't want to take away from our night.

"Yeah, you do, now go enjoy with your future wife." Dad gives me a little push in her direction.

We mingle for a while and Winry shows off her oval shape diamond ring. Soft music plays in the background and I'm feeling romantic. I scan the patio for Winry and find her with her sisters.

"Excuse me, care to dance with me, fiancée?" I hold out my hand for her.

"I would love to." She takes my hand, and I lead her over where there is plenty of room.

I give her a spin then pull her into me. "Are you having a good time?"

"Yes, I still can't believe it. We are getting married," she exclaims. "I love you."

"I love you too, buttercup." I hold her in my arms, swaying to the music.

In my arms, I have my all, my everything, my future. No matter what life throws at us, I know I want to do it all, feel it all, with her by my side.

THE END

Acknowledgements

Krischan, thank you for always supporting me and every crazy idea I have. You are the reason I started writing and without your encouragement and support, there is no way Feel It All would have come to be. You are my rock, my love, my everything. I love you.

Maverick and Lena, I hope you always follow your dreams and never settle for anything less than what you deserve. I want you to grow up and be unapologetically you and know that it is all a part of the journey.

Mom and Gracie, thank you for being my inspiration for the Bennett sisters. Our life has not been easy, but I would do it all over as long as I have you two with me. Each struggle has shaped us into who we are, and I know I wouldn't want to be anyone else. "Though one may be overpowered, two can defend themselves. A cord of three strands is not quickly broken," (Ecclesiastes 4:12).

Dad, I did it. I'm an author. Thank you for always looking out for my best interests and passing down the "writer's gene" down to me. Your poems inspire me, and I hope you find your love for writing again.

Tammy and Brandon, you two entered into my life I guess rather unconventionally, and I could not be happier about it. You accepted my family as it is and made it whole again.

Alyson, thank you for being a superhero to my kids and always being there for me when I need you. We are two kindred spirits, thank you for being a second mom to me.

A special thank you to Momma Tina, you read the raw, unedited Feel It All and your encouragement kept me going. Thank you for cheering me on chapter after chapter.

To my small town in Tennessee, despite what I said in high school, you are a great town. The support I have been shown by the community has been nothing short of amazing.

Lastly, to my readers. If I could hug you through this book I would. I'm eternally grateful for you. Writing Feel It All has been an incredible journey and it means the world to me that you took the time to read it. I pray that each one of you knows how truly amazing you are. I love you all. From the bottom of my heart, thank you!

About the Author

Mollie and her husband are high school sweethearts. She has two children and three big dogs who sometimes also act like children. Her husband has been her biggest supporter on her writing journey and his encouragement is one of the primary reasons she started writing. Her mother and sister served as the inspiration for the sister dynamic in this book and plans to turn it into a series. When not writing, Mollie enjoys going on walks, reading, exercising at the gym, and having a good glass of wine while taking a bubble bath.

Printed in Great Britain
by Amazon